RIVERBEND FRIENDS™

Real, Not Perfect
Searching for Normal
The Me You See
Chasing the Spotlight

THE ME YOU SEE

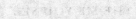

The Me You See

RIVERBEND FRIENDS™

Jill Williamson

CREATED BY

Lissa Halls Johnson

FOCUS
ON THE FAMILY.

*A Focus on the Family Resource
Published by Tyndale House Publishers*

Cover design by Mike Harrigan. Interior design by Eva M. Winters.

Interior illustration of musical note copyright © streptococcus/Adobe Stock. All rights reserved. Interior illustration of emoji icons copyright © Marc/Adobe Stock. All rights reserved.

For manufacturing information regarding this product, please call 1-855-277-9400.

For information about special discounts for bulk purchases, please contact Tyndale House Publishers at csresponse@tyndale.com, or call 1-855-277-9400.

ISBN 978-1-58997-706-8

Library of Congress Cataloging-in-Publication Data can be found at www.loc.gov.

Printed in the United States of America

27 26 25 24 23
 7   6   5   4   3   2

Chapter

1

"Pancakes at seven o'clock."

My eyes flashed open. Someone stood over my bed, looking down. Fire shot through me as my brain put two and two together.

"Sebastian!" I pulled my blankets up to my chin. "No coming in here without knocking!"

"I did knock, Isabella Valadez," my brother said. "Pancakes at seven o'clock."

I glanced past Sebastian to the digital clock on my nightstand. It was 7:04. He'd probably been knocking since 7:01.

"I'll be downstairs in five minutes," I said.

Sebastian didn't move. His eyes—such a light brown they were almost hazel—were fixed on my bedspread. My brother didn't like making eye contact. His normally frizzy curls were wet and tightly matted together. He'd showered and dressed himself already.

"Go downstairs and wait for me, Bash." I stifled the *¡Ahora!* I wanted to tack on. Anger never worked on my brother. I softened

1

my tone, reminding myself he wasn't trying to annoy me. "Get out the flour and the comal, okay? That will help me make them faster."

"Get out the flour and the comal. Make them faster." Sebastian wandered out of my room, leaving the door gaping.

"Sebastian!" I yelled after him. "Shut the door behind you. *¿Por favor?*"

He stepped back into the open doorway. "Okay, yes, Isabella Valadez. Shut the door behind me." He turned his back to the door, reached behind him, and closed it.

My head fell back against my pillow. My brother was the most *impaciente* person in the world. He was twelve, but because he had autism, my parents acted like our move last summer nullified Sebastian's independence. Now that we lived in a city, they said someone had to always be watching him. Since Mamá and Papi both worked full-time, Leo was in college, and Claire had robotics *and* a job, that someone was usually me.

I lay under the warm covers, wishing I could doze another hour or three. Captain Marvel gazed at me from the poster on my wall. My whole family was obsessed with the franchise, but with her intelligence, strength, and kindness, Captain Marvel was my favorite. *How would she handle a brother like mine?* No question there. She'd get up and make the kid breakfast. After checking her cell phone, of course. There could be an important message from Nick Fury.

I reached for my phone. Checking it was the first thing I did each morning. I had to know what was going on out there—what I was missing. Cyber-stalk my crushes. All the important aspects of a girl's life.

To my great disappointment, there was nothing going on. At least not with my squad. They'd been gone all winter break. They were still gone. And I was still here with Sebastian. Every day. Making him pancakes for breakfast and peanut butter and honey sandwiches for lunch. Wishing I could go someplace where people my age were hanging out. Cute people. Boy people.

With that thought, I thumbed over to Cody Nichols's Instagram. He lived at the end of my street and was the whitest white boy I'd ever crushed on. I couldn't help it. He was a total Captain America with peachy skin, blond hair, and the sweetest brown eyes. Sadly, Cody had friend-zoned me from day one. He friend-zoned everyone. I don't think he actually dated. Cody never posted on his feed, but he usually had a story up. Nothing today, though.

Next up was Zac Lloyd's page. His real name was Isaac, but everyone called him Zac. He was a senior and a white boy, too, but he was so tan his skin was as brown as mine. We'd make a striking entrance to prom. He was super hunky. I'd started saying *hunky* after watching an '80s movie with my mom. It made me laugh at the time, but now I think it's perfect for describing boys like Zac. Especially since he looked a lot like Matt Cornett, who played E. J. on *High School Musical: The Musical: The Series*, which was my current favorite because, duh, #musicals. Zac was on my sister's robotics team and ran track, but his most notable trait was something I called "The Dazzle." Zac had the most incredible hazel eyes that sparkled. All. The. Time. When those hazel eyes were directed at someone—even accidentally, which had happened to me twice, swoon—they had the power to captivate. Think Flynn Rider's smolder, only I didn't think Zac could control it. It was simply who he was.

I have crushed on Zac ever since I first laid eyes on him at church. He attended sporadically with his dad. Multiple times I've tried to calendar his appearances without success. So far stalking his social media was the best I could do to chase after the man I loved.

Actually, I thought he had a girlfriend, so there was that little problem too.

Oh. And also, the fact that he didn't know I was alive. But I was a glass-three-quarters-full kind of girl, so I didn't count those things as obstacles against our future marriage.

He, too, rarely posted pics of his face, which I found somewhat annoying. Last night he'd posted a football meme I totally didn't get. Me and sports don't mesh so well. I lingered a bit, gazing at the two pics in his feed that actually showed his face and those mesmerizing eyes.

I closed out of Instagram and was about to thumb over to Snapchat, when I remembered I didn't have time. In about three minutes Sebastian would return to demand his breakfast. I sighed and rolled out of bed, knocking about a dozen stuffed animals onto the floor. I shoved my feet into my monkey slippers, put on my bathrobe, and padded downstairs.

—⁓—

"Pancakes at seven o'clock," Sebastian said when I finally placed a plate of five pancakes in front of him. "It's 7:28, Isabella Valadez."

"Sorry to disappoint you, bro," I said, fetching the honey and the butter dish. I set them on the table in front of his plate. "I worked as fast as I could." Considering I'd been dead asleep twenty-four minutes ago, I thought I'd done rather well.

Scowling, Sebastian reached for the honey. He must have been starving because normally he would have reminded me of my error another three times before letting it rest.

My little brother's brain worked differently from mine. His brain liked things done on schedules. His brain took your words literally and did everything possible to hold you to them. Thankfully, his brain also liked pancakes. My nana always said the way to a man's heart was through excellent pancakes. I guess that meant little brothers too.

I returned to the stove and started my own short stack, adding an array of chocolate chips to each one and popping a few in my mouth while they cooked. Sebastian occupied, I checked Snapchat—which was barren. I scrolled through Instagram again, liking several foodie pics from some of my favorite bakestagrammers: cookie dough cupcakes from @cakenessbakeness and some adorable hedgehog cupcakes from @tastytreats56. I liked those so much I took a screenshot so I could make them for Shay. She was the only one of my squad who appreciated animal-themed cupcakes. Tessa wasn't picky about her cupcakes but preferred chocolate–peanut butter anything. And Amelia? I once made her a banana crème cupcake that she liked so much she stood up in the middle of the cafeteria and sang "Food, Glorious Food" from *Oliver!* at the top of her lungs. That was Amelia. Loud and ostentatious but extremely lovable.

By the time I shut off the burner, Sebastian had finished his food and was lost in the world of dragons. He was obsessed with the Wings of Fire series and had read the books at least five times. *I should probably grab his plate and clean up my cooking mess.* Instead, I carried my food to the living room couch, burrowed under a blanket, and ate my breakfast.

Pancakes never used to be on the menu in the Valadez household until we'd moved to Riverbend, which was where my papi grew up. He was third-generation Mexican American, so his mamá cooked way more American dishes than my Abuelita Ortiz. Nana Valadez had always made pancakes when we spent the night at her house, and Sebastian loved them so much, they'd become our daily breakfast ritual.

I slid my fork across my sticky plate and scooped up my last bite. The bittersweet, buttery goodness melted in my mouth. So yum.

I pressed my cell's home button. Nothing. Not one answer from all the texts I'd sent out yesterday. *Where was everybody?*

Dumb question. I knew exactly where my friends were. Shay had been busy helping her aunt at the bookstore up until Christmas Eve. Then she'd gone to her grandparents' and wasn't returning until the day before school started. Amelia practically lived at her church during the holidays. If she wasn't helping run something or performing something, she was babysitting or sitting in the audience. Now that Christmas was over, she was off visiting her humongous extended family. And Tessa, the one person I could usually count on seeing at least twice a week at church, had gone skiing with her mom. Skiing. The mere idea of so much athleticism made me shudder.

What I didn't understand was why they weren't texting me back. All those places had cell service.

Christmas used to be my favorite holiday. When we'd lived in Williamsport, the whole town had celebrated Christmas with caroling hayrides, truck parades, and holiday bazaars. After Christmas, we would go to Posen to stay with Abuelita and Abuelito Ortiz until Three Kings' Day. Mamá's parents were Catholic and celebrated Christmas differently than we did. I loved it because it always felt like having two Christmases. Now we lived too far away to drive up for Three Kings' Day. Besides, Mamá had to work at the clinic. Always.

Riverbend hadn't been completely void of celebrations, though. I'd gone to four bazaars and the tree lighting downtown, but I'd gone alone. By myself. There ought to be a law against that. I'd wanted to spend the break with my squad, but everyone was too busy. So I'd resorted to binge-watching YouTube cooking videos and *Cupcake Wars* on Netflix.

I did have two fun things happen. Zoe, a youth leader at my church, had hosted a girls' night at her apartment. With Tessa out of town, I'd hung out with Lauren, another sophomore, and Becky and Morgan, two eighth graders who volunteered with me in the church nursery. Zoe made us watch *Anne of Green Gables*, a super-long old movie that turned out to be pretty chill. I also went out last Saturday to the bookstore Shay's aunt owned and read to the kids, but that had been the extent of my adventuring.

Thankfully, winter break was almost over. I'd be with my people again soon.

I grabbed the remote control and clicked on the TV. Noise burst from the speakers. I jumped—panicked—and fumbled for the mute button as the blaring sounds of *Cupcake Wars* assaulted our ears.

"Sorry!" I called out, but it was too late. Sebastian went into ambulance mode, which was what I called his high-pitched wail. He shoved his book off the table and kicked it, sending it gliding over the floor until it smacked against the back door.

I managed to press mute, and the room went silent but for my brother's howling. Sebastian had two moods: good and bad. He could flip from one to the other with little provocation. Loud or sudden noises were one of his triggers, which was why we usually watched TV muted with subtitles. I don't know who had put the volume up that loud, but if I ever found out, I would make the offender do the chicken dance and post it on Instagram.

I watched my brother carefully. He was standing by the kitchen table, moaning, palms over his ears, fingers curved around his head. His elbows touched in front of his face like a large beak. I called it *elbow face*. At least his volume had subsided.

"Tell me about Marvel, Bash," I said.

He rocked from foot to foot, and for a minute I thought he was going to ignore me. Then he wandered my way, still in elbow-face mode, and began to mumble, "*Iron Man*, May 2, 2008. *The Incredible Hulk*, June 13, 2008." Whenever Bash got stressed, I tried to get him to list the Marvel movies by year. He had an excellent memory for facts, and reciting them calmed him down.

He edged closer and then passed by the couch, headed for the baby grand piano. He didn't play—hated the sound of the piano, actually—but sitting underneath was his favorite place to play video games. Sure enough, he let go of his ears and crouched, continuing to say his Marvel movies.

"*Iron Man 2*, May 7, 2010. *Thor*, May 6, 2011." He crawled to his spot beneath the piano, sat cross-legged, and picked up his Nintendo Switch. As it loaded, he continued to recite. "*Captain America: The First Avenger*, July 22, 2011. *The Avengers*, May 4, 2012. *Iron Man 3*, May 3, 2013."

I relaxed, proud of my brother. He used to be so much harder to deal with, but his new teachers here in Riverbend were helping him learn to manage his own behavior. They believed he could learn independence to be able to one day care for himself and live and work in society. I was all for that. I loved my brother, but I did *not* want to babysit him for the rest of my life.

I picked up my phone and thumbed my way back to Instagram. Zoe had posted a picture of herself on the balcony of her apartment, Bible in lap, Cookie Monster coffee mug in hand. I'd have to make her a Cookie Monster cupcake sometime. The thought came to me that I might have turned off my notifications on Snapchat, so I went to check. No notifications popped up, which made me sure there must be something wrong. But when I got to the settings, I was let down again. They were on. I just hadn't received any Snaps.

Whhhyyy? Where was everyone?

The question inspired me. I found a picture of an adorable, frowning puppy and snapped to all of my followers, "Where is everyone?" Inspired by my misery and hoping to draw some pity comments at the very least, I crafted a similar post for my Instagram stories.

There. Maybe now someone would connect.

Cupcake Wars ended, and I made myself grab my plate and get off the couch. I abhorred cleaning, but I grabbed Sebastian's plate and carried both plates to the sink—actually rinsed them off and put them in the dishwasher. I stood there, annoyed that I was even thinking about washing the batter bowl.

"*We love you, Miss Hannigan!*"

Panic spiraled through me as my custom text message alert

blasted from my phone, along with a small thrill of hope. I desperately wanted to hear from just about anyone, but I did not want to send Sebastian into ambulance mode again. As I ran to the living room, I practically tripped over my own feet. I slid across the hardwood floor in my monkey slippers, snatched up the phone, and swiped just as Sebastian said, "Text message, Isabella Valadez!"

"Thank you," I said.

I silenced my phone, thankful my text alert hadn't been loud enough to throw him. My older brother, Leo, had loaded a bunch of Broadway musical ringtones onto my phone last year for my birthday. Best present ever. *Annie* was one of my favorite movies, and the "*We love you, Miss Hannigan!*" line was short enough to make a good text alert. I liked my ringtone better—it was a couple of lines from "I Feel Pretty" from *West Side Story*—but no one ever called me. Everyone texted. So I heard the *Annie* line most often.

I checked my messages. Seeing *Mamá* at the top of the text was a total letdown.

> Mamá: Need to stay late. Can you start dinner?

These days my mamá always worked late, but I never shied away from an opportunity to cook. I texted back: Sure ☺

> Mamá: Was going to make mole. There's some chicken in the freezer. If you take it out, it should thaw in time. You can use the instant pot too.
> Me: I'm on it. ☺☺
> Mamá: Thanks, Mija. Sebastian ok?
> Me: He's playing video games
> Mamá: Ok. Hasta luego.
> Me: Love u
> Mamá: Love you too.

Authentic mole took about two hours from start to finish, but the Instant Pot could make a cheater mole that still tasted great.

Abuelita Ortiz would never approve of such methods, but she didn't have to eat it.

I set my phone alarm for 3:30 to remind me when to get started, then went to the kitchen to do the prep work. I found the chicken in the freezer and pulled it out. I washed my hands and put the chicken in a bowl to thaw in the fridge. Then I grabbed the mole paste from the cupboard and started the sauce. Mole paste on its own never tastes quite right, so I put the paste in the blender and then added half a chopped onion, chunks of dark chocolate, a garlic clove, tomato puree, sesame seeds, raisins, salted peanuts, and a couple of cans of chicken stock. I pureed this until it was smooth and then set it in the fridge too. Later, I'd put the chicken in the Instant Pot, pour on the mole sauce, and set the pot cooking.

That done, I went back to my spot on the couch and started another episode of *Cupcake Wars*. The show had barely begun when Sebastian started screeching.

I ran to the piano and knelt so I could see him. He had his hands over his ears and was rocking back and forth like a bobble-head, his Switch on his lap.

"What's wrong, bud?" I asked, grabbing the Switch.

"Lost!" Sebastian yelled.

The screen was black. I pressed the power button and it started up. "Did it crash?"

"Lost, lost!"

It annoyed Sebastian how the auto save function in *Minecraft* froze his game while he was building, and he had a bad habit of turning it off. Every once in a while the game crashed, and Sebastian would lose days of work. He was building the Avengers tower, and he'd been at it since before Thanksgiving.

Sebastian rolled onto his knees and shoved me.

"¡Ay!" I said, righting myself.

He crawled past and ran toward the stairs.

I set the Switch back on its charger, then climbed out from under the piano. I grabbed the Wings of Fire book and headed upstairs. I found Bash in his room, under the blankets on his bed, rocking and moaning. From the weird shape of his head under the blankets, I could tell he was in elbow-face mode. He thankfully hadn't started destroying the place. Wailing and kicking his book like he had this morning were mild reactions compared to a full-blown episode. It had been a while since we'd seen the kind of destructive behavior from him when he broke things and injured others.

"Tell me about Marvel," I said.

The groaning switched to a growl.

I decided to give it a try, though I was always wrong on purpose since he couldn't stand it and had to correct me. "Let's see . . . *Iron Man*, May 20, 2010."

"No!"

I fought back a smile and went on. "*The Incredible Hulk*, June 3, 1992, I think?"

"Wrong, Isabella Valadez. Wrong, wrong, wrong."

"Then came *Guardians of the Galaxy*, right? But I can't remember the date."

Sebastian started to speak in a rush. "*Iron Man*, May 2, 2008. *The Incredible Hulk*, June 13, 2008. *Iron Man 2*, May 7, 2010 . . ."

As he went on, I stayed put, watching and waiting. That he was still under the covers meant he wasn't pushing or biting me, which was a major pro. I still had a scar on my hand from an episode he'd had three years ago.

". . . *Thor*, May 6, 2011. *Captain America: The First Avenger*, July 22, 2011 . . ." When he was done reciting them all, he pulled the blanket off his head, revealing tousled hair and red eyes. He was grinning, though, so I figured we'd made it through. Again.

"You did it," I said. "Bash, you're so smart."

He grinned. "I did it, Isabella Valadez. I am so smart."

I held up his book and smiled. "Wings of Fire?"

"Okay, yes. Wings of Fire." He snatched the book and opened it. I waited another ten seconds and then slipped from his room and back downstairs, relieved I'd gotten off easy twice today.

Chapter 2

THAT NIGHT we were sitting around the table—everyone but Mamá, who was still at work. Clarissa, my older sister, whom everyone called Claire, was sitting beside me. Sebastian was at the end of the table, opposite Papi.

Sebastian and Claire were built like Papi, all slender and small—small eyes and mouths and hands. Leo and I resembled Mamá. We three had meat on our bones and then some. We also had big eyes and bigger smiles, but our hair was the biggest of all, curly and lots of it. Papi and Claire had straight hair—Papi's short and neat, Claire's shoulder length with bangs. Sebastian had curly hair, but Papi kept it cut short so it never got too wild.

"When will Mamá be home?" Claire asked.

"Sometime after eight," Papi said.

"Mamá is very busy," Sebastian said.

"That's right, *mi hijo*. Your mamá works hard helping people at the clinic."

Claire slumped in her chair. "I wanted to ask you both something important."

Papi met her gaze. "Ask us what?"

"Well, you know Kick-Off is this coming Saturday, right?"

"Where they announce the robot challenge," Papi said.

"I can go?" Sebastian asked. "I can go, too, right?"

I watched Claire, eager for her answer. The Kick-Off was a potluck breakfast for the robotics students and their parents. Even though Claire ditched me almost every day during winter break for her robotics friends, and even as boring as it sounded, I didn't care—I was dying to go anywhere.

"Only if Mamá or Papi come too," Claire told Sebastian.

"Or me," I said, because I was practically Sebastian's legal guardian these days. But most importantly, Zac Lloyd would be there. Perhaps he would see me, and we could have a moment. He'd forget all about that Ensley girl and only have eyes for me.

"That's what I wanted to talk to you about." Claire bit her bottom lip. She looked nervous. *My sister. Nervous.* Which was weird since she normally marched around like a drill sergeant. "Coach needs a place for the team to gather after Kick-Off so we can brainstorm robot conceptualizations and create a strategy for the season. It's usually at his place, but he lives up Knight Ridge and the roads are icy, so he asked if anyone else might be able to host this year. I said maybe we could."

A tingle ran up my arms. *Claire wants to invite the robotics team to our house. To invite Zac Lloyd.*

Papi frowned. "This is Saturday?"

"In two days, yes."

"How many people are we talking about?"

"Twenty-three," Claire said, wincing.

My stomach zinged again. *Zac in my house. Zac Lloyd.*

"What time?"

"From about twelve-thirty until probably five?" More wincing from Claire.

"So we don't have to feed them. Just let them take over the living room?"

"Well . . . Mr. Lucas said he'd donate sandwich stuff. We only need a volunteer to put everything together." She looked at me. "Maybe Izzy would like to—"

"Yes," I said eagerly. "I could make cupcakes." *A cupcake for Zac!*

Claire grinned. "I thought you'd say that."

Papi seemed to be thinking it over. "Do I have to supervise? I'll be home, but I had planned to work on the car." Papi had been restoring a 1965 Ford Mustang, bit by bit on the weekends for the past three years. It started as a project with him and Leo, but with Leo off to college, Papi was on his own now.

"Mr. Lucas will be here," Claire said. "Mrs. Mosely too. And I'll clean up any messes."

"I should hope so," Papi said.

"So? Can they come?" Claire gazed at Papi like a hungry kitten.

Papi pondered the question. Mr. Lucas not only went to our church, but he was also a history teacher at Northside High and the head coach of Claire's robotics team. Papi loved him. Surely he'd say yes. He finally shrugged. "I don't see why not."

I clamped down on my squeal. Didn't want to appear eager. Arouse suspicion.

"Okay, great." Claire was smiling now but still seemed uncertain. "What about Sebastian?"

Papi's expression pinched, and we all glanced at Sebastian, who had finished his mole and was reading the Wings of Fire book that lay open beside his plate.

"Nana has been wanting to have him over so he can ride his new bike on the trails behind her house," Papi said. "I'll see if he can spend the afternoon with her and Tata."

Claire squealed. "Thank you, Papi! You don't think Mamá will mind?"

"She's working Saturday, so no, I don't think she'll mind."

Claire was visibly giddy. I hadn't seen her so happy since the day she found out she'd made the robotics team when we first moved here. Suddenly, I, too, had something besides school to look forward to. *Zac Lloyd was coming to my house! Would be sitting in my living room. Would be eating the food I served. Might even speak to me.*

I smiled. Now I was giddy too.

———m———

After dinner, I texted Tessa my news.

> Me: Guess what? Claire's robotics team is coming to our house for a planning meeting this Saturday. She asked me to play hostess. Get the food ready and everything. Make cupcakes. Entertain you know who.

When I'd seen Zac for the first time at church, I'd been with Tessa, who grew up here and knew everyone. She said Zac was new to Riverbend, like me. She asked her boyfriend, Alex, for help, and Alex had reported back that he thought Zac liked Ensley. And I'm pretty sure I saw Zac and Ensley holding hands in the cafeteria in early December.

So, yes. Zac probably had a girlfriend, though I'd only seen them together that one time. And, no, I didn't know him. I'd never even spoken to him. Just drooled regularly from afar and had stumbled into the path of two Dazzles. But that was going to change. Zac and I were going to have a conversation. Which would lead to him falling madly in love with me.

It was going to be perfect.

An hour later, Tessa replied to my text with one measly sentence.

Tessa: **Be careful, Iz. He's taken.**

Ugh. I loved Tessa, but she could be so annoying sometimes. Always acting like everyone's mother. Total glass-half-empty.

Me: **Always!** ☺

———ᵚᵚᵚ———

Saturday finally arrived. Claire left before I was out of bed. Kick-Off for FIRST Robotics was an international event. It started somewhere on the East Coast and was broadcast live all over the world, so Claire's team had to be at the school early to set up for the potluck breakfast.

Papi and Sebastian went to the potluck, but since I was the designated lunch hostess, I had much to prepare. Last night Mr. Lucas had brought over platters of meat and cheese he'd ordered from Costco. He'd also brought a tub of potato salad and two bags of chips. I would set out all that later, but right now, it was cupcake time. I was slowly becoming known at Northside High for my cupcake decorating.

Today, I decided to keep things simple-*ish*. While I was at it, I got out my tripod and recorded a video for my Instagram stories. I'd been neglecting my followers and couldn't afford to waste such a perfect opportunity.

I made four dozen cupcakes, half chocolate, the other half lemon. While the cupcakes were baking, I drew a stencil in the shape of a robot gear and cut it from a mylar stencil sheet leftover from a Halloween project I tried last fall. I used an X-Acto knife on a cutting mat to remove the inner holes and gear shapes from my stencil. It turned out super cute. Since our school colors were blue and gold, I made yellow frosting. I would pour blue sugar crystals through the stencil to make the gears.

Claire had said the theme for robotics this year was "Dragon Horde," so I also found a tutorial online for adorable piped buttercream dragons. They were a lot more challenging than the stencil, so I practiced on wax paper with plain frosting until I could nail the technique.

In the end, I decorated two dozen cupcakes with the robotics gear stencil and the other two dozen with buttercream dragons. I got out my cupcake stands—I had two—and arranged my dessert at the end of the counter. I also put out the plates, napkins, forks, and cups. It was still a little early to put out the sandwich trays, so I made a banner that said "Dragon Horde Team 1015" and hung it from the front of the kitchen counter. That in place, I set out all the food. Everything was perfect. I was ready to party.

Granted, this wasn't a party, and it wasn't about me. Still, I couldn't wait for Claire and her robotics friends to show up. She had texted forty minutes ago to say they were done and heading over. I positioned myself at the front windows to wait. So far no one.

I glanced back at the spread I'd set out on the island. Frowned at the chip bowl that was sitting too close to the counter's edge. I walked to the kitchen and shifted it so it was even with the plate of sandwiches. Better.

I had just finished adding ice to the lemonade in the hammered-glass beverage dispenser when I heard voices outside. I ran to the front windows and peeked past the edge of the curtains. Claire's truck sat in the driveway—people pouring from it like clowns from a tiny car. My heart skipped a beat, and my eyes sought out Zac's perfectly coifed dark-brown hair.

Nada.

A blue car pulled in behind Claire's truck, and I waited to see who was inside. Still no Zac, and now the front door to the house was opening.

I ran back to the kitchen island to assume my role as hostess. Joy and concern warred inside me. People were coming. Soon they would be eating my cupcakes! *But what if Zac didn't show? What if he missed seeing my adorable creations?* I went to the cupcake stand and found the best one. I set it on a plate and hid it behind the toaster.

The sounds of a dozen voices in our house thrilled me, and I kind of wished I could join in the fun. They were talking robotics, though. It might as well have been Japanese for all I understood.

"It's a foul if the robot touches the upper mechanisms on the scale," some guy said.

"But not the bottom?" asked another.

"What defines the upper mechanism?" This from a girl I recognized but didn't know.

"The beam and the arms are all part of the upper mechanism," the first guy said. "The robot can't touch any of that. But it's okay if it touches the pans while it's releasing a cube."

"That's not so bad, then," said the second guy. "We just need to build an arm or elevator or something to lift the cube high enough to reach the pan."

"We could make a launcher," the girl said.

"No launchers!" like, three other people said at once.

See? Japanese.

The door opened again, bringing a gust of cold air inside as another five people entered and took off their shoes, adding them to the growing mound beside the door. My gaze jumped from one face to the next, increasingly disappointed each time I didn't see my hunky future boyfriend. I did recognize Michael Torres, Austin Yager, and Samar Bhat—all from my PE class. I did a quick head count. There were fourteen people here so far. There were probably at least two more carloads on the way. Zac would probably show up anytime.

But he didn't. Several more groups of people arrived, bringing with them the two robotics coaches and still no Zac.

I took in the crowd, intrigued by the faces present. Claire had been involved with robotics since we moved here last summer, but I'd paid little attention to who was on the team besides Claire's two besties, Natalie and Ryan—and Zac, of course. I recognized a bunch of people from the halls of Northside High School. Some I even knew by name. Luke and Kyle were in Claire's grade. For sophomores, there was Micah from Algebra I, Gavin from Biology, and the three boys from PE class. A lot of boys on the team, actually, but I counted seven girls, not including Mrs. Mosely. Claire kept her robotics roster stuck to the fridge with magnets, and I made a game of trying to match the names and faces I didn't know. Too often my gaze found Isaac Lloyd's name in the middle of the list, and I *might* have memorized his home address.

Claire wandered over. "You ready?"

"Yep," I said, heart heavy. I so desperately wanted to ask about Zac—*What if he's sick? I could make him soup!*—but I held my tongue. Claire had things to do, and this was not the time.

She discovered my cupcake stands at the end of the counter. "Izzy! Oh, my goodness! These are so cute." She was grinning big as she leaned in to admire my handiwork. It had been a while since I'd done anything to make my sister smile, and it felt great.

"You're amazing, Iz. Thanks for doing this. I'm going to say something and then send them over. Okay?"

"Okay." I smiled, wanting to appear happy but inside I was . . . so . . . disappointed. *Oh, Zac. Wherefore art thou,* mi amor?

"Hi, everyone!" Claire said, her voice near shouting.

The room quieted.

"Welcome to my house." This she said in a normal speaking voice. "My sister, Isabella, has set out lunch for us, and she made the most adorable cupcakes, too. Can we thank her for her hard work with a round of applause?"

Claire began clapping, and everyone joined in. Some of the kids darted close and gushed over my cupcakes. Highlight of the day so far. I beamed and did a little curtsy.

Claire dismissed everyone to get food, and the robotics team surged toward me. Everyone was really nice, and I received lots of compliments on my cupcakes, unsurprisingly. They *were* totes adorbs, after all. When Michael came through, I couldn't help talking to him in Spanish. His family was from Guatemala. There weren't many Hispanic students at Northside High, and Michael and I liked to practice our Spanish with each other.

"*¿Qué onda, Miguel?*" I asked.

"*No mucho,*" he said. "*¿Qué hay de nuevo?*"

"*Bueno, no mucho.*" I handed him a plate.

"*Gracias*, Isabella."

Once everyone had food, the group got right to work. They'd come to design a robot, and that's what they were going to do. I, on the other hand, after I refreshed the lemonade and salads, had nothing to do. I pulled out my phone and sent a text to my squad on our group thread.

Me: Kick-Off party going great.

I sent a couple of pics of the cupcakes and one of the robotics team all gathered in the living room.

Amelia texted back: Cupcakes look YUM!
Me: Thanks! ☺

That was that. At least someone had responded.

I turned my attention to the robotics meeting. Ryan was talking.

"Since you get the most points for pellets on the scale," he said, "that's where we should put our focus."

"But we shouldn't discount the horde," Claire said. "Those will add up."

"We need a way to pick up the pellets and lift them really high," Natalie said.

"Like putting them on a shelf?" Samar asked.

"We need an elevator." This from a boy I didn't know.

"Elevators are too expensive," Ryan said. "The pellets don't weigh much."

"I say we do something new this year," Claire said. "Something that will set us apart as risk-takers and innovators."

"Do you have an idea in mind?" Mr. Lucas asked.

"What if we built a stationary robot?" Claire said. "It would have arms and a rotational mechanism that allowed for a 360-degree turn radius so the arms could extend every direction to grab pellets. If we started in the center, we'd be in position to quickly store the pellets in the horde for extra points."

"Our allies could bring us pellets," Natalie said.

Ryan's forehead crinkled. "It actually could make sense not to move."

"Let's troubleshoot Claire's idea," Mr. Lucas said. "I've heard some compelling reasons for a stationary robot. Does anyone have some drawbacks?"

The door opened, breaking my attention from the robotics talk. And there he was, standing in my doorway, kicking off his slate-blue Vans.

Zac Lloyd.

Chapter
3

I STARTED TOWARD ZAC. Claire was getting up too, but I waved her to sit. "I'll show him the food," I said casually, like I wasn't completely desperate to be the one to greet the *chico guapo*.

She sank back to the floor, not missing a beat with her idea. "Three points per pellet in the horde, guys. Ten on the scale."

"Welcome," I said to Zac, sounding every bit the confident hostess, but inside it felt like I was floating and falling all at once. "I'm Izzy, Claire's sister."

I purposely left out the *little*.

Zac finished removing his shoes and glanced up. His eyes met mine, but then he looked me up and down in that way boys do sometimes. My stomach zinged at his scrutiny. "Nice pandas," he said, smirking at my leggings.

"Aren't they cute?" I twisted and turned, admiring them from my view. "You hungry? The food is over here." I didn't wait for an answer. I spun in a half circle and pranced toward the kitchen, because everyone knows teenage boys are always hungry. Also, because I had just struck several poses in front of Zac Lloyd and was feeling quite foolish.

As we crossed to the kitchen behind the congregated robotics team, I was very aware of the sound of Zac's stockinged footsteps behind me. *Was he still checking me out?* I hoped I didn't have powdered sugar all over my pants.

I slid around the end of the island and leaned on the opposite side of the counter, facing him. I kept my voice low so we wouldn't disrupt the meeting. "So there's lemonade, sandwich stuff, potato salad, chips, some fruit, and dessert. Go ahead and help yourself."

"Thanks."

Ahh. Even his voice was hunky.

He filled a cup with lemonade, set it on the counter, and then picked up a plate. He arranged two slices of white bread, but when he glanced up, his gaze locked on the cupcake stand. "There are dragons on the cupcakes!" He picked one up. "Have you seen these?"

"Yes, actually," I said, amused. "I made them."

Those hazel eyes of his widened. "You made these? How?"

I shrugged one shoulder. "Cake decorating is kind of a hobby of mine."

"That's incredible. I can really eat this?"

"Yep. Actually, I have the best one hidden." I retrieved my perfect dragon and handed it to him.

He examined it. "You're right. This one *is* perfect."

"It's yours. I saved it for you."

"For me?"

"Mm-hmm."

His eyes crinkled and his mouth twisted in the most adorable way. "Have we met?"

"You're Zac," I said. "You go to my church. Sometimes."

"Faith Community." He tipped his head back, as if relieved to have made a connection that had been bugging him. "That's why you look familiar."

I sucked in a stealthy gasp through my nose. *I looked familiar. To Zac Lloyd.* The refrain for "I Can Hear the Bells" from *Hairspray* rang through my mind. I smiled. Blinked. *Both were good, right? Boys liked girls who smiled and batted their eyes? How was it I didn't know how to flirt?*

I needed help! But my squad was MIA. I was on my own.

"I should probably stop talking to you so you can join the discussion." I motioned to the living room and knocked over his cup of lemonade. Light-yellow liquid flooded the counter. "Oh, stars! I'm so sorry." I spun around and pulled a half-dozen paper towels off the roll, then whipped back and shoved them onto the spill just as Zac did the same with a bunch of napkins he'd grabbed from beside the plates. Our fingers touched. I didn't move away. Neither did he.

I looked up, and his eyes were on mine. Melt me like butter—this boy had eyes like marbles, all sparkly and greenish brown. He grinned, and it was like he'd flipped a switch. Flynn Rider might have perfected the smolder, but he had nothing on Zac Lloyd's Dazzle.

Zac could Dazzle me anytime.

His cold, wet fingers slid over my hand, curled around the sides, and gently lifted. "I got this," he said, taking the soppy paper towels away with his other hand.

Both of Zac's hands on my hand at the same time. I seriously felt like I was having a heart attack.

He finally released me and set about mopping up the rest of the spill. "I'm not worried about missing anything," he whispered. "They never listen to me, anyway."

"Why not?"

"You have a trash can?"

I held out my hands, and he relinquished the soppy wad of

napkins and paper towels. I tossed them into the trash underneath the sink, then turned on the water and started to rinse my hands. Before I could finish, Zac came around the counter and joined me, our hands under the stream of hot water, his arm touching my arm. He was so tall and wore some kind of spicy cologne that tickled my nose and made my stomach perform the "Mexican Hat Dance." I picked up the hand soap and moved it to his side of the sink.

"Thanks," he said, taking a squirt.

I'd never washed my hands so thoroughly in my life.

All too soon our hands were clean, and Zac was back on his side of the counter. He was watching me though. I never thought I'd like having someone stare at me, but the intensity of Zac's gaze made me feel . . . I don't know, pretty? Irresistible, maybe? As my face slowly grew warmer, I dug for the right words—any words, actually—to finish our previous conversation. "Why don't they listen to you? The team?"

He shrugged and said, "I'm a programmer. My ideas come later. I don't really understand all that CAD stuff. I always want to build a launch cannon, and every year that's the wrong idea."

I laughed, recalling how I'd already heard the team reject launching mechanisms. "Why a launch cannon if you know it's wrong?"

Another grin, this one crooked and completely adorable. "I like making stuff fly." He picked up the dragon cupcake I'd given him and pretended to fly it in the air between us.

I laughed, and he joined me. *We* laughed. We. *Together.*

"So I can eat this? Really?"

"That's what it's for."

He frowned. Adorable expression number 147. "It's too cute to eat, though."

I had to agree. "He *is* pretty adorable."

Zac set the cupcake down on the counter between us. "I can

only do this on one condition." He reached behind him and pulled a cell phone from his back pocket. "I will immortalize the dragon by taking a picture and posting him all over social media."

My cupcake made viral by Zac Lloyd? Yes, please. "If you think that's necessary."

"Oh, it's necessary, baby."

While I recovered from him calling me "baby," he used his phone to snap a couple of pics of the cupcake. I couldn't help but notice he had the exact same phone and case as Amelia. It was slate gray with a little pocket on the back that could hold a driver's license or school ID. "My friend has that same phone case," I said. "Did you get it at that place in the mall?"

"Kiosk. At the bottom of the escalators," he said.

"Yeah." Our eyes met, and we stared at each other. This was chemistry. It had to be. I'd heard about this but had never experienced it until now. Our stare started to grow a wee bit awkward, but I wasn't going to be the first one to look away.

Zac finally broke our connection, glancing down as he picked up the cupcake. "You sure it's okay to eat him?"

"I'm sure."

"Okay, sorry about this, Pete." He started pulling one edge of the cupcake paper.

"Pete?"

"He looks like the dragon from that Disney movie."

"*Pete's Dragon*," I said. "I love that movie. But the dragon is named Elliott."

"That's right. I knew that. My dragon is Pete, though."

I chuckled. "If you say so."

"I do."

He said, "I do." Those were wedding words!

Zac peeled off the cupcake paper, set it on the counter, and opened his mouth. He did this slowly and watched me, eyebrows raised. "You're absolutely sure."

"Yes! Just eat him."

"All right." Now he turned the cupcake to face him. "Pete, buddy. This isn't my fault. She's making me do this."

I smirked.

He bit the cupcake in half, eating the head of the dragon. He chewed, frowned, said "Mmm," and licked his lips.

Embarrassed to be staring at him while he was eating, I glanced away and caught Claire watching us.

"Dragon never tasted so good," he said.

I smirked. "Eat a lot of dragon, do you?"

"Oh, all the time. Dragon bacon is the best."

"Dragon bacon?"

"The strips are as big as scarves. The kind you wear in winter. Huge." He motioned with his hands, and I couldn't help noticing how his arm and chest muscles shifted under his snug shirt.

"That's some big bacon," I said.

"You have no idea." He ate the second half of the cupcake in one bite.

"Aren't you going to eat lunch?" I asked.

He continued to chew, and only after his throat bobbed from swallowing did he say, "I start every meal with dessert."

"A sweet tooth, huh?"

"Well, I *am* sweet. At least that's what people tell me."

"What people?"

"Girls, mostly. I can't help it if the ladies love me."

I rolled my eyes as if I didn't believe him for a second, but inside I didn't doubt it at all. He couldn't help looking the way he did any more than I could help staring at his completely unfair hotness. Not that I was complaining about my front-row seat.

He picked up his phone and set about uploading his pictures of Pete the Cupcake to Snapchat.

"What's your Snapchat, Izzy?" he asked. "So I can tag you."

"MissIzzyValadez." Then I spelled *Valadez* because people

often forgot the second *a*, and I didn't want to risk Zac not finding my profile ASAP.

"*Ss* or *Zs* in Izzy?"

"I-z-z-y," I said, nervous to be exchanging info with Zac Lloyd, the hunkiest of all senior boys.

His thumb flew over his phone, and I was impressed with his speed. His addiction to social media must be worse than mine. In less time than I could have pulled up my own profile, Zac was done on Snapchat and already posting to Instagram. "What's your Instagram handle?"

"Same as Snapchat," I said.

"I got you," he said. "You'll follow me back, right?" He shot me a little pout.

"Sure," I said, like it didn't really matter. But it *so* did.

Zac Lloyd was following me on Snapchat *and* Instagram, and he wanted me to follow him back. I fought the urge to squeal.

"Mr. Lloyd." Mr. Lucas came up behind Zac and put a hand on his shoulder. Zac was almost a head taller than the history teacher. "How about you come join the group?"

"Yeah, sure," Zac said, pocketing his phone. "Just let me get my food." He picked up his plate—which still only had bread on it—and finished making his sandwich. He grabbed a handful of chips, skipped all the salads, and helped himself to two more cupcakes. "Later, Izzy," he said, flashing me one last Dazzle and a wink that made my insides dance again.

And . . . curtain.

I was so overcome with energy from flirting with Zac, I decided to back off, lest he think I liked him. I made a pact with myself not to even look in his direction again unless he came to talk to me first. I set about refilling the food bowls and platters and rearranging the cupcakes so the outside of the stand looked full. Then I ran up to my room to check my phone and see what Zac had posted.

Sure enough, he had tagged me on Instagram both on his

profile and in his stories with #toocutetoeat across the top of the picture. He'd also followed me.

I grabbed Fiesta, my tan-and-white stuffed cat, and hugged him. "He followed me! What do you think?"

I moved my thumb to follow Zac back but stopped myself. I didn't want to come off as too eager. I needed to play it cool. I decided to wait until later tonight to follow him, after he'd left. *I mean, I had a life, right?* I wasn't desperate or needy. I was a busy girl, helping my sister with her party. As hostess, I had things to do.

I opened Snapchat, and several notifications jumped out at me. All from Zac. He'd posted the cupcake pic and tagged me. He'd also sent me a friend request and a private snap of him eating a different cupcake. He must have taken that one since I'd come upstairs. Unfortunately, I'd blown it by looking at it because Snapchat would tell him it had been seen. I chose not to respond to anything. Yet. But I most certainly would later.

When I came back down, Claire met me in the kitchen.

"Want me to put away the meat trays?" I asked. "They've been out for over an hour now, and I think everyone is done eating."

"Fine," she said, grabbing my arm and dragging me toward the dining room.

"*¡Ay!*" I pulled free. We were out of sight of the living room, so I didn't mind giving her a death glare. "What's wrong with you?"

"Me?" she said, scowling. "I could ask you the same."

"What did *I* do?"

"Coach could hardly get the group to focus on the robot design because they were all too busy watching the *Izzy and Zac Show* in the kitchen."

My mouth fell open.

"Don't act all innocent," she said. "I know you better than that."

"You're *loca*!" I said.

"Look, I appreciate all you did to help today, I really do, but now I need you to make yourself scarce for the rest of the afternoon so we can get some work done."

"You're kicking me out?"

"Everyone is here to build a robot. We need to focus. Zac too."

"He said there was nothing for him to do until you guys decide what to build."

Claire rolled her eyes. "While that's completely untrue, we can't decide anything with you two distracting everyone."

I pouted. "I was just being nice."

"Sure, you were."

"You're a jerk, Claire." I pushed past her, ran back through the kitchen and up the stairs to my room, fighting back tears. I closed the door, then fell onto my bed, grabbed Fiesta, and pulled a pillow over my head.

I couldn't decide if Claire was right and I had thrown myself all over Zac or if my sister was overreacting. Mr. Lucas *had* come to pull Zac away from the kitchen, so maybe there was something to Claire's accusations. Maybe Zac and I *had been* distracting everyone. *Oh, I sincerely hope not because that would be so embarrassing!*

But everyone had been talking. It wasn't like I'd heard any huge moments of silence in the house since they'd come in. I also don't remember anyone but Claire looking at us—until Mr. Lucas had shown up.

I moved my pillow and sniffed, revived by the fresh air. I locked eyes with Captain Marvel. She wouldn't let some older sibling push her around. I hadn't done anything wrong. This was just Claire being bossy old Claire. Same as always.

Chapter

4

I was sitting on my bed, earbuds in, watching one of my favorite YouTubers decorate a cake when Claire texted me.

> Claire: We're leaving. I put the meat in the fridge. Mr. Lucas said we could keep it. You can come down and clean up now.

Oh, could I really? Her text made me so mad I deleted it without responding. I just wouldn't come down at all. Claire could clean up the mess herself when she got back. She'd promised Papi she would.

I glanced at the time on my phone. It was 5:34. Twenty-six more minutes before I would let myself go on social media and respond to Zac. I returned to my video and watched two more after it. Before I got the chance to go social with Zac, however, there was a knock on my door.

I hit the space bar, pausing my video. "Yeah?"

My bedroom door opened, and Papi walked in, Sebastian behind him. Both were eating cupcakes. It was funny how alike they were. They were even wearing the same outfits today: navy-blue robotics T-shirts, jeans, and sneakers.

"I'm assuming you made these?" Papi raised the cupcake toward me. It was a sugared gear one. I was pretty sure all the dragons were gone.

"Yep," I said.

"You're very creative."

Sebastian echoed our papi. "Very creative, Isabella Valadez."

Their praise made me smile. "I know."

Papi snorted. "A little humility goes a long way, Isabella."

"Yeah . . ." But I was riding a confidence high after having snagged the attention of a hunky senior boy today. And painfully forcing myself to wait before groveling at his feet.

"Any food left?" Papi asked.

"There should be sandwich stuff," I said. "Claire said she put the meat and cheese tray in the fridge. Mr. Lucas said we could keep it."

"My thanks to Mr. Lucas. Where's Claire?"

"She left with everyone else."

"She say where she was going?"

"Nope. Just took off." And no way was I going to cover for her after her snotty attitude.

"I remember a time when my children asked for permission before going anywhere."

"I guess Claire thinks she can do what she wants."

Papi gave me a look. "Claire isn't the only child in this house who does what she wants."

I shrugged. "With you and Mamá working all the time, we *niños* have to fend for ourselves."

Papi paused, considering. "I suppose that's the sad truth." He turned his attention to Sebastian. "What do you say we get some dinner to go with this dessert?"

"Okay, yes. Let's get some dinner, Dañel Valadez."

Papi shot me a funny expression. About two years ago, Sebastian started calling people by their full names, and no matter how hard Mamá and Papi had tried, they could *not* get Sebastian to make an exception for our parents or our grandparents.

"Enjoy your dinner, Sebastian Valadez," I said.

My brother smiled. "Thank you, Isabella Valadez."

Papi steered Sebastian out of the room, but before he closed the door, he poked his head back in. "Don't encourage him."

"*¿Qué?*" I said, faking an innocent expression. It was good acting practice, after all.

When Papi finally shut my bedroom door, I checked the time on my phone: 6:04.

Zac time!

I hopped on Instagram first. Pretty much everyone I knew lived on Snapchat, but I preferred Instagram with its coordinated picture posts and my larger number of followers. I tortured myself a little longer by ignoring the notification that said I had one new follower and set about posting the pic I'd taken this morning of the cupcakes. I took my foodie pics on our kitchen counter, which was white quartz. I liked its clean look as a background to my colorful cuisine. My aesthetic was top notch, and the dragon cupcakes made an adorable addition to my feed. I copied and pasted the caption I'd written in my Notes app during the robotics meeting and shared the post.

Enough stalling. I clicked on my notifications and saw @zackylloyd had followed me. I followed him back and then moseyed over to his account. His profile picture was of the back of his head—dark hair perfect. I wondered if that hair was soft. His bio said only: *"You know who I am."* I rolled my eyes. *Confident much?* He was following fourteen others who followed me, Claire and Cody among the names. He had 307 followers and was following 1,526. That surprised me. I had 2,674 followers and was only following 225 people. Weird how many he was following, though unsurprising he had so few considering the lameness of his posts.

With the exception of my adorable cupcake, the pictures in his feed were unimpressive. Besides the football meme that still eluded me, he had a picture of his Vans-clad feet, a raccoon, and several pictures of his friends making faces—bugged-eyed, tongues hanging out. There was also an overabundance of memes: one about farting, one about free pizza, and a picture of a red sports car that he captioned, *"You will be mine. Oh, yes. You will be mine."*

Yep. His was undoubtedly a boy's account.

The realization that my account was more popular than his gave me a little rush of pride, which was dumb considering my followers were mostly foodies who liked the pics I posted. Plus, I'd been working hard this past year on posting consistently and making sure everything matched my aesthetic. I'd gotten pretty good at using the right hashtags to find other people with accounts like mine, so I knew that had made a difference too.

I twisted my lips, thinking through what I was going to write. Then I clicked on his picture of my cupcake in his feed and added the comment: *"R.I.P. Pete."*

I clicked on his stories, where he'd also shared the cupcake pic, and left a similar comment. Then I jumped on Snapchat and answered his messages there. Added him as a friend. Done and done.

I fell back on my bed, stared at the popcorn ceiling, and recounted the day, reliving the spilled lemonade moment and how it felt when he had held my hand.

Would he even speak to me again? I hoped he wouldn't pretend we'd never met. I hated it when guys did that. Maybe I should be the brave one and say "*Hola*" when I saw him. I shot down that idea as quickly as it came. Conversation at school seemed like a line he'd have to cross first. I wasn't that brave.

Okay, so that wasn't exactly true. I was brave. I just wasn't stupid. Talking to Zac at school in front of his friends would put him on the spot, which sometimes made boys panic and play dumb just to save face. I might be completely humiliated. I embarrassed myself enough on a daily basis just by being me. I didn't need any help.

"*We love you, Miss Hannigan!*"

I checked my phone.

A text from an unknown number: this izzy?

I frowned. I knew better than to answer texts from people I didn't know, but the timing felt too coincidental. My heart began to hammer inside my chest. *Could it be Zac?*

I answered: who is this?

Please be Zac. Please be Zac. Please, oh, please, oh, please!

Mystery number: zac lloyd

Oh. My. Stars. I fell back against my pillows and stuffed animals and screamed, "Ahhhh!" while stomping one foot against my mattress.

My phone buzzed again. I quickly sobered and sat up to read the text.

Zac: we tlked tday at ur house

Like I could forget The Dazzle. The hair! How cute that he thought forgetting him was even possible. I needed to play this cool.

Play-it-cool me: Oh, hi. How'd you get my number?

Zac: got it frm natalie taylor

My cheeks burned. Oh my stars. It really was Zac. And he'd tracked down my number!

> Play-it-cool me: If you wanted my number, why didn't you ask?
> Zac: u were bzy

What now? What now? I picked up Fiesta and looked him in the eye, nose to nose. "What should I say?" I got the impression Fiesta told me I should keep playing it cool.

> Play-it-cool me: Did you forget something? At my house?
> Zac: didn't forget nutin just wnted to tlk

To meeeee?!? He wanted to talk to me! I could *not* stop smiling.

> Play-it-cool me: What about?
> Zac: food
> Me: Okay . . .
> Zac: what else u can cook or bake or whevr
> Me: I can cook anything.
> Zac: evn sushi?
> Me: I never tried to make sushi but I could if I wanted to.
> Zac: how?
> Me: Look up instructions online.
> Zac: ur pretty izzy
> Zac: just wnted to tell u so

My stomach fluttered. *Oh my. Oh my.* I threw myself onto my back and screamed at the ceiling. Zac Lloyd said I was pretty. *Best. Day. Ever.*

> Play-it-cool me: Thank you?
> Zac: srry. that was prolly weird huh?

> Me: A little. Do people go around telling you you're handsome?
> Zac: smetimes

I didn't doubt it one bit.

> Zac: what r u doing rght now?

I don't know why, but I lied.

> Me: Cleaning up the kitchen.
> Zac: srry we left a mess
> Me: It's no big deal. It's part of the gig and I volunteered to help.
> Zac: which was very nice of u
> Me: Thanks. What are you doing?
> Zac: lying in bed thnkng bout u

My eyes popped. Okay, so that was a lot intense. It kind of gave me a weird vibe, so I decided not to respond right away.

I really wanted to respond.

I grabbed Fiesta and hugged him. "Help me! I have no self-control."

My phone buzzed.

> Zac: actually i gotta go.
> Zac: c u later

Ah. Well, that settled that. I stared at the screen, wondering if he was really done talking. Two full minutes passed by, so it appeared he was.

> Me: Okay bye.

Then I brought up the group text between me, Tessa, Shay, and Amelia.

Me: You will NOT BELIEVE what happened to me today.

Me: Claire asked me to help feed the robotics team while they designed the robot at our house. And guess who spent forever talking to me in the kitchen?

Me: Zac Lloyd that's who.

Me: And guess who asked Natalie for my cell phone number and texted me just now?

Me: Zac Lloyd that's who! Ahhh!!!

Then I uploaded a gif of Elmo doing a wild and crazy dance.

And would you believe it? Within ten minutes all three of my friends—friends who'd been too busy to text me all week—they responded.

Tessa: ☺

Shay: Which boy is this?

Amelia: Did he forget something at your place?

Tears prickled my eyes. I couldn't believe it. None of my squad had found any time to text me back the past few days—Tessa's motherly watchdog comment and Amelia's cupcake affirmation excepted—but here they all came with their negativity about the one person who'd been nice to me all winter break.

A minute later, another text came through.

Amelia: Isn't he dating Ensley?

Okay, maybe. I kind of thought she was his girlfriend. I flipped over to Instagram and looked up Ensley Barnette. When I couldn't find her, I went to Mika Lawrence's profile. Mika was a junior, super popular, and in concert choir with me. She'd been nice to me at the beginning of the year and friended me and everything. Through the list of people Mika was following, I was able to find @barnette.ensley.cheer. Her profile pic was of five girls in cheerleading uniforms. Her bio said: "Junior. Cheer is life. ❤ @zackylloyd ❤"

Well, rats.

My phone buzzed again.

> Amelia: What about Cody the Cutie?

I growled and looked to Fiesta. "Can you believe this?"

Fiesta couldn't.

I didn't bother to answer. In fact, I deleted the text thread altogether. I didn't want to see their names on my phone at the moment.

But Amelia's comment did make me start thinking about Cody Nichols. I pictured him and Zac side by side and wasn't sure I liked the obvious conclusions that jumped out at me. Cody was light and sun. Zac was night and stars. Cody was boundaries and friendship. Zac was mischief and flirtation. If Cody was Captain America, who was Zac? Iron Man? I supposed it fit his interest in robotics.

I stared at the poster on my wall, feeling conflicted. I was a Captain America girl. I'd never been an Iron Man girl. But what do you do when the Captain isn't interested but Iron Man maybe is? And what if Iron Man *was* interested but had a girlfriend?

I didn't know.

That night, I lay in bed, listening to "Without Love" from *Hairspray* from my musicals playlist, feeling pathetic and sad. I was tired of living without love. *How long do I have to wait for a boy to notice me? To like me back?*

"*We love you, Miss Hannigan!*"

The words interrupted my song and about gave me a heart attack. I grabbed my phone and paused the music. Speaking of Iron Man . . .

Zac: whatcha doin?

After I had recovered from the shock of getting texted at—I glanced at the time—11:38, I texted back: Listening to music.

Zac: wht kind?

So I told him about my love of musical theater. About *Dear Evan Hansen* and *Hairspray* and *Newsies* and *Annie* and all my other favorites. He told me he liked to play video games. My video game knowledge started with Mario and ended with *Minecraft*. Zac liked something called *The Elder Scrolls* and shooter games and said we should play sometime. Uh. No. We somehow got onto the topic of cosplay, and Zac said if he ever went to a comic con, he'd dress up like the Joker. I said the Joker was creepy and he should dress up like Iron Man or Star-Lord from *Guardians of the Galaxy*. Zac said he would dress up like Star-Lord if I dressed up like Gamora. This conversation went on and on and filled me with a rush of electric energy that seemed incapable of running out. I wanted to ask him about Ensley, but it never seemed the right moment. Besides, I didn't want him to stop talking to me. *Was it bad to text a guy who had a girlfriend?* My squad would say yes. Claire would say yes. Captain Marvel would say yes. Yet I didn't stop. Instead, between texts, I googled the question to see if I could find an alternate opinion. Turns out, the internet is filled with a ton of nonexperts with a lot of negative ideas. I'm just saying.

I woke to the sound of "Good Morning" from *Singin' in the Rain* blaring in my ears. My alarm song. *Time for school?* That didn't seem right. My eyes stung. I shifted, couldn't move my arm, and found my cell phone's charging cord tangled around my wrist. I blinked a few times, momentarily confused as I worked to free myself from the cord. *What day is it? Why is my phone going off? It's still winter break, isn't it?*

Refreshing my phone revealed a text thread between me and Zac Lloyd. The last few messages were a clue as to why I couldn't remember what was happening.

> Zac: what do u thnk?
> Zac: helloo?
> Zac: izzy?
> Zac: where you go girl?
> Zac: hellloooo???

My stars. I'd fallen asleep texting Zac Lloyd. I dropped my phone and pressed my hands to my cheeks. *How embarrassing!* I couldn't believe I'd drifted off on him like that. I hope he didn't think I thought he was boring.

Okay, so that wasn't exactly fair. Considering Zac's last text to me had come at 2:37 this morning, it was totally reasonable that I'd conked out. I'd had a long day with all the baking and hosting and texting a hot guy who had a girlfriend.

I picked up Fiesta. "What do I do? I don't want to be the other woman!"

"Then don't be," I imagined Fiesta saying as he looked at me sternly. I was too ashamed to look to Captain Marvel, knowing what she would say about such a thing.

I suddenly remembered what day it was and why my alarm had gone off. It was Sunday. I had church today, and on Sundays I set my alarm early to beat Claire to the shower, so I'd also have time to make pancakes. I jumped out of bed, grabbed my phone and my bathrobe, and stumbled out of my room.

Chapter

5

FINDING SOMEONE to sit with in church usually wasn't a problem. The sanctuary had a section the teens had taken over, so I hardly ever sat with my parents and grandparents, and they didn't mind as long as 1) I wasn't sitting in the balcony, 2) I was paying attention, and 3) I took good notes on the sermon. Key word: *good*. Doodles didn't count as notes.

Tessa wasn't back from her ski trip. Two days ago, her absence would have filled me with angst, but today I was secretly thankful. I wasn't ready for the Zac lecture she'd give me. I needed more time to figure this out. Or work up the courage to ask Zac about Ensley.

There was no sign of Lauren, another sophomore from Northside High that Tessa and I often hung out with. I saw Alex, Tessa's boyfriend, but he was sitting with a bunch of guys, and I wasn't brave enough to sit with them without Tessa.

Still, I was determined not to sit with my family today, mostly because Claire was still giving me death glares like I'd broken some kind of sisterly code when I'd slaved away to host her robotics party then dared talk to one of her guests. The nerve of me, right? Well, I didn't dare tell her Zac had asked Natalie for my number. I was pretty sure she'd freak if she knew he'd been texting me.

I ended up sitting with Becky and Morgan. A lot of sophomores would never hang out with middle schoolers, but I liked people of all ages, especially those who liked little kids. The music started, and the worship team began to sing. I admired Zoe's box braids and fashion sense as she crooned into the microphone. I could never pull off that gorgeous orange dress like she could. Those black leather ankle boots, either.

Pastor Joe's sermon was about being content with your life. I liked it because I was a happy person. I'd never been overly jealous of anyone. Today, however, I kept thinking of Ensley Barnette and how I wished she'd up and move to Texas. Such negative thoughts were unlike me, so I worked hard to get all of pastor's advice in my notes.

Pastor Joe wasn't really talking about jealousy, though. He gave five tips for contentment in the new year. I filled in the blanks and drew pictures of cupcakes and kittens in the margins of my bulletin, which only brought up another area of my life in which I wasn't content. Pets. As I started drawing kitten number five, I told myself I needed to be happy to be around the animals of my friends—Shay's dog and cat and Amelia's dog.

After church, we went to lunch at the Peachtree with Nana and Tata Valadez. The Peachtree was kind of an everything restaurant that had excellent burgers, decent Mexican food, and a variety of homemade pies I was known to drool over. I was in the middle of eating my bacon cheeseburger when my nana asked Sebastian about his big day tomorrow. When Sebastian didn't answer, Nana turned her attention on me.

"Isabella, are you ready to help Sebastian with his new"—Nana stumbled, looking for the right word—"privilege?"

As if I had a choice in the matter. "Yes, Nana," I said.

"What?" Tata asked. He was hard of hearing and, despite Nana's insistence, refused to get hearing aids.

"Sebastian is going to ride his bike to and from school from now on," Nana told Tata.

"What's that got to do with Izzy?" Tata asked. "She doesn't go to the middle school."

"Tell Tata the plan," Mamá said to me.

"I'm going to be waiting at home after school for Sebastian," I said. "To make sure he gets there safe."

"Why wouldn't he?" Tata asked. "It's only a few blocks."

"I will get there safe, Lorenzo Valadez," Sebastian said.

Mamá ignored Tata and Sebastian and kept on me. "That doesn't mean in the kitchen making cupcakes or filming videos. That doesn't mean on the computer uploading videos or watching YouTube." On the table beside her plate, her phone began to buzz. She peeked at the screen and sighed. "That means in the living room, curtains opened, where you can see the front door. Excuse me, I have to take this." She picked up the phone and left the table. "Hello, Sean, what's up?"

Stars, she's intense. What I wanted to say was, "Am I allowed to go to the bathroom?" I took another bite of my cheeseburger.

"Claire won't be sticking around," Papi added. "You'll be on your own."

Claire's shift at Pizza Brothers started at 3:30. From there she went to robotics until 9:00. Her full life and my lack of one was the reason I'd been chosen as Sebastian's caregiver. "We'll be fine. It's not a big deal."

"It's a big deal for Sebastian," Mamá said as she returned to the table.

"Is everything all right, Josefina?" Nana asked.

"*Sí,* just some conflicts at the clinic."

"Mamá," I said, not willing to end this without getting to say my piece. "It was no big deal in Williamsport for Bash to ride his bike to Papi's florist shop after school. What's the big deal now?"

Mamá took a bite of her salad, chewed, and waited until she swallowed to answer me. "Sebastian doesn't know our town yet," she finally said. "I don't know what he'd do if he got lost."

"He'd ask someone for help," I said. "He's capable of that."

Papi chimed in. "He is capable, Izzy, but we need to make sure the move hasn't thrown him before we cut him loose to ride home to an empty house."

I wondered what Bash thought of everyone talking about him like he wasn't here.

"How will you know when he gets to school in the mornings?" Nana asked.

"Mr. Jamison will text me as soon as Sebastian arrives," Papi said. "But we'd have no way of knowing when he got home without Izzy helping out."

Papi was always saying things like that, as if I'd valiantly volunteered to "help out." I think it was his way of acknowledging this situation wasn't fair.

"No friends over either," Mamá said as though continuing from where she left off.

I fought the urge to roll my eyes. Mamá didn't have Papi's way of framing my new responsibility as a help to the family. In our culture, family came first. A daughter did what she was told. *Fair* didn't even register.

"It's not like any of my friends would come over anyway," I said. "Everyone is too busy having a life."

"Izzy," Papi said. "You have a wonderful life."

I liked my life just fine, but I wouldn't use the word *wonderful* to describe it. I mean, I liked two guys, one who had friend-zoned me and the other who maybe had a girlfriend. When you factored in my indentured servitude as my brother's keeper and the fact that my sister and friends had no time for me in their lives except to boss me around, my life was barely mine. *When would I get to make my own choices?* It might be time to start looking into colleges on the West Coast or in Zimbabwe.

—◆◆◆—

Sunday afternoon I was in my room watching a YouTube cake decorating video when I got a text from Zac.

> Zac: u home?

The thrill that ran through me was quickly followed by a heavy dose of shame. I shouldn't be getting all tingly over some guy who was taken. Frankly, he really shouldn't be texting me, either.

Still, I wrote back: Yes.

> Zac: come downstairs
> Me: ???
> Zac: im at ur house

I stared at the phone, shocked. *Had Zac come to visit me?* I flew to my dresser to check my reflection, gave my hair a fluff and combed it out with my fingers.

My phone buzzed again.

> Zac: izzy come down plz?

I ignored the nagging thoughts about Ensley as I made my way down the stairs. The smell of microwave popcorn and the sound of voices drifted up to me. Then Claire's voice, above the others.

"That will make the frame too heavy," she said.

Ah. The robotics team had returned, which meant Papi had taken Sebastian somewhere.

I paused. Knowing why Zac was here changed things. First, it meant he wasn't here to see me and therefore wasn't cheating on his girlfriend. He was likely bored. Still, Claire wouldn't want me around. She'd made that clear yesterday. But this was my house too, and I wasn't about to let Claire tell me where I could and couldn't go in my own house.

I peeked into the living room to get an idea of who was there. I counted seven people, all students. Claire was on her knees in the middle of the floor, her back to me and the couch. Natalie knelt on her left, Ryan on her right. They were leaning over a huge sheet of butcher paper, pencils in hand. Across from them, Luke sat cross-legged, inspecting the drawing. Noah and Kyle stood behind Luke, inserting their opinions. Zac sat alone on the couch, his feet kicked up on one of the reclining sections, a bag of microwave popcorn in his lap.

I made my move, crept toward the circle of furniture, and leaned on the back of the couch. "Hi," I whispered, hoping Claire wouldn't hear.

Zac twisted around, and his face lit up. He offered the bag over his shoulder. "Popcorn?"

I reached in and took a few pieces. Greasy, orange non-butter from the edge of the bag streaked the back of my hand. I ate a piece of popcorn and nodded toward the others. "What are they doing?"

"Trying to finalize the design."

"Shouldn't you be helping?"

"They don't need me."

"Then why did you come?"

"I wanted to see my favorite chef."

Oh-kay . . . Forgetting the fact that I was a baker, not a chef, his words had me melting like the greasy, orange non-butter. Zac's eyes seemed electric somehow, like they could see into my soul. I had to look away to keep from drooling. As I watched Claire and her friends, from the corner of my eye I could see Zac looking at me. My cheeks burned.

"Want to play Uno?" I asked, still keeping my voice low.

"What's Uno?"

"It's a card game. Don't tell me you don't know how to play Uno?"

"Okay, I won't." He grinned.

"It's almost the same as Crazy Eights," I said.

"I have never played a card game in my life," he said.

"Oh, my stars, Zac. That's terrible! Okay, I'm going to teach you. Come on."

I tiptoed back toward the stairs and into the den, which was out of sight of the living room. Zac followed. I grabbed Uno off the game shelf.

"What's with the doughnut pants?" he asked as I sat down at the card table.

I glanced at my leggings. They were black, printed with bright-colored glazed cartoon doughnuts, many with sprinkles.

I shrugged. "They make me smile."

He waved a hand at my black knit T-shirt dress and claimed the seat on my left, rather than sitting across from me. "Why are you wearing leggings when you have a dress on?" he said. "You could go without and leave your legs bare." He reached out and rubbed the back of his knuckles over my thigh. Electricity sizzled all through my body.

"I like leggings," I managed to say without purring like a cat. "Not only are they incredibly comfortable, but they also come in so many fun patterns, it's really quite amazing."

"Amaze me," he said. "What other kinds do you have?"

"Oh, my stars, so many. You saw the pandas yesterday. I also have kittens, unicorns, hearts, paw prints, sharks, camo—a few colors of camo, actually. Blue camo and pink camo and regular camo. I also have a ton of solid colors. I have some Christmas ones, too, though I put those away until next year."

"They're kind of wild, don't you think?"

"That's why I like them." *That and they allowed me to get away without shaving my legs regularly.* "Some people think my leggings are tacky, but I don't care. I like who I am, and I won't change for anyone."

Zac was staring at me, and the corner of his mouth quirked up in a lazy smile. "That's awesome. So many girls are fixated on being just like everyone else, you know?"

"Exactly, and I think that's sad." Those hazel eyes were electrifying me again, so I dealt the cards and taught him to play Uno. When I won the second game, and Zac made a huge deal of shouting, "Unfair use of Draw-Four cards!" Claire stepped into the archway to the den, Natalie right behind her. The glare she gave me sent a different kind of electricity through me, like she was the Wasp and she'd just used her powers to sting me. I pretended not to know she'd seen me, but she was not to be deterred from staking her claim on Zac's time and attention.

Chapter
6

"ZAC, WE COULD USE a programmer's opinion of our schematic," Claire said.

He arched one eyebrow. "Ask Natalie?" he said, which made Natalie laugh in this overly loud way and turn a super-confused expression on my sister.

"Natalie is already helping," Claire said. "We need a second opinion."

Natalie clicked her tongue. "Claire!"

"What?" Claire said. "A good team continues to evaluate and get feedback and improve," she said. "We need everyone's input. You're supposed to be helping us."

"She's right," Zac said, dropping his cards on the table. He got up, grabbed my hand, and tugged. "Izzy, come and look at this schematic with me."

I tried not to look at Claire as Zac dragged me past her and out of the den. He towed me all the way to the living room, stopping at the drawing on the floor, us standing side by side. The way his large hand felt wrapped around mine and the heat his touch sent throughout my body completely fogged my mind.

"Okay, we're here. Sell us on this design," Zac said, still holding my hand, which was now trembling. *Stupid hand.* I told it to stop, but it would *not* listen.

"Izzy doesn't know anything about robotics," Claire said.

"Precisely," Zac said. "An outsider's opinion is just what we need."

I snapped out of my hormone-induced fog and did my best to inspect the drawing on the floor while avoiding looking at Claire, though I could almost feel the steam shooting out of her ears.

Ryan, however, jumped right into a pitch, the words rushing at me like too much Japanese. "Our concept for this year's bot will have a four-sim, single-speed, west-coast drive-gear box. Frame dimensions are twenty-eight inches by twenty-two, made of two-by-one aluminum box tube with bumpers to protect six pneumatic wheels."

The word *wheels* surprised me. "The robot is going to move? I thought it was going to be stationary this year." I looked at Claire, recalling how she'd pitched her idea, but she was looking at the floor.

"It was a good idea," Luke said, "but we weren't going to be able to rack up enough points for ourselves that way. We need to be more versatile."

Ryan went on with his description of the design, pointing to the drawing as he went. "Fully extended, the arm will be seventy-two inches long. It will bend in three places and have a set of claws on the end so we can pick up pellets. It will either suck the pellets through an intake tube on its back, swallowing the pellets into an inner chamber we're calling the belly. Then we can drive the bot to the horde and spit out the food to earn points."

"*Or* we can hold the pellet in the claw," Luke said, "raise up the arm on a cascading chain lift, and drop the pellet on the scale."

"Right," Ryan said. "You get more points for pellets on the scale, but you can load pellets in the horde faster, and those points will add up."

"The arm is made of the same two-by-one tubing?" I asked.

"Yes," Ryan said.

"How heavy will the claw be? And the pellets?"

"About two pounds, probably," Ryan said. "The pellets should only weigh about a pound each."

"How high is the scale?" I asked.

"Five feet off the ground, unless the other side has more pellets loaded," Ryan said, "so then it will probably tip as high as seven or eight feet."

"Wouldn't a six-foot arm be kind of unwieldly when it's fully extended, especially if it's holding a pellet?" I asked.

"It might be," Ryan said. "We'll have to test it."

"What if you ditched the claw?" I asked. "And instead of *swallowing* the pellets you pick up, you use the vacuum to suck the pellets from the bottom all the way up through the hose and then spit them out at the top and onto the scale?"

Silence as the team considered my idea.

"I actually really like that," Luke said.

"Won't work," Claire said. "The pellets would get stuck in the hose."

"Not if the vacuum was strong enough," Ryan said. "If we could eject pellets onto the scale as fast as we could suck them up, we'd earn a ton of points."

"It sounds a lot like a shooter," Claire said.

The team groaned.

"No. No. It's not a shooter," Ryan said, an intense look on his face. "If we keep the vacuum at the right power level, it won't shoot pellets so much as push them, nice and easy."

"It's the same concept, Ryan," Claire said.

"I respectfully disagree," Ryan said. "We wouldn't be launching pellets through the air; we'd be ejecting them slowly, like emptying a septic tank."

A chorus of "Ewww!" rang out, and Natalie hit Ryan with a pillow.

Ryan raised his hands to defend himself. "I believe this idea merits a discussion with Mr. Lucas."

I took that moment to slink away to the kitchen and help myself to a glass of water. When I turned around, I found Zac had followed me.

"That was a great idea, Izzy," he said. "You should join the team."

"Robotics is Claire's domain," I said.

"Not all of robotics is about building the bot," he said. "You could join the programming subteam with me."

I wrinkled my nose. "I don't like coding. I did a week of it in my eighth-grade computer science class, and that was enough for me."

"There's also a marketing subteam. They work on costumes and fundraising and planning meals for competitions."

Which sounded equally boring. "I don't know," I said. "I'll think about it."

"If you were on the team, we could sit together and cheer at competitions."

I drank some more water, hoping the glass would hide my blushing cheeks. *Did Zac Lloyd like me?* It seemed like he did. I wanted to ask him about Ensley but didn't have the guts. I felt like I was in junior high, crushing on a boy in secret, afraid to say anything out loud because finding out he didn't like me would be too devastating. Maybe I could write him a note.

Do you like me? Circle one: YES NO

So not happening. Yet I couldn't deny that this hunky senior boy who commanded The Dazzle had been talking to me a lot lately. In any normal world, that would mean he liked me.

I stayed downstairs until the robotics team left, and all that time I couldn't help but notice—because: electricity—that Zac seemed to go out of his way to touch me. A hand on my arm or leg, bumping his shoulder against mine, tugging a strand of my hair, sitting so close on the couch our arms and legs touched. Being near him so enamored me, I forgot to go to Thrive Night at youth group, which was a special Bible study group that met on Sunday nights for kids who wanted to deepen their faith. I didn't even realize I'd missed it until Tessa texted.

Tessa: You coming tonight?

Oopsy.

Me: Sorry! I had to help Claire with another robotics gathering at our house.
Tessa: Aw, well, I missed you. See you tomorrow at school!
Me: Yay!
Tessa: You're weird for being excited about school.
Me: What can I say? I miss my people.
Tessa: ❤

I might have forgotten about Tessa and youth group, but I hadn't forgotten about Ensley Barnette. I wanted so badly to tell Tessa all about what was happening with Zac, but I knew she'd be like, "Yes. Flirting with someone else's boyfriend is wrong." She'd tell me to ignore him. But I couldn't! Zac was the first boy to ever pay this kind of attention to me. So until I knew for sure about him and Ensley, I had to keep my feelings to myself.

When Claire left for work that night and I was home alone, I turned on the computer in the den. On a whim, I went to

Facebook, which was logged into Mama's account. I found Ensley right away. She had the exact same profile picture of her and the cheerleaders as she had on Instagram, but it was much larger and brighter on the big monitor. *What was it about cheerleaders that left a non-cheerleader feeling bad about herself?*

Ensley actually seemed to use Facebook. At the top of the page was a post from Mika about the TV show *Glenwood*. As I scrolled down through posts from her friends, I came upon a picture of her and Zac from December. It was a selfie she'd taken of him kissing her cheek. I scowled and scrolled back to the top. That's when I saw it.

Relationship: It's complicated

My breath hitched as I gaped at those two little words. *Were she and Zac not getting along?* I clicked on her pictures. In every single one, she looked like a model. Ensley was petite and blonde, yet curvy the way boys liked. She had flawless skin and hair so straight and frizz-less, she could have walked out of a shampoo commercial. She wore lots of dark eye makeup and had pouty lips that made it look like she was ready to kiss just about anyone who might happen by. Her real beauty was in her smile, though. It completely lit up her face. She had perfect teeth. Perfect everything. I normally didn't compare myself to other girls. I liked the way I looked. But something about Ensley made me feel small, even though I was taller.

Most of the pictures were of her and her cheer friends. Sometimes they were in their uniforms. Sometimes not. There was one of her and an older lady. Mom, perhaps? A family picture. Her and another girl, hugging each other. Ensley sitting on a horse. Holding a suitcase and looking back over one shoulder. Ensley and some guy wearing a cowboy hat. Posing with Pluto from a Disney park. She and two other girls, all wearing black-rimmed nerd glasses with tape in the middle. Drinking iced coffee with a friend. Sticking out her tongue. (Ugh. Of course, she even had a cute tongue.) My favorite was her cuddling a brown rabbit with huge floppy ears. Stars, that rabbit was adorable!

I made myself get off the computer. Creeping on Ensley had left me feeling all wrong inside. I needed flesh-and-blood people, but I had no idea where my family was. I wanted to talk to my squad about Zac. Since I couldn't, I made myself some dinner and ate it alone in the living room while watching *Cupcake Wars* on Netflix. By the time my parents got home, they were overwhelmed trying to get Sebastian ready for bed. Turns out they'd been at Nana and Tata's house, ended up staying for dinner, and had forgotten to let me know.

I was exhausted after having stayed up so late last night talking to Zac, so I decided to put myself to bed and be done with this day. It seemed no one would miss me, anyhow.

I was fast asleep when the cast of *Annie* woke me. Squinting at the time on my phone, I saw it was 10:30 p.m.

> Zac: u up?

It felt *so* nice to get attention from such a hunky guy—even more so now that I knew he and Ensley *might* be over. I had school tomorrow, though, and if last night was any indication of Zac's texting patterns, I needed to set some ground rules.

> Me: Yes, but I can only talk until 11:00.
> Zac: a curfew?
> Me: I'm tired from last night when we talked so late I fell asleep on you!
> Zac: didnt rlize I ws so boring
> Me: You're so not! ☺ I was tired from being on my feet all day making cupcakes. And I have school tomorrow, so . . .

> Zac: who nu bking was so xhausting?
> Me: Um . . . I did. ☺
> Zac: u should be on one of those bking tv shos
> Me: That would be AMAZING. ☺☺☺
> Zac: u use a lot of smiley faces when txting
> Me: I'm all about the smiley faces. ☺☺☺

I signed off right at eleven, then had to mute Zac's texts—because he was *still* texting me even though I'd set ground rules and said good night. Which, in all honesty, made me grin. I kind of liked being irresistible. I finally plugged in my phone on the other side of the room from my bed. That way when the alarm went off in the morning, I'd have to get out of bed to shut it off. Plus, I wouldn't be tempted to keep looking at my phone to see what else Zac was saying.

Proud of my clever and mature choices regarding texting a boy, I shut off the lights and climbed into bed, excited for school tomorrow, where I'd see my people. And Zac.

Was it foolish to even dream Zac would be as nice to me at school as he had been at my house? And if it was over between him and Ensley, and if he was friendly, did that mean he might want me to be his girlfriend?

Guess I'd have to wait and see.

Chapter
7

As I MADE MY WAY across campus Monday morning, I couldn't help but walk with a little spring in my step. I was so glad to be back at school. If anyone heard me say that out loud, they would have thought I was crazy. I couldn't help it, though. The sight of so many faces made me feel better about life. I caught myself scanning those faces for Zac and berated myself for being a silly girl. Just because he'd been nice to me this past weekend didn't mean he would be now that school was back in session. Isaac Lloyd had a bazillion friends—all of them popular and/or upperclassmen. He'd probably only been nice to me out of sheer boredom.

I waved to Deputy Packard as he stopped the drop-off traffic so we could cross the lane. He was our school resource officer, and part of his job was directing traffic before and after school.

When I got to the foyer, I spied Shay standing outside the main office. We had World History first hour, so we usually met up here. She saw me coming and waved. I ran up and hugged her, briefly lifting her off the ground. My hug made her stiff like a flagpole, but I hoped after all this time, she would be used to them by now.

"Whazzup?" I asked.

Shay shrugged, her posture slouched as usual. She was wearing a Green Tree Farm T-shirt, jeans, and her dirty cowboy boots. "Nothing much. I get to start working at the barn more regularly soon. They're going to start giving lessons."

I squealed. "Maybe I can get some lessons." *Though not likely. Because . . . Sebastian.* "How are Stanley and Matilda?" Stanley was Shay's brindle greyhound, Matilda her tortoiseshell cat.

That got me a real smile. "They're good. Stanley is back on his feet, though moving slow."

Stanley had been hit by a car over a month ago. "Poor guy," I said. "I miss him. Matilda too. I need a snuggle visit."

"They always love seeing you," Shay said, giving me her warm smile. Shay might be introverted and quiet around strangers, but she was incredibly awesome. After all she'd been through in the past year, it was impressive that she was even standing upright.

"How did it go with your grandparents?" I said, almost afraid to ask. Her aunt had made her go see them over break. They weren't the nicest people.

Shay sighed. "It started out okay. They were trying. They really were." She winced. "I just don't think we're ever going to be close, which is sad. But it's also okay, you know?"

I didn't. I couldn't imagine being estranged from either set of my grandparents. "I'm sorry" was all I could think to say as we headed up the stairs toward our class on the second floor of the humanities wing.

"How did the robotics thing go?" Shay asked.

I wanted to say, "Amazing! Wonderful! I have a new friend in Zac Lloyd!" but I held back, not ready to trust my squad with the full story. Because it wasn't a story. Not yet, anyway. Whatever happened next depended entirely on Zac. So I left him out of my recap. "It was okay, I guess. I got some good experience as a hostess. Thinking about asking Mr. Lucas for a recommendation if I ever apply for a job with a caterer."

"You're so smart to think of that," Shay said. "It must be weird, having a teacher who goes to your church."

"Not really. Mr. Lucas is cool, and his kids are adorable. I get to play with them when I work in the nursery or help with the preschool class. You should come more often."

Shay tucked a wisp of her honey-blonde hair behind her ear. "I think we might. Aunt Laura joined a Bible study with Carrie and some of her friends. She's been inviting us to come."

Carrie was Tessa's mom. "Yay! It would be awesome to see you there. Oh! My dragon cupcakes were a hit. I uploaded a video to my IGTV and already have 142 views, which was more than I got on the Santa cupcake video."

"That's great. You should send me the link. I'll watch it *and* give you a like."

"Thank you! I'll send it later." I couldn't believe I'd forgotten to send the link to my squad. Normally I would have done that by now. I pondered how much power a cute boy had to throw a girl like me out of her normal patterns. It was a little scary.

We slowed to a stop when we reached the crowd waiting outside the classroom. Mr. Lucas must not be here yet.

Shay leaned against the wall and folded her arms. "My aunt said you came to the bookstore dressed up like a mouse."

I grinned. "Yeeaahh . . . I totally did. *If You Give a Mouse a Cookie*." Shay's aunt had a sign-up sheet for volunteers to read to kids on Saturday mornings in her bookstore. Since my winter break was the most boring ever, I was like, yes please.

"Wish I could have seen it." A slow smile grew on Shay's face. "She said you brought cookies too."

"How could I not? They were in the title of the book, and I desperately needed more projects to help pass the time."

Shay met my gaze, something she didn't do often. "I'm sorry none of us were around."

"Yeah, I'm not going to lie. I was pretty much dying without you girls."

Shay chuckled. "Well, it's nice to be missed."

I growled and narrowed my eyes, but I was totally joking.

Shay shook her head, used to my antics. "Did your brother ride his bike to school today?"

"Yep. All must have gone well because I didn't hear anything from Papi. He would have texted if the plan was off, so it appears Operation Sebastian Watch is still a go."

"Lucky you."

"I know, right?"

As we entered Mr. Lucas's history class, a girl named Katerina stopped Shay to ask her something about the bookstore. I released a deep sigh. One down, two to go. Shay was the least nosy of my three closest friends. Amelia would want a play-by-play because she liked to know everything about everything. I could probably distract her with Broadway talk, and she'd forget all about Zac Lloyd. But Tessa would definitely wonder if there'd been any further contact with Zac, and she would not be so easily sidetracked.

I took my usual seat in the middle of the room. Not so close to the front that I'd get called on all the time, but not so far back I'd be sitting with the boys who were always goofing off. I usually sat between Shay and Lilliesha.

"Hey, girl," Lilliesha said. "Where's my cupcake?"

I gasped and clapped my hand over my mouth, saying, "I totally forgot! I'm so sorry!" the words muffled by my hand.

She frowned so deep, it made creases on her forehead. "You forgot my cupcake. After I had to stomach two dozen pictures of dragons and gears clogging up my Instagram? That's cold." She pointed a long fingernail my way that was painted silver to match a huge pair of hoop earrings.

"I'm sorry," I said. "It was a crazy weekend. The robotics team came to our house twice. Plus, my parents have been on me about Operation Sebastian Watch. I don't know what they think is going to happen."

"If there's trouble to be found, Sebastian can find it."

"He's not like that," I said, shaking off the prickles climbing my arms.

Lilliesha's expression said she thought otherwise. "You're a saint to take care of him like you do."

"He's my brother," I said, anger rising. "I'd do anything for him." I sounded self-righteous, but inside conflict brewed. I was such a hypocrite. I didn't want to have to watch Sebastian. My parents had decreed I would, and that was that. But when people acted like he was some kind of burden on my family, that made me so angry I could spit.

Shay slipped into the seat on my right, and Lilliesha shot me a pair of raised eyebrows, which were usually a precursor to some serious attitude. Before she could say anything, Mr. Lucas began class.

"Good morning!" he said, rubbing his hands together like they were cold. "I hope you all enjoyed winter break."

"Can we talk about what we did on break instead of doing work?" Jason Corina asked from the back row.

"While I would love to hear what each of you did over winter break, we don't have time to discuss that in class today. However, we aren't going to do work, either."

Cheers rose up, especially from the back row.

"Instead we're going to talk and read."

"Aw!" This from someone behind me.

"Today," Mr. Lucas said, "you are going to discover some of the ways the world is different because of imperialism. You'll start by reading a blog entry written by a man in a formerly colonized country; then we'll discuss—first in small groups, then later as a class—how the article made you feel and what present-day examples you identified as to how people in less-powerful countries are influenced in their thinking by more powerful countries."

Ugh.

We read about some guy in Nigeria who was mad that Nigerians went to America and started acting like Americans and caring about things like American fashion and pop culture. He didn't want his people to forget who they were, where they came from, and what mattered to them as a culture. It was actually pretty chill.

In English, Mr. Oster passed out copies of *To Kill a Mockingbird*, which we were going to start reading, so that was kind of a bonus. I preferred reading a book to writing boring essays.

Then came my least-favorite class on the planet earth: PE. As quickly as possible, I changed into my shorts and T-shirt, then went back into the gym. Mrs. DeLeon was one of my favorite teachers. She was super-pregnant with her first child, and I admired how she expertly dealt with so much obnoxious behavior on a regular basis. The class had thirty-five students on the roster—mixed grades—and three-quarters of them were annoying boys.

Mrs. DeLeon always had us sit in alphabetical order on the baseline at the start of each class while she walked by and took attendance. She started with Samar Bhat at one end of the gym and slowly made her way down the line to Austin Yager. Weird that our line started and ended with two robotics freshmen who happened to be besties. Since my last name was Valadez, my place was at the end of the line with Austin on my left and Michael Torres on my right.

"*Hola*, Isabella," Michael said as I sank into place in line.

"*Hola, Miguel*," I said. "*¿Qué onda?*"

"*Nada*," he said. "*¿Tuviste una buena semana?*"

"*Sí fue bueno. ¿Tú?*"

"Hey, it isn't nice to tell secrets," Sarah Kate Thompson said, focusing her bubbly attention on Michael. She was a tiny freshman with spiky pink hair and a nose ring. She spent most of her time flirting with Michael.

"We're not telling secrets," Michael said with more than a little attitude.

"We just like practicing our Spanish," I added to ease his sting.

Her eyes went wide. With that hair, she looked like a shamed Pokémon. "I just wondered what you were saying. That's all."

In other words, she was jealous I'd been monopolizing Michael's time. I certainly didn't want to give anyone the wrong idea where Michael was concerned. He was nice and all, but there was no electricity between us. "Michael asked me if I had a nice week. I told him I did and asked how his was."

"Oh," Sarah Kate said. "Well. Um. How was your Christmas, Michael?"

"*Bueno*," he said, grinning like a middle-school boy.

Sarah Kate knew that word. "Mine was good too," she said.

"Thompson . . . Torres . . . Valadez . . . and Yager," Mrs. DeLeon said as she walked past, marking us present on her clipboard, a red kickball tucked under her arm. At seven months pregnant, she always dressed in the most adorable maternity workout clothes. Today she was wearing a seafoam-colored half-zip hoodie with black-and-gray-camo leggings. So cute.

She tucked the clipboard under her arm and tossed the ball to Michael. "Okay, kickball! A through L on offense. M through Z on defense. Let's set it up!"

Michael took off for the center of the gym while I headed toward my regular spot in the outfield. My position there not only kept me out of the way of most of the action, but it also gave me a good view of Captain America—ahem, my adorable neighbor, Cody Nichols. His last name put him on my team, and he always ran around right in front of me, chasing the ball and throwing it to get people out. He was a jumper. A guard on the basketball team and a pole vaulter, he was extremely light on his feet.

Best. Show. Ever.

Okay, not really. *Newsies* was the best show ever, but Cody did well for a one-man act. I'm just sayin'. I bet he was a good dancer, too.

The only good thing about PE, besides talking Spanish to Michael and watching Cody jump, was that when it was over, I got to go to drama class—the best class of my entire life. Drama was held in the multipurpose room, which had an old stage along the wall opposite the door. It was smaller than the auditorium stage—just a few steps off the ground—and instead of theater seats, the space was filled with mismatched furniture. There were couches, love seats, a couple of recliners, beanbags, and a bunch of wingback chairs, none of them matching. There was even a hot-pink stiletto chair that looked straight out of an '80s music video. I put my cell phone in the shoe organizer Ms. Larkin kept by the door. Amelia's gorgeous red curls caught my gaze. *Amelia, here already?* She was usually late for just about everything. I headed toward where she was sitting on the love seat in our favorite spot in the room.

Amelia exuded a boldness I admired. Like me, she didn't care what people thought of her fashion sense, and she always looked amazing. Today she was wearing an oversize Ramones T-shirt, black-and-white houndstooth pants, and a red cardigan with big navy-blue flowers on it.

"Whazzup?" I said, giving her a side hug. "You're early." Amelia was Ms. Larkin's TA, but she usually sat with us, doing homework for other classes or joining us for various activities.

"Only because I lost my phone last class and Mr. Oster gave me a pass to go look for it." She squeezed me back. "Life is sadly no different from how it was before winter break. Any more developments with Zac?"

See? I knew she'd be curious. I so wanted to tell her all about it, but I spotted Tessa and Shay waiting in line at the shoe organizer and reined myself in.

"You know what I noticed about Zac?" I said. "He looks like Matt Cornett from—"

"*High School Musical: The Musical: The Series!*" she finished for me, her eyes wide. "I never thought about it before, but you are totally right. Wow." She grinned, her eyes a little glassy. I figured she was picturing Zac and Matt side by side in her imagination, and the effect of a double Dazzle was pretty much hypnotizing.

Tessa and Shay approached while Amelia was still lost in Dazzleland. Tessa claimed the beanbag, so Shay sat on the rocking chair. This was our little spot in the multipurpose room; we'd staked our claim on it last fall.

"Welcome back, kiddos!" Ms. Larkin announced from her place, center stage. "Please find your seats, and we'll get started."

Those not in their seats yet kicked it into high gear. I jumped up and threw my arms out to the side, looking down on Tessa. "Hugs?"

She tilted her head and smiled at me, like I was oh so predictable. "But I'm already in the beanbag, Izzy."

"That's okay. I got this." I squatted and hugged her where she sat. She patted me awkwardly with one hand while laughing and batting my hair out of her face with the other. Satisfied, I returned to my seat.

"What about Shay?" Tessa asked. "Doesn't she get a back-from-Christmas hug?"

"I got mine before first hour," Shay said, raising an eyebrow.

Tessa tipped back her head and laughed. "Of course you did," she said.

"Many of you have asked me about the spring show," Ms. Larkin said, drawing our attention. "Some of you more than once." She glanced at Amelia.

I did, too, and chuckled when Amelia's cheeks turned pink.

Ms. Larkin went on. "I'm sure you're all excited to hear what I've chosen, but I'm going to make you wait a bit longer."

A chorus of groans rang out, Amelia's the loudest.

"Don't despair. I will make the announcement a week from today at the start of this class, standing right here, center stage." She pointed at her feet, which were hidden under the hem of her flowy red-and-white dress.

"Why make us wait a week?" Amelia asked, her frustration evident.

"Because anticipation increases interest," Ms. Larkin said. "Even waiting one week to make the announcement will create a buzz within this school that will make our production all the more successful."

"Makes sense," Amelia whispered and nodded, her crazy red hair bouncing. It didn't take much to get Amelia on board with anything drama-related.

Tessa glanced at Amelia, then at me. She grinned. I grinned back. I loved drama, but drama was Amelia's life. Like baking was to me.

"Now, to get you all back into the practice of the theater arts, we are going to discuss objectives," Ms. Larkin said. "How can you know the objective of the character you are going to perform?" When no one raised their hand, Ms. Larkin called on her TA. "Amelia? Could you give the class an idea?"

"Look to the needs of the character. What the character needs informs his or her objectives. As I become the character, I must do what I have to do to achieve my objectives."

"Say more about this," Ms. Larkin said. "Give us an example."

Amelia twisted her lips. "Well, take the musical *Annie*. Annie needs her family and believes they're still alive, so her objective is to find them. This informs her actions several times in the show. Twice when she runs away and a third time when she tells Daddy Warbucks about her parents, and he offers to help her find them."

"Intriguing. Can a character have more than one objective per scene? Marcus?"

"Uh . . . I think so," Marcus said. He was sitting on a lime-green armchair against the back wall. "But probably each objective will have its own action."

Ms. Larkin continued the discussion, then wrote the following on the whiteboard: *I need _____, so my objective would be _____, and to achieve this, I would do _____.*

"In a moment, I'm going to have you get out your journals," Ms. Larkin said. "I want you to think of a character in a musical—any musical you like. Then come up with a scene. Once you have that, write this sentence in your journal and fill in the blanks with what you think that character's need, objective, and action would be for the scene you have in mind. If you get stuck, remember Amelia's example from *Annie*. Once you've finished, find a partner, then take turns acting out each other's scenes. Stage fighting only, kiddos. I'm looking at you, Marcus."

The class laughed.

"You may begin," Ms. Larkin said.

I withdrew my theater journal from my backpack. I knew right away I wanted to do *Newsies*, but it was harder to come up with a scene than I thought.

Tessa dragged her beanbag over to the couch, dropped it at my feet, and then fell into the squishy, squeaky pleather. "I don't think I even know any musicals besides *Annie*," she said.

"Sure you do," I said. "You know *Mary Poppins* and *Cinderella* and *Beauty and the Beast* and *The Lion King*. All the Disney ones."

"I do like *Beauty and the Beast*," she admitted, frowning at the sentence frame she'd copied in her notebook.

I considered the play *Newsies* and settled on the scene near the end of the show where Jack has been called into Pulitzer's office, bribed, and blackmailed. If Jack helped Pulitzer, he'd be given enough money to leave town, but if he didn't help, Pulitzer would send all Jack's newsie friends to the refuge. I decided Jack Kelly's deep need was family, so his objective would be to protect his newsie brothers from Pulitzer, and to achieve this he'd have to try to end the strike so they would be safe.

I filled in my blanks and then read it again. I felt satisfied with my choice. I glanced at Tessa, then at her notebook. She had written "Belle needs to *protect her father*, so her objective would be to *rescue her father*, and to achieve this, she would *offer to take her father's place*."

Tessa caught my gaze. "Do you think I did it right? I feel like the need to 'protect her father' might be wrong. I keep thinking how she says in the song she wants adventure."

"Characters can have more than one need," I said.

Once everyone was done, Ms. Larkin had us act out our scenes as best we could without any actual lines to read. She would be walking around to observe us.

"I'll go first," Tessa said.

"Really? Why?" Tessa hated acting.

"Because Ms. L. is over there, and I'll be done by the time she gets over here. Then she'll be watching you, not me."

I laughed. "Got it. But we're still both going to be acting for both scenes. We need two people. You're going to have to be my Pulitzer, and I'll be your Beast."

"Oh, right." Tessa frowned.

Tessa did her best as Belle, and I played both the Beast and her father, which was actually pretty fun. We switched before Ms. Larkin got to us. Tessa had never seen *Newsies*, and Shay had never seen Amelia's choice, *The Sound of Music*. A crime, in my opinion. So Amelia and I were acting out *Newsies* when Ms. L. came our way, which was funny because Amelia hated *Newsies*, but she was nailing the part of Pulitzer.

When we finished, Ms. Larkin applauded. "An excellent performance by both of you. Well done."

We laughed, and I wondered if I could use this sentence frame in some way to make things work out between me and Zac. I needed *a boyfriend*, so my objective would be to *make Zac fall in love with me*, and to achieve this, I would have to . . .

That's where I was stuck.

The bell rang and took away my chance to figure it out. It was time for lunch. Time to see if I would get a peek at that Dazzle today.

Chapter

8

THE CAFETERIA WAS a mass of people, noise, and general cheer as 800-some hungry teenagers stuffed their faces. We made our way to our regular table and sat down. I took charge of the conversation straightaway in hopes of keeping the topic away from Zac Lloyd.

"So?" I asked as I unpacked my lunch bag. "What did everyone get for Christmas?"

"I got a new ski jacket and boots," Tessa said.

"And a ski trip," I added, still unable to comprehend why anyone would find skiing fun.

Shay was smiling at Tessa, elbows on the table, chin in her hands. "Did you have a nice trip?" she asked.

"I did," Tessa said as she unwrapped her tuna sandwich. "The snow was perfect."

Amelia leaned across the table. "Did Alex give you something?" Amelia was as boy crazy as me and always wanted all the details about Tessa's love life. Probably trying to live vicariously and all that. We single girls did what we had to in order to cope.

"Yes," Tessa said. "Since he knew about the ski trip, he gave me a hat and scarf and gloves that matched my jacket."

"Aw!" Amelia and I said at once.

"How'd he know what your jacket looked like?" Shay asked, typical for a girl who always picked up on the details.

"He asked my mom ahead of time. Plus, he said he didn't like me walking home from swimming with wet hair and no hat." She smiled, blushing, and focused on the salad and sandwich in front of her.

"So sweet," I said. "Did your dad get you something?"

Her smile vanished. "Technically, he did, though I think he's trying to manipulate me."

"How so?" Amelia asked.

Tessa squeezed her eyes shut. "He got me a puppy."

I gasped.

Shay squealed and leaned forward, nearly squashing her peanut butter sandwich. "What kind?"

Eyes opened again, Tessa rolled them and fought a smile. "I knew you girls would freak out when I told you."

"But why is a puppy manipulation?" Amelia asked.

"It's just, my mom has always been allergic, which means the puppy has to stay at Dad's house. So it's *technically* mine, but it's really Dad and Rebecca's."

Shay frowned. "I'm so sorry. That's hard . . . and unfair."

It really was. *After what he did? Using an adorable animal to try and bribe Tessa to spend more time with him? Rotten.*

After an awkward moment of silence, Shay, wearing her endearing expression, said, "Well, what's it look like? Boy or girl? Did you name it?"

"It's a girl," Tessa said, "and her name is Hermione. She's a Sheepadoodle, which is a cross between a sheep dog and a poodle, and she's absolutely adorable." Tessa was smiling, so it was clear the problem wasn't with Hermione but with her dad. Last fall, he'd divorced her mother for his pregnant girlfriend. The whole thing was pretty much awful. Worse than all that, he acted like he'd done nothing wrong, like it was perfectly normal for husbands to cheat on their wives and abandon their families to start new lives with other women. It still made me growl when I thought about it too much.

"Wow," Shay said. "A designer dog. Expensive."

"A puppy right before the baby?" Amelia said. "That seems weird."

"Yeah," Tessa said, her lip curling. "Don't get me started on all the ways Dad has been trying to buy my forgiveness and affection."

"Well, I'd love to meet Hermione sometime," Shay said.

"Me too!" I said. "Puppies are the best."

Tessa's expression shuttered. "Well, seeing as I've only seen Hermione twice, I doubt that's going to happen. Like I said, she's really more Dad and Rebecca's dog, and it's not like I'm planning a sleepover at their house or anything with the baby coming."

"In March, right?" I asked.

"March 17, yep," Tessa said. "Last time I was over there, they were working on the nursery. I just can't go back right now. It's too much."

"Well, at least things are good with Alex, right?" Amelia asked, expression ever hopeful.

Tessa's smile returned. "Yes, Alex and I are doing great."

Amelia stood to look around the room. "Then why doesn't he sit with us?"

Tessa grabbed her sleeve and yanked her down. "Because we are two different people with different friends, and we don't need to spend every moment together."

Amelia made a face, like Tessa and Alex were crazy for not walking the halls like Danny and Sandy from *Grease*.

"Enough about me," Tessa said. "What about everyone else?"

"Nothing exciting to report." Shay shrugged. "My aunt gave me some books. My grandparents gave me some cash."

"Oh, poor you," Amelia said, rolling her eyes.

"Did you get your singing lessons, Amelia?" I asked.

"No," she said, pounding a rapid staccato on the table with the side of her fist. "I *asked* for singing lessons. I *asked* for tickets to a show at U of I, preferably *Dear Evan Hansen*, but I would have loved any show."

I winced. "What did they give you?"

"Tickets to a worship concert at Crossroads Christian Center."

"Oh, Amelia," Tessa said, resting her hand on Amelia's arm. "I'm sorry."

"It's fine. I just want to prepare, you know?" Amelia brushed a tear away and sat up taller. "The spring musical is coming," she said, her voice more confident, "and I want the lead."

"You don't even know what show it is," Shay said.

"It doesn't matter what the show is," Amelia said. "The lead is the lead."

"What do you think it will be?" I asked.

"Well, last year we did *Seussical*. And two years ago, they did *Shrek*, which is a bummer because I would have made a perfect Princess Fiona."

"What part did you play in *Seussical*?" Shay asked.

"Oh, I wasn't in the show last year," Amelia said, sighing heavily. "We had a family emergency, and I missed auditions."

"Oh no!" I said, horrified. "You must have been so disappointed."

Amelia shook her head, like she didn't want to talk about it. "I was, but there's always this year."

"Do you think it will be something I've heard of?" Tessa asked. "I am *so* not in touch with musicals."

"Me either," Shay said, and I tried not to giggle. The theater was about Shay's least favorite thing, ever.

"Almost certainly," Amelia said. "There are so many musicals high schools perform."

"Like what?" Shay set the crusts of her peanut butter sandwich on her paper lunch sack and dusted the crumbs off her hands.

Amelia started rattling them off. "*Mary Poppins, Cinderella, Alice in Wonderland, Honk!, Annie, The Music Man, Singin' in the Rain* . . . I could go on and on."

"I love the classics," I said. "What about *Newsies*? Please tell me that's a possibility."

Amelia sighed heavily. "Unfortunately, it is. Though Northside did *Newsies*, like, three years back, so Ms. Larkin might not want to repeat it so soon."

"Are you certain it will be a musical?" Shay asked.

"The spring show is always a musical, yes," Amelia said. "You know, she might go more modern. Something like *Legally Blonde, High School Musical Jr., Mean Girls* . . ."

"I would die for *Hamilton*," I said.

"You haven't even seen it," Amelia said.

"I don't care. I love the music so much," I said.

"What music do you love so much?"

I tensed. The voice behind me was male and *very* familiar.

We all turned at the same time, and there stood Zac Lloyd, behind me to my left, gazing down at me, Dazzle in full force.

"*Hamilton*," I said, trying to play it cool. "It's a musical."

"About Alexander Hamilton, sure. I've seen it."

Amelia squeaked. "You saw *Hamilton*?"

"In Manhattan last summer," Zac said, as if he went to New York all the time. "I went to visit my mom. Seeing a show was on her 'must do' list for me. Since *Hamilton* was the best, that's the one we went to."

"And was it?" I asked, flooded with jealousy.

He shrugged, a smirk tugging at the corner of his mouth. "It was cool."

"Cool?" I shoved his leg, because that was what I could reach.

He laughed and stepped back, looking down at me. "Hey, now."

"What a waste," Amelia muttered, suddenly grumpy. That girl could jump moods faster than a frog on lily pads.

"You want to sit down?" I asked.

"I already ate." He lifted his hand, showing off an empty cardboard food tray holding an empty soda can. He put his hand on my shoulder and squeezed. "Tomorrow, look for me, okay? We'll sit together."

"Okay," I managed to squeak.

He grinned—one last Dazzle—and then walked away. I watched him until he was out of sight, my shoulder still tingling from his touch.

When I turned my attention back to our table, Tessa, Shay, and Amelia were staring at me, all three open-mouthed. I couldn't help it. I squealed and stomped my feet under the table. No point in keeping my feelings a secret anymore. If Zac was going to talk to me at school, he had to be on the outs with Ensley. I was *all* in.

"Izzy . . ." Tessa said, tipping her head, an expression like a worried mama bear on her face.

Nope. I was done holding back where Zac was concerned. He knew my name, he'd spoken to me at school, he'd *touched me* at school, and tomorrow, I would eat lunch with him.

—⟋∿⟍—

Claire was waiting inside her truck when I reached the parking lot. I climbed in, and she instantly started backing up.

"In a hurry, are we?"

"Kind of," she said.

I checked my cell phone, felt my belly flip at the sign of a text notification, but it was only a thumbs up from Amelia in answer to my last text.

"Nothing from Zac?"

I glanced at my sister, who had steered us out onto the main road. "What?"

"Natalie told me she gave him your number. She and I got into a fight about it in physics class."

"Why?"

"I don't think she should have given it to him. I think she should have asked me. *He* should have asked me."

"Why?"

"Because I'm your sister. We're family. And I don't think Zac should be texting you."

I was about to say, "Why?" when I caught myself sounding like a parrot and added a little differentiation. "Why not?"

"He and Ensley broke up, like, three days ago," she said. "I don't like him rebounding with my baby sister in my own house. I feel responsible."

Too much all at once. Until that moment, I hadn't realized how much a statement could totally annoy me and simultaneously be the equivalent of sweet nothings. "Then I should be thanking you," I said, grinning.

"Izzy, don't be stupid."

That hurt. "You don't think I can handle myself?" I asked.

Claire blew a raspberry. "Not really."

Okay, now I was 100 percent annoyed. "Excuse me?"

"I get the impression Zac has a lot more experience with all this than you have."

"Because of Ensley?"

"Partly, yeah, but also . . . just a feeling."

"And this *feeling* is based on your massive experiences with boys?" *Zing!* Probably not a very nice thing to say to a sister who'd never had a boyfriend or even been on a date. But I wanted to remind her that she really didn't have any research to back up her vague *feeling*.

Instead of zinging me back like I expected, Claire glanced at me, and I could tell she was actually worried. "Just be careful, okay? That's all I'm saying."

Her fear defused my anger somewhat, but now all I could think about was what kind of experience Zac might have gathered while dating Ensley, which was kind of . . . eww.

Claire pulled into the driveway, but she didn't shut off the truck—didn't even put it in park.

"Aren't you coming in?"

"No. Thanks to you, I'm going to meet Ryan and Luke at Pizza Brothers to talk about the new vacuum hose."

I winced. "Sorry I messed up your design."

"You didn't mess it up. It was a good idea, actually. And if anyone can pull it off, it's Ryan and Luke."

"Well, I'm glad, then. See you." I got out of the truck, and Claire drove away, leaving me standing in the driveway. Right away I texted my squad.

> Me: **Claire says Zac and Ensley are broken up. He's fair game!** ☺

I went into the house, dropped my school stuff on the living room couch, and ran to the bathroom. When I came out, I grabbed a granola bar and a juice pouch from the pantry, then flopped onto the couch to see if my squad had responded.

> Amelia: **Whoo hoo! I say go for it!**
> Shay: **Poor Ensley. She must be sad.**
> Amelia: **Who dumped who? If Zac was the dumpee, Izzy can cheer him up.**
> Me: **I plan to! And I don't know what happened with Ensley.**

I turned on an episode of *Cupcake Wars*, poked the straw into my juice pouch, and enjoyed my snack. While I was eating, more texts came through.

> Tessa: You don't want to be his rebound girl. You should take it super slowly until you're sure he's emotionally ready for another commitment.

Of course Tessa would say that.

> Amelia: Are guys ever emotionally ready for anything?

That made me laugh, and I almost choked on my granola bar. I was planning to reply, but the texts came faster than I was able to type.

> Shay: Commitment? Izzy, do you really want him to be your boyfriend? Do you know him well enough? Why can't you two just be friends?
> Tessa: That sounds wise, Shay. It worked for me and Alex.
> Amelia: 😩 Ignore them Izzy. It's clear he likes you.
> Tessa: I just think you should be careful. That's all.
> Shay: Me too. ❤

Ugh. So annoying. I turned over my phone and tried to enjoy the show. In no time, a second episode had started, and Sebastian still hadn't arrived. A quick look at the clock told me he was definitely late. My pulse rose a bit, and I stood and walked to the door. He was likely fine, but I needed to be sure.

I pulled on my TARDIS hoodie so I would have a place for my phone, which I shoved into the front pocket. Then I rode my bike toward the middle school. I was glad Amelia was on my side about Zac, but it bothered me how negative Tessa and Shay were being. I recalled some advice Mr. Oster had given our English class today. We'd started revising the essays we'd finished before Christmas and had to trade them with three partners. Mr. O. had said we didn't have to make any changes to our essays we didn't want to make, but if all three of our readers gave the same critical feedback, we'd be wise to listen to the masses.

Claire, Tessa, and Shay made three votes for "be careful" in regard to Zac, so if I followed Mr. O.'s advice, I'd be wise to listen. But here was the thing: I didn't really want to be careful.

Because Zac was hunky and had The Dazzle.

Because Zac was tall and smelled like a spicy forest.

Because Zac had been super nice to me.

Because Zac had said I was pretty.

Because Zac was Zac—popular and well-known and even though he'd dated Ensley, things hadn't worked out. Now he seemed to like me, Izzy Valadez, a girl no boy had ever liked before, as far as I knew. Even better, I liked him back. A lot. There was no way I would not be giving this opportunity all the effort and attention I possibly could. *If it didn't work out, so what? But why couldn't I give it a shot? What was so dangerous about that?*

I found Sebastian sitting on the cement beside the bike rack, arms around his knees, rocking back and forth. My heart sank. I swung my leg over the back of my bike and jumped off, running it to a quick stop. I shoved the front wheel into the bike rack and went to stand beside my brother, careful to give him his space.

"What happened, Bash?" He didn't like emotion. Just the facts.

"He locked my bike. Locked it."

"Who did?"

"Matt Vega locked my bike. Matt Vega."

I frowned, examining the chain and padlock currently securing my brother's bike to the rack. A longer glance at my brother revealed his own U-lock poking out from one side of his lap.

"Why would he do that?" It was the wrong question, but

Sebastian must have been out here long enough to have cooled down somewhat because rather than trying to push over the bike rack or shift into ambulance mode, he answered.

"He wanted to park in spot number one. I was here first, and I wanted to park in spot number one."

Ah, the maturity of sixth grade boys. I took a deep breath, thinking this through. I seriously doubted Sebastian would leave his bike here overnight. I tested my theory with a question. "I guess we'll have to leave it and walk home, then."

Sebastian released a deep-throated wail and lunged at the rack, threading his arms around the crossbar of his mountain bike.

"All right," I said. "Let me see if someone in the school can help."

I went inside. Even though we'd only moved here six months ago, and I'd never gone to Riverbend Middle School, pretty much everyone here knew me. I was the emergency contact on Sebastian's paperwork, after all. With Mamá and Papi working, I was the one who had walked him home from school last fall. I was the one who rushed over to talk him out from under the desk when he was in one of his moods. Making sure Sebastian's new bike worked out was in both our best interests. The boy needed independence, and so did I.

I leaned against the counter at the school's front desk. "Hi, JoAnn," I said. "We have a little problem with Sebastian."

Her eyes widened. "What happened?"

"Someone locked up his bike. Do you know a Matt Vega?"

Her brow creased, and she humphed. "We all know Matt Vega. What'd he do?"

"He put his own lock on Sebastian's bike, so we can't get it out of the rack. Sebastian has been sitting there since school was out."

"Oh, that poor boy." JoAnn reached for the phone. "I'll call Gary and have him bring out some bolt cutters."

"Thank you," I said.

Gary was one of the custodians at Riverbend Middle. He was short and wiry, and was wearing jeans that bagged out at the knee.

"Well, this is new," he said when he arrived, frowning at the bike lock. "I keep telling these kids not to waste their money on cable locks, now here I am cutting through one like a bike thief."

Sebastian didn't move, but his eyes flickered to watch Gary in action. The custodian opened the bolt cutters and they bit through the cable lock in one quick snap. He pulled the chain, and it clinked against the rack and the bike as it came loose.

Sebastian's face lit up, and his stiff posture relaxed.

"There you go, Mr. Valadez," Gary said. "One liberated mountain bike. You know, this is a mighty fine-looking bike. I've got to say, I'm glad to see you use a U-lock. U-locks like yours won't be beaten by any bolt cutters like mine, and that's a fact. No one's going to rip it apart with their bare hands or smash it with a hammer, either."

Sebastian got to his feet. He hung his U-lock over the handlebars and pulled his bike out of the rack, ready to roll.

"Thank you," I told Gary as Sebastian rode away. "We appreciate your help."

I jumped on my bike and rode after my brother, wondering if he'd ever be able to live a normal life—wondering if I would. I instantly felt guilty for such selfish thoughts. Sebastian couldn't help how his brain worked. He deserved the best life had to offer, and I would do whatever I could to make sure he got it.

Chapter
9

As I STEPPED INTO Ms. Larkin's drama classroom on Tuesday, I wasn't sure how to act. I mean, I fully intended to sit with Zac at lunch, and Tessa and Shay probably thought that was down-right foolish. It made me feel naughty, like I was doing something wrong. I didn't like that feeling, so I decided to pretend everything was normal.

I jogged over to where the three of them were sitting, Amelia and Shay on the love seat, Tessa on a beanbag. I fell onto the rocking chair and kicked back.

"Hi!" I said, all perky.

Shay offered me a warm smile. From Amelia I received a half wave-smile combo as she continued to talk nonstop to Shay about stage lighting. Amelia was wearing a black beanie today, and it made her look like some kind of old-timey movie director.

Tessa was rummaging through her backpack. I could tell she

was bothered. It could be she'd lost something in her backpack. It could be something with her dad. But it could also be about me. I needed to keep us busy so she wouldn't have time to lecture me before Ms. Larkin started class. I jumped up from the rocking chair, dropped my bag in the seat, and then walked toward the shoe organizer as if I'd forgotten to put away my phone. Okay, I did. But I forgot on purpose, so I could come back. I'm clever that way.

Deep inside I felt this nagging pulse, like some kind of red light flashing a warning that Tessa wanted to lecture me. She was smart and had experience with boys. I had no experience with boys. Logic said I should listen to Tessa. But the boy I liked was not only talking to me, he was also texting me and asking me to sit with him. *Me!* It felt so good to have that kind of attention. I couldn't help it. I wanted that more than I cared about Tessa's two cents.

Ms. Larkin began as I was making my way back to my seat. "Yesterday we talked about character objectives," she said. "An actor must discover what his character wants so he can understand what motivates his character to make decisions and take action. The character's wants are closely tied to the character's emotions. You must understand a character's wants if you are to accurately portray that character's emotions."

Before long, we were in pairs, discussing our character's objectives. This time I partnered with Amelia to avoid any chance Tessa might take to sneak in a lecture. This plan worked seamlessly while class was in session, but as soon as the bell rang and we were all headed toward the exit, Tessa found her chance.

"Are you really going to sit with him today?" she asked as we filed out the door and into the hallway. Her flip-flops smacked the tile floor as we went.

"Um, *yes*," I said with a whole lot of "*Duh*" attitude, and then added in a kinder tone, "For today, anyway. I mean, you and Alex don't sit together every day, and you're dating. I'm not dating Zac yet, but I'm going to sit with him today because he's adorable and he asked me to."

Tessa sighed in that way mothers do when they are fighting the urge to tell their kids they're making all the wrong choices in life. "Well, we will miss you. I hope you have a nice time."

That sounded sincere, so I responded with, "Thanks, I plan to," and a mischievous grin.

Tessa and I parted ways in the cafeteria as she headed toward the salad bar and I went through the entrée line with Shay. We exited the line and walked toward the table where Zac and his senior friends usually sat. When I saw he wasn't there, my steps slowed.

"What are you going to do?" Shay asked, still at my side.

"I'm not going to sit there without him," I whispered.

"Then come sit with us," Shay said.

I wanted to turn in a circle and scan the cafeteria for a tall, dark, and handsome figure, but I didn't want him to catch me looking for him.

"You know? I think I'll get some salad today," I said.

"You? Vegetables?" Shay asked.

"I eat vegetables." I stomped toward the salad bar. "Sometimes."

As I scooped a small helping of lettuce onto my tray, I watched Shay continue on to our regular table. She glanced at me, like, three times, her face etched with concern.

I added another pinch of lettuce, grabbing only three more little leaves. I really didn't want any salad. I wanted to stall. I inched down the salad bar and added some peas, some carrot shavings, some garbanzo beans, some pinto beans, a huge pile of cheese, and then drowned it all in three ladles of Thousand Island dressing.

Now what?

"Oh, croutons," I said, spying the crusty squares on the other side of the bar. I slipped around, and was just adding a pile to my salad, when someone tapped my shoulder.

"Hey, girl."

Relief coursed through me at the sound of that hunky voice. "Hi," I said with a glance in Zac's general direction. "Getting some salad."

"I'll wait," he said.

He'll wait. *Swoon.*

I grabbed another crouton, then dropped the tongs. "Done," I said.

"Right this way," he said.

We approached Zac's table, which was only half full. Shawn Edwards, a baseball jock who shaved his head, was sitting across from Ross Miller, a short, scrappy guy who I thought also played baseball. The two of them were locked in what looked to be an intense conversation.

Zac slid onto the seat beside Ross, and I sat beside him. The boys didn't even pause.

"I'm telling you," Ross said. "That what Mika said."

"Please," Shawn said. "Who told you Mika say that? 'Cause I don't buy it for a second."

"My sources are my business," Ross said, "but I've no reason to doubt."

"Your sources are jacked, man." Shawn bit into his pizza. "Ain't no way Mika say that, and ain't no way it's true."

"Yeah? Well, where's your girl, then?" Ross said. "Why ain't Teresina here?"

"I ain't her momma," Shawn said. "And it ain't my turn to watch her."

"I'm telling you, man. She's stepping out."

"Just shut it, you hear me? I'm done talking about this." He turned to Zac, and they knocked knuckles. "How you doin', man?" His eyes flicked past Zac to me. "Who this?"

"This is Izzy," Zac said, and then tucked right into his cheeseburger.

Shawn perused me in a way that made me wonder if he had x-ray vision. "Izzzzy," he said. "That short for somethin'?"

"Isabella," I said.

Ross leaned forward to look past Zac. *"Ee-sah-belll-lah."* He flicked his tongue like some kind of wannabe opera singer. "You Latina, then? You got that look."

I didn't know what "that look" meant, but I didn't want to play skin-color games with anyone. "I'm human," I said, then stabbed my fork into my pile of drowning lettuce.

"I hear that, girl." Shawn, who happened to be black, offered me his fist across the table, and I tapped it.

"Hey, you know Teresina Lyman?" Ross asked me.

"No," I said. "Does she go here?"

"Now I know you didn't ask a stranger about my business," Shawn said.

"What?" Ross said. "It was just a question."

"You better shut your mouth, fool."

Well, this was fun.

A group of girls joined us. I was relieved to see Mika Lawrence from concert choir, but I didn't know the others. One had dark curly hair with blue streaks. The other was blonde and . . . *Oh, my stars.* It was Ensley. I tried to keep my expression neutral. Pretend I didn't know about her and Zac's complicated, recently ended relationship. She didn't look at me, so that made things easier.

"Yo, Mika!" Shawn slid down the bench until he was across from her. "You hear from Sina today?"

Mika didn't even look at him. "Maybe."

"What 'maybe'? Why you don't tell me?"

"Because it's none of your business who I talk to."

"Come on, girl. Why you gotta play like that?"

She finally graced him with a look similar to the one Mamá gave Papi when he left the toilet seat up. "If you want to talk to Teresina, go talk to her. But leave me out of it."

"You put yourself in the middle when you started talking trash about me."

Mika turned toward me. "It's Izzy, right?"

"Yep, that's me."

"Who brings you to this table?"

The question drew the attention of everyone around us, including Ensley, whose expression made me think she'd eaten something rotten.

"I'm with Zac," I said casually.

All eyes shifted from me to Zac.

"*With Zac?*" Ensley said, her tone dripping with disdain.

Shawn snorted.

Ross stifled a laugh.

"Yo, listen up," Shawn said. "A friend of Zaky's is, you know, a friend to us all."

"Yeah, man," Ross said. "Thanks for *exposing* us to your new friend."

This sent him and Shawn into a fit of snorting laughter I did not understand.

"You guys are pigs." Ensley glared at Zac, grabbed her food, and left. The dark-haired girl left with her. *Ouch.*

Shawn's smile faded. "What'd I say? I was just welcoming the new girl."

"Give it a rest, guys, okay?" Zac said.

"What'd I do?" Shawn looked legitimately puzzled, while Ross was still laughing. "Seriously, man. What?"

I couldn't help wondering what Ensley knew about the boys' laughter that I didn't. Unless she was just mad Zac had invited me to lunch. Tessa's warning about being Zac's rebound girl flitted through my mind, but I pushed away the annoying thought.

In an effort to make peace, I pulled a Ziploc of cookies from my backpack and slid it down the table. Food was a great peacemaker. "Cookie?"

Shawn's eyes lit up. "Don't mind if I do." He took one.

"Yeah, thanks." Ross took one too.

"Izzy is a chef," Zac said.

"More of a baker, actually," I said.

"Girl can bake anytime she wants," Shawn said over a full mouth. "You bring the sweet things right on up in here, Izzy girl, and I will help you put them away. Right into my mouth."

The guys laughed, and I couldn't help but smile. I still felt like I was missing a million inside jokes, but they probably had nothing to do with me.

I turned and gazed at Tessa, Shay, and Amelia at our regular table. Alex was sitting with them today, and they were all laughing. I wondered what was so funny. I wished I could be in two places at once.

The rest of lunch went by with Mika on her phone, Ross and Shawn trying to predict who would make the NFL playoffs this year, and Zac talking to me about movies and music and food. It was so easy to talk to him. Despite the laughing thing with Ross and Shawn, and Ensley's departure, we didn't have a single awkward moment.

The bell rang. Zac bumped his shoulder against mine. "Text me later?"

"You first," I said.

He flashed me The Dazzle and then left, heading toward the senior hallway.

I grabbed the Ziploc and put it on my tray, which was empty but for the pile of salad, now missing only the croutons and some of the cheese.

Across from me, Mika threaded one strap of her backpack over one arm. "I know you didn't ask," she said, "but I'd be doing all of womankind a disservice if I said nothing. Be careful with Zac."

"You hear this, man?" Shawn said to Ross. "Always talking trash when a guy isn't here to defend himself. Like with me and Sina. It's messed up."

"Whatever." Mika rolled her eyes and lowered her voice. "It's just . . . Ensley only took off because she thought Zac wanted to work things out. Then he invites you to sit here. He's sending mixed messages. Girls get confused."

Did she mean me? Or Ensley? "Thanks for the warning," I said, because Zac *had* ignored Ensley just now, and I'd seen her relationship status, so I didn't doubt there was some miscommunication going on. But as I headed into geometry class, I felt defensive. My squad already disliked Zac. If I told them what Mika had said, they'd have an actual reason to distrust him, and I wasn't ready for them to write him off. I decided to keep Mika's warning to myself.

—◆◆◆—

When Zac texted that night, I wasted no time in getting to the bottom of Mika's warning.

> Me: What happened with you and Ensley?

When no answer came, I started to worry I'd crossed a line or something. Then finally:

> Zac: we were a bad fit 2 alike.
> Me: How?
> Zac: we're both only kids bssy & set in r ways we both alwys wanna be rght
> Zac: 2 cntrol freaks dnt make the best mtch
> Me: Mika said you told Ensley you wanted to work things out.
> Zac: wow whn mika say that?
> Me: Today at lunch.

Zac: 😳 srsly

Zac: i did wanna wrk it out but that was bfre we had a bg fght ovr brk

Zac: u no wht I like bout u, izzy? u just cme out & say what's on ur mnd. ensly was so confusin i nvr nu wht she wnted frm me

Me: So, you two are officially broken up?

Zac: yep 1000% over

Well, that was pretty clear, but Zac wasn't done.

Zac: i gotta be honst iz. I like u

Zac: i feel like we got this major cemstry ive nvr flt w/anyne b4 like mgic

Zac: but I dont wanna ruin whats going on w/us cause of drma w/ens so i get it if u dont wanna hang w/me

Wow. This time I didn't answer right away. He felt the chemistry too. Said it was like magic. I understood that. Everyone thought Michael and I should go out since we're both Hispanic and spoke Spanish, which was the stupidest logic I'd ever heard because I didn't like Michael like that. There was no flutter when we locked gazes. No chemistry. With Zac, it was different.

I decided to respond in a super mature and confident way.

Me: I like you too. Why would Ensley's drama affect us?

Zac sent back a gif of a cartoon rabbit with his heart beating out of his chest.

I took a moment to breathe and read back over our text exchange. Stars, this seemed clear to me. Zac and I were going to give this thing a whirl and see what happened.

I whooped and hugged Fiesta. "I'm going to get my first kiss,

Fiesta. I'm sure of it!" I tossed the stuffed cat in the air and caught him, then looked to my Captain Marvel poster. Her expression said it all. "Higher, further, faster, baby."

I responded out loud with a salute. "Sir, yes, sir!" As far as Zac and I were concerned, I was all in.

Chapter
10

Zac texted me every night that week. He told me all his favorites. Junk food: Doritos. Video game: *Elder Scrolls*. Movie: *Titanic*, which totally surprised me. I talked about my favorite YouTubers and #bakestagrammers, and he raved about my online following, calling me famous. Shockingly, he knew a lot about musicals. Turns out *Hamilton* wasn't the only Broadway show he'd seen in the Big Apple. He'd seen so many! *Cats*, *Wicked*, *The Phantom of the Opera*, *The Lion King*, *Mean Girls*, and *Dear Evan Hansen*. It *so* wasn't fair, since he was completely indifferent about the fact.

> Zac: its wht ppl do in nyc
> Me: Yeah, but those are the best musicals.
> Zac: mom alwys asks whts most ppulr & buys
> tkts so she can brag

Zac also told me about his cat, Lola, who was about to have kittens. I made him promise to tell me when they were born because I had to see those baby preciouses.

Having Zac to talk to was amazing, but the more we talked, the less I texted my squad. I mean, they texted me, but I had the tendency to ignore the group thread when Zac was on. Thursday night, however, Zac had gone somewhere with some friends and said he'd be MIA until after eight. Sebastian had an incident at dinner and had thrown such a fit, he'd knocked the pizza off the table. Papi sent me and Claire to our rooms and handled it himself, which was a relief. I'd been on Sebastian overload lately. Since I knew Zac was busy, I texted the girls about Sebastian and was surprised when they all answered within minutes. They showered me with hug emojis and kind words about my brother. I smiled at my Captain Marvel poster. *See? We girls get it. We need one another.*

The subject shifted to Ms. Larkin's latest assignment: the personal connection monologue. She wanted us to share with the class about a musical that spoke to us in some way. As usual, Tessa and Shay were freaking out since musicals were far from their favorite.

> Shay: I guess I don't understand what she wants.
>
> Amelia: It's not a big deal. You can find something to relate to in almost any musical. Last year for this assignment, I talked about Thoroughly Modern Millie because, well, my name! Plus, Millie moves boldly to NYC to follow her dreams. There are some major disconnects too, which I also talked about. You can choose to point those out or not. It's up to you.
>
> Tessa: For example . . . ?
>
> Amelia: Well, in TMM, Millie wants to marry for money and there's some racial problems with the musical. But I still connect with Millie.
>
> Tessa: *sigh* The problem is, I don't know very many musicals.

Me: I'm doing West Side Story and connecting it to being Mexican and immigration.

Amelia: Ms. L will love that!

Me: ☺

Tessa: Help me, Amelia. Tell me what to watch, and I'll watch it.

Amelia: Okay, thinking . . . Hold on.

Shay: I might talk about Fiddler on the Roof. I always liked that movie.

Tessa: What would you say about it?

Me: *singing* Tradition! ♫♫

Shay: I don't know. Something about my faith?

Me: But it's all about how the world is changing and girls getting married without their father's permission. That doesn't sound like you.

Shay: Yeah I guess not.

Amelia: Okay I'm back. So Shay I agree Fiddler is not a great fit for you but you could totally do Dear Evan Hansen. Tessa you could do Come from Away.

Shay: I haven't seen Dear Evan Hansen.

Me: You don't have to see it. There are enough clips on YouTube.

Amelia: Izzy's right. Evan is shy and feels alone and there is a song called Waving Through a Window that's all about watching life through a window instead of engaging with people. Google articles about the meaning of the musical and you'll find what you need.

Shay: But I engage with people. And life. I'm just picky about who I spend it with.

Tessa: Yup. You are far from being a loner.

Shay: Besides, I thought a lot of people already signed up for Dear Evan Hansen

Me: It's true. I think there are like five people doing it.

Amelia: Ms. L said she didn't care as long as you made a connection.

Shay: I don't know . . . I'd rather do something more original.

Tessa: Okay, I googled Come from Away. What is the connection to me?

Amelia: I was thinking about the pilot, Beverley Bass. She was the first female captain of a commercial airline, and she sings a song called Me and the Sky—look it up on YouTube. She was brave and driven in chasing her dreams in a male-dominated industry. Defying the odds. I thought you could relate her flying to your swimming. My two cents. Take or leave. ☺

Tessa: ❤

Tessa: Watching now.

Zac: hey babe

I glanced at the clock. It was 7:45.

Me to Zac: You're home early! ☺

Zac: missed u

Me to Zac: 😊

Shay: What about The Lion King? Because my dad was killed by a drunk driver, which is kind of a betrayal like Scar killing Mufasa. Then I got sent away to live someplace else . . . I guess it's not really the same.

Amelia: The Lion King would totally work, Shay! It doesn't have to be perfect. As long as you can explain your connections.

Zac: 😉

Whoa. Zac had never sent me a kissy emoji before. How bold should I be? I felt giddy and a little bit naughty.

> Me: Are you sending me kisses Mr. Lloyd?
> Zac: 😘😘😘😘😘😘😘

Oh my stars. How to respond to keep the kisses coming? Should I send one back? Before I could decide, he sent another text.

> Zac: ur so pretty izzy
> Zac: i luv how ur hair is all wld arond ur face

Strange how such badly spelled words could make a girl blush, even when she was alone in her bedroom.

> Play-it-cool me: I've never been much of a pony-tail girl. They give me headaches.
> Amelia: Ooh! New idea for Shay. Beetlejuice. Lydia feels invisible because her mom died and her dad doesn't want to feel anything and says she's just being moody, which totally makes me think of your grandma. Look up the song Invisible.
> Me to girls: Beetlejuice is a great idea!

Then I silenced my squad's text thread so I could focus on the conversation with Zac.

> Zac: u go. wht u like bout me?

Oh-kay. That totally sucked the wind from my sails. Had he said what he said to me because he meant it? Or because he was fishing for compliments?

> Me: I've always been impressed with your stellar spelling skills.
> Zac: haha I turnd off spll chk cause it changd my wrds & no one spks 4 me not even apple

Zac: hey u wanna ply borderlands?
Me: Still no. I'll play Minecraft.

Zac sent a gif of a cartoon man pointing a water hose to his head with water on full stream.

Truly, I think Zac had a bad case of senioritis. He rarely studied or did homework. He was all about making mischief. In class. In the hallways. Via text. I don't know how many times I'd told him I didn't want to play online shooter games, yet he still tried to talk me into it. Same with watching horror movies. Yesterday, he'd invited me over to watch *Death Night* even though 1) I'd told him I abhor horror movies, and 2) I'd already said no twice.

Zac: imma come ovr 2morro aftr school k?

My breath caught. *Now he wanted to come to my house?* I would prefer that, actually, but sadly, it wasn't an option.

Me: You can't. I have to watch Sebastian.

As I waited for Zac's reply, several more texts came through on my squad's thread. Amelia still helping Tessa and Shay with the musical assignment. No one seemed to have missed my exit.

Zac: dont u wtch ur bro evry day?
Me: Yep. Every weekday.
Zac: i'll hlp. im good w/kds

Aw! If only.

Me: I'm not allowed to have anyone over while I'm watching my brother. Besides, Sebastian doesn't like strangers.
Zac: wow that sucks
Me: It's usually only for a couple hours until Papi gets home.

Zac: u nevr had a frind ovr when ur bro is home? ever?

Me: Tessa has been here a few times, but Sebastian knows her from church.

Zac: i go to ur church!

Pfftt! Sure he did.

Me: You hardly ever go to church. And you've never met Sebastian.

Zac: i'll come on Sunday and meet him

Me: Okay!

But I had serious doubts Zac would show up.

Chapter

11

ONE THING I COULD COUNT ON with Zac was that he wouldn't text me before 3:00 on the weekends. He must sleep the day away or something. So, when I heard the orphan's cry to Miss Hannigan around ten Saturday morning, I knew it wouldn't be Zac.

It turned out to be Tessa on our group text.

> Tessa: Wanna all meet up for coffee and shopping downtown today?
> Me: Yes!!!

I was the first to answer, but both Shay and Amelia said they were game too. I hadn't gotten together with the girls outside school since before Christmas, and I was giddy to see them. We met at Grounds and Rounds, the coffee shop downtown. Shay was wearing her hiking books with a T-shirt and jeans, her hair in a ponytail. Tessa looked adorable as always in a cotton baby doll dress and leggings. And Amelia was our bright star, wearing her rainbow cardigan over a Rolling Stones T-shirt and a tiered red skirt that reached below her knees and revealed chunky black shoes.

While we were waiting in line for our drinks, Amelia followed up on the text conversation from last night.

"Did you two decide what musical you're doing?" Amelia asked.

"*Beetlejuice*," Shay said at the same time as Tessa said, "*Come from Away.*"

Amelia beamed. "Perfect. You'll both do great."

The barista called my name. I grabbed my drink and claimed the couch and wingback chairs in front of the fireplace. I took a picture of my hot chocolate, opened Instagram, and posted it with the caption: "Hanging with my girls at @groundsandroundscoffee."

I jumped over to check Zac's page, excited when I noticed he'd posted something new. Until I saw it was a picture of a dog's backside. Boys were so weird.

I sipped my hot chocolate, purposely sticking my nose in the whipped cream. I could feel the cold moisture on the tip of my nose as I sat back and waited for someone to notice.

Amelia was speculating over Ms. Larkin's musical announcement this coming Monday. "It hope it's *The Sound of Music*," she said. "It's my favorite oldie."

Tessa's gaze met mine and then shifted to my nose. She let out a snort and hid her smile behind her hand.

Amelia's head jerked toward Tessa. "What? What's so funny?"

"Izzy, you have whipped cream on your nose," Shay said, motioning to her own nose.

Tessa lost it. I feigned surprise, but my heart swelled at the joy that came from making people laugh.

I dabbed my napkin between my eyes. "Did I get it?"

Shay shook her head and touched her index finger to the tip of her nose. "It's lower."

"Izzy!" Amelia said. "Will you be serious for ten seconds?"

"What?" I asked, still very much in character.

"Oh." Shay slapped her thigh. "She knew it was there, didn't she?" she asked Tessa, who nodded while still laughing. Shay rolled her eyes and chuckled softly.

I dabbed the whipped cream from my nose, still not even cracking the tiniest smile. "What part would you want in *The Sound of Music*?" I asked.

"Maria, of course," Amelia said. "I did some research online about the best songs to sing while auditioning for Maria, and I've narrowed it down to 'Getting to Know You' from *The King and I* or 'A Spoonful of Sugar' from *Mary Poppins*. What do you think?"

I frowned, like I was seriously considering the matter, but I sensed that familiar underlying tension that arose anytime Amelia started talking about getting the lead in the spring musical. I understood why she wanted the lead, but without knowing the show, how could she get her heart set on it? What if the lead was a boy? I wouldn't put it past her to get a wig and try out for Jean Valjean in *Les Misérables*.

"I don't know *The King and I*," Tessa said.

"It's kind of a weird one," I said, "but that's a good song, and a good fit for *The Sound of Music*. Plus, I doubt anyone else will choose it since *Mary Poppins* is better known."

"That's what I was thinking," Amelia said, pushing her soft curls over her shoulder so she could sip her coffee without battling her hair.

After coffee, we made our way along the quaint downtown shopping area. We ended up at Paprika's, the best kitchen store in the world. It's so full of products, if you bump something, you risk knocking down every display in the building like dominoes. While the girls admired some cookie jars up front, I gravitated toward the baking area and was soon drooling over an ergonomic Williams Sonoma piping gun. I wanted it. But to be honest, the barrel would be a pain to clean. Plus, to switch colors, I'd have to clean it every time. Piping bags were easier for my colorful creations.

"Making cupcakes again?"

Cody Nichols was standing beside me, wearing his royal blue Paprika's store apron over a red T-shirt, a patriotic look that hearkened toward Captain America. I hadn't even heard him approach, but now that he was there, I recognized that clean boy smell. It was much softer than the cologne Zac wore, but every bit as pleasant.

"Not today," I said, returning the piping gun to its place on the table.

"Riku still talks about your cupcakes," Cody said with a smile, which sent some dormant butterflies fluttering about my stomach. I hadn't realized Team Cody butterflies were still down there.

"I'm glad he liked them! Birthdays are the perfect excuse for making cupcakes," I said. I was especially proud of the ones I'd made the Nichols' Japanese exchange student, featuring his favorite anime characters.

Amelia stepped up on my other side. "Izzy makes cupcakes almost daily."

"Weekly," I said.

"She's Instagram famous, you know," Amelia said. "For baking and stuff."

Cody's brown eyes met mine. "Really?"

I wrinkled my nose. "I just like posting pics and videos of what I make."

"Are you on Instagram, Cody?" Amelia asked.

"Sometimes." His gaze left mine and focused just behind me. "Hey, Tessa."

Tessa and Shay arrived, arm in arm.

"Isn't your birthday coming soon, Cody?" Tessa asked.

"End of February," he said, reaching up to straighten a stack of coasters.

Tessa nudged me. "You should make him a cupcake."

"No," Cody said. "That's okay."

"You'd be doing her a favor," Tessa said. "She's always looking for excuses to practice."

"It's true," I said. "I like to bake."

Cody raised an eyebrow, and I berated myself for such a lame line of speech. *I like to bake? What was I, five years old?*

"What kind of cupcake would you make him, Iz?" Amelia asked.

Nothing like having your friends put you on the spot. "Well, I could always go the safe route. Color them blue and gold and put your basketball number on the top. It's 42, right?"

A nod. "Yeah."

Like staring into the sun made one blind, looking too long at Cody's cuteness threatened to render me speechless, which made me feel like I was somehow cheating on Zac. I looked away and fought to say something coherent. "Riku said you like frogs, so I could make you a frog cupcake." An idea popped into my head. "Don't you also like *Diary of a Wimpy Kid*?"

He rubbed the back of his neck. "Back when I was in middle school."

"No," I said, refusing to allow him to be embarrassed. "You never outgrow a favorite book series. And it would be fun to make cupcakes with different cartoon faces, all black and white. I could do Greg and Rowley and Fregley and Patty. Even Rodrick. What do you think?"

His eyes widened. *Gah. Cuteness multiplying.*

"How would you even do that?"

"Easy," I said. "They'd be frosted white, and I'd use black piping to draw the characters. I'd have to print pictures of their faces since I don't remember them that well."

"Put a reminder in your phone, Izzy," Amelia said. "So you don't forget."

Cody shook his head. "You don't have to do that."

But I was already pulling up my calendar app. "February what?" I asked.

A shy smile graced his face. "February 28," he said.

I put it into my phone, well aware of how fast my heart was pounding in my ears. I told myself I liked Zac, but my body didn't seem to care. It was happy for Cody's presence. Hormones to blame no doubt. Stars.

"Well, I've got to unload some new freight," Cody said. "Have fun out there."

We said goodbye and then made our way out to the street. My gaze settled on the sign for La Petite Boulangerie just down the street. The French bakery was another favorite of mine.

"I need a crème puff," I said.

"Mmm," Tessa said. "I wouldn't mind a chocolate peanut butter macaron."

"I don't know, Izzy," Amelia sang. "If you're truly giving up on Cody, does that mean he's fair game?"

I frowned. "Why?"

"Because he's cute, that's why."

"You're seriously saying Zac isn't cute? Have you forgotten his E. J. hotness?"

"Eww," Tessa said.

"Oh, he's cute, all right," Amelia said, "and he knows it. Cody on the other hand. His hometown sweetness is pretty appealing. I wonder if he likes freckled redheads."

The nerve of that girl. "Why don't you ask him?"

"Maybe I will."

"Good," I said, knowing she never would. Amelia acted confident, but around boys, she definitely wasn't. At least not when she was talking about herself.

We reached the crosswalk and waited for traffic. "Zac said he's coming to church tomorrow," I told Tessa. "He wants to meet Sebastian."

"Sebastian doesn't like strangers," Tessa said.

"Which is why he wants to meet him." *Was she even listening?*

"You didn't invite him to your house, did you?"

See? This was exactly why I didn't tell Tessa things. "You know I'm not allowed to have anyone over but you," I said. "He just wants to meet Bash."

Come Sunday, however, Zac didn't show at church. Thankfully, Tessa kept her opinions on the matter to herself. When Zac texted me later, I asked him why he hadn't come.

> Zac: ack! izzy im so srry totally forgot to tell u

I sighed and picked up Fiesta. "He forgot. What do you say to that?" I pushed down Fiesta's forehead until it wrinkled. "I heartily agree."

This was the first time since this whole Zac thing started that I felt doubt creep in. Nobody was perfect. Still, I'd believed him when he'd said he wanted to meet Sebastian. I wanted him to want to meet my brother. To care about the things I cared about.

> Zac: thr ws a chang in plns w/my dad took me 2 an art thing in chicago so I was out o town w/hm this wknd

I could hardly fault him for being with his father.

> Zac: nxt week ill set my alrm. u forgiv me?

I grinned at the phone.

> Me: Of course.
> Zac: ❤❤❤
> Zac: u set ur alrm for nxt week 2 ok? remnd me
> Me: Sure. I can do that.

In the span of a half day my respect for Zac had fallen a few notches but then bounced right back up. Relationships were a lot more complicated than I'd ever imagined they could be.

—◈—

"We begin our time together today with an important announcement," Ms. Larkin said Monday morning in Drama.

The class burst into applause, everyone eager to learn Ms. L.'s choice for the spring musical. Amelia scooted to the edge of the couch, so overcome by excitement, she almost slid right onto the floor. She caught herself on the arm of the love seat just in time.

Ms. Larkin waved us to settle down. "You've all been patient, and for that I thank you. As I hoped, your anticipation was contagious. Just this morning Mrs. Ventrella inquired about our play. I told her she had to wait until after this class since I promised that you'd be the first to know."

Jaiden wolf-whistled from the stiletto chair. "Way to go, Ms. L.!"

"Thank you for your enthusiasm, Mr. Andrews."

A chuckle wisped over the class. I admired Ms. Larkin's restraint. That she wouldn't even tell the school principal was impressive.

"Without further ado, I announce the spring musical will be . . . *Peter Pan*."

Gasps rose around me, none louder than the one from Amelia, followed by her whispered, "Brilliant." The class cheered again.

"*Peter Pan* is a wonderful production with a great deal of parts, and it will appeal to a broad audience," Ms. L. said. "I believe it will also strengthen our theatrical community and reach beyond these walls to inspire our school and the city of Riverbend."

She went on to talk about the different roles, which she would post on the RHS Theater website soon, and encouraged us to read them thoroughly as we considered which part we might audition for six weeks from today.

"Auditioning for the production is mandatory for this class," she added.

Tessa gasped, and Shay looked like she might pass out. I was sitting beside her on the couch and scooted closer to lend my support.

"That is not to say everyone will be given a part," Ms. L. continued. "However, participation is a must, so if your audition does not result in a role, you will have to sign up for stage crew, set design, or marketing."

Then she, shockingly, made us go back to our lessons on character motivation, as if any of us could concentrate after that announcement. When the bell finally rang, the four of us clustered together on our way to the cafeteria.

"I like *Peter Pan*," Tessa said. "But I do not want to audition for anything."

"Me either," Shay said.

"I want to be a Lost Boy," I said, remembering how adorable they were in the Disney movie. "Think I would get a raccoon tail?"

"How about you, Amelia?" Tessa asked. "What part will you audition for?"

"Peter, of course," she said, stepping forward to fill her tray.

Tessa glanced at me, her look of unease matching the one I felt growing inside. *Was Amelia serious?* Amelia, with her size, height, and shocking red hair, was *not* the right look for Peter, a boy who could fly.

"Won't someone like Gage or Chad get Peter, though?" Tessa asked.

"The role of Peter is often played by women," Amelia said. "Chad is way too tall, and Gage is not experienced enough to pull off a lead."

I got some pizza, and by the time I settled at our table, Amelia was still talking *Peter*.

"For the monologue portion of the audition," she said, "I'm

thinking the scene between Peter and Tinkerbell will be most powerful. When he rejects her. Comedy is easier than drama, so it will be important to show I can handle the range of the part. My guess is Ms. L. will have us read something much lighter, like the first conversation between Peter and Wendy when he's chasing his shadow or one of the duels against Captain Hook."

I took a bite of my pizza to avoid having to look at Amelia.

Tessa, ever the diplomat, came up with something wise to say. "I suppose we should all be open to any part," she said, "though I'll die if Ms. Larkin casts me at all."

"Don't the leads go to upperclassmen?" I asked. "I heard that about *Seussical*."

"The leads in *Seussical* were upperclassmen, yes," Amelia said, "but I don't think any qualified underclassmen auditioned."

"Did she make the whole drama class audition last year?" Shay asked.

"Nope," Amelia said. "She held auditions after school, and that's why I ended up missing them. If they'd been during school hours, I would have been there. This year is going to be different. I can feel it. I *am* Peter." She closed her eyes and took a meditative breath, in through her nose, and out through her mouth, lips pursed as if blowing on a bowl of hot soup. When she opened her eyes again, she said, "I was meant for this part."

I caught Tessa's uneasy glance as I took a bite of pizza, now chewing slowly with worry for Amelia, who clearly had her heart set on the lead. Like I always say, I'm a glass-three-quarters-full girl, but this just felt weird.

Tessa managed to change the topic to new movies, one of which was a musical about a girl during the Great Depression.

"I wanted to go Friday night," I said. "But Papi was out of town, and I had to watch Sebastian until late."

"Your brother doesn't like musicals?" Shay asked.

"He doesn't like the theater period," I said. "It's too loud, and crowds freak him out."

"Isabella." Zac stepped over the bench beside me and sat down, straddling the narrow seat so he was sitting perpendicular to me.

My eyes widened, and I managed to say, "Hi," without sounding like a total freak.

He tilted his head and flashed me The Dazzle. "You ditched me today."

I felt my cheeks heat, but I ignored my traitorous body and acted like I didn't know what he was talking about, though I was secretly flabbergasted. I hadn't realized he'd expected me to sit with him permanently. "Ditched you for what?"

"I had to eat lunch with Ross and Shawn," he said. "I had nothing pretty to look at."

Amelia made a choking sound, and when I looked her way, she started coughing and took a drink from her water bottle. Tessa and Shay were giggling.

"You ditched me on Sunday," I said.

He had the decency to look ashamed. "You forgave me for that."

I held my annoyed expression for one . . . two . . . three . . . more seconds, then grinned. "I'm teasing. We were just discussing Ms. Larkin's big announcement."

"Right, right," he said. "The spring musi-calle. Tell me it's *Chicago*."

I rolled my eyes. "It's *Peter Pan*."

"Oh," he said, nodding. "I like that one too. Pirates are awesome."

"I'm sure Ms. Larkin will be relieved to have secured your good opinion," Amelia said.

"Mock if you will," he said. "But my friends and I can make or break anything in this school if we put our minds to it."

That shut up Amelia in a hurry. My jaw dropped. Tessa

and Shay both sat up straighter and threw each other a look of astonishment.

I slugged Zac's arm, but he caught my fist and held on. "*Zac*," I said. "Promise me you'll use your power for good and help promote the play?"

"I promise, fair Isabella," he said, kissing my hand.

Stars! I laughed and pulled free, delighted at how absolutely adorable he was. For the sake of my squad, though, and to keep Zac on his toes, I said, "You're a nut."

"A hunky nut, though, right?" he asked.

I fought a smile and lost. "Totally hunky."

"Ugh, that word," Tessa said, rolling her eyes.

Zac got up and leaned on the table with both hands. "Sit with me tomorrow?"

"Sure," I said.

"You're welcome to sit with us, too," Tessa said.

He grinned. "Thanks." He grabbed my hand and squeezed, then walked away, holding on until the last moment when our fingers slipped apart.

Amelia, watching him go, sighed dreamily. "Has he kissed you yet?" she asked.

"No," I said. "I totally would have told you."

"Just checking," she said. "Because I want to hear all about it when he does."

"Maybe I'll kiss first," I said.

All three girls stared at me, eyes wide like I had just said I was going to come to school tomorrow in my underwear.

"What?" I said. "If the opportunity arises, I'm taking it. He said the cutest thing last night." I pulled out my phone to show them.

Amelia yelped, eyes fixed on my cell. "My phone!" She leapt from the table, patting the pockets of her cardigan. "I must have left it in the Drama room." She took off, a streak of red hair, pea-green cardigan, and plaid red pants.

"I shudder to think about her as a mom someday," Shay said, which made me laugh.

"Well," Tessa said, not about to let Amelia's exit ruin her chance to shower me with wisdom. "I give Zac extra points for not having made a move yet," she said, "but try to remember this has only been going on for a week."

"Ten days," I corrected.

"Which is why I still think you should move slowly."

I wanted to say, "*Sí, Mamá*," but I held my tongue. Not even Tessa's pessimism could get me down after that little visit.

Chapter

12

After Drama on Tuesday, I carried my lunch tray toward the table by the windows where Zac sat with his friends. Ms. Larkin had kept us late, talking about the soul of a character, so the table was already pretty full. Zac was surrounded by his guy friends, with Mika and some other cheerleaders sitting opposite. No sign of Ensley.

Zac spotted me and stood. "Izzy!" He shoved Ross's arm. "Move down, dude."

Ross slid down the bench, leaving a spot open for me beside Zac. I squeezed into the narrow space. Zac and I were both wearing short sleeved shirts today, and our arms touched. That and his spicy cologne sent tingles through my body.

"What are you doing this afternoon?" he asked, his voice husky.

"Watching Sebastian, like I do every day."

"Right, right. What about after that, once your parents are home?"

I shrugged. *Was he going to ask me on a date?*

"Because you should come to robotics with Claire," he said.

"Why?" I asked.

"The team needs someone with your creativity," he said.

"I don't know." I re-situated a piece of pepperoni that had nearly fallen off the side of my slice. "I don't think I can commit to that many nights out."

"Marketing only meets on Wednesdays," he said. "Come on, Iz. Robotics is boring without you there."

Never in my life had I had a sliver of interest in robotics, but I loved that Zac wanted me there. "I have youth group on Wednesday nights."

"That's right," he said. "Well, at least think about it. Maybe you could alternate. One Wednesday with us, one with the church." He grinned.

I was starting to think Zac knew exactly what kind of effect his Dazzle had on girls.

"I'll alternate if you do," I said. "You come to youth group with me every other week."

He winced. "Can't. Not during the build season. Mr. Lucas would kill me. Programmers are at meetings five days a week right now to get the bot ready for the competition."

He wasn't exaggerating. This I knew from Claire. I took a bite of my pizza as a buffer against the pressure Zac was wielding. It didn't matter what he asked. His propositions always came with a magnetic pull, and when it was something I didn't want to do, I struggled to resist. Breaking eye contact was always the first step. Which brought my gaze to Mika, who was looking at me from where she sat across the table.

"I heard the drama class is putting on *Peter Pan*," she said. "Brie is so excited."

Brie was a junior who was in my PE class. I think she was also in Drama 2. "Is she going to audition?" I asked.

"Totally," Mika said. "She'll make a great Peter."

The audacity of her statement felt like a slap, but I thought about petite Brie, who often showed off her gymnastics training by doing handsprings in PE class. Brie, whose head came up to Amelia's shoulder. And Amelia, who completely filled most doorways. Mika was right. Brie would make the perfect Peter Pan. My chest felt tight, and I glanced across the cafeteria to where my squad was sitting, spotted that glorious head of red curls.

Poor Amelia.

———⁓———

After dinner, Claire and I were in the kitchen, tag-teaming to get the dishes done. She was loading the dishwasher while I did the pans, so when my phone started buzzing, my hands were covered in soapy water.

Claire got to my phone first. "Zac says he wants to play a game."

My pulse rose. "What game?"

"He didn't say. I hope it's not inappropriate."

I clicked my tongue. "Why would you say that?"

She shrugged.

"Whatever." I scrubbed the frying pan harder. The sooner I was done, the sooner I could get my phone away from Claire, escape to my room, and find out what Zac wanted.

"You don't have to get all mad," Claire said. "I was kidding."

"Sure you were."

"It's just . . . I see you sitting with him and his friends at lunch. Do you know what him and Ross talk about in class? They're pretty crude."

I rinsed the pan and shoved it toward her to dry. "I'm not doing this with you."

She took the pan. I avoided making eye contact as I wiped

down the sink and dried my hands. I grabbed my phone and headed for the stairs.

"Good night, Izzy," she said, her tone all small, probably trying to make me feel guilty.

It wasn't going to work. "Night, Claire," I called, then ran up to my room, shut the door behind me, and leapt onto my bed. I opened my texting app and Zac's message.

> Zac: wanna play a game w/me? its fun
> Me: It's not a video game, is it?
> Zac: lol no kiss marry kill or wld u rather

Hmm . . . Kiss, Marry, Kill seemed like it could get us in trouble in a hurry. I thought up a good question for Would You Rather?

> Me: Would you rather lose the ability to read or lose the ability to speak?
> Zac: read cuz I cld hve somone read 2 me
> Zac: wld u rather be able 2 contrl animls w/ur mind or be able 2 talk 2 animls
> Me: Talk to animals, of course! ❤
> Me: Would you rather have edible spaghetti hair that regrows every night or sweat out maple syrup?
> Zac: ur gross uhm swt mpl syrp cuz id smell sweet
> Me: Dogs would follow you everywhere and lick you.
> Zac: u could lick me. ☺
> Me: 😬
> Zac: kk wld u rather wear fncy cloths w/no makeup or comfortbl cloths w/fncy makeup?
> Me: Comfortable clothes.

Zac: kewl

Me: Why cool?

Zac: was just thinkin how gorgeous u are & how hot u would look w/mascara

My stomach fluttered. I loved when he said things like that.

Me: What's so gorgeous about me, anyway?

Zac: evrythng babe! ur hair is my fvrite. u shld wear it dwn more. plus u hve dark eyes. mascara wld bring out ur eyes evn more. ur gorgeous now but u cld be drop dead sexy

So much to soak in with that last text. I didn't know if I liked the word *sexy*, though. *Did I want to be sexy?*

Me: I've never been much into makeup.

Zac: its prolly a pain yeah? enhances beauty tho

Pffft. Spoken like a boy who didn't have to wear makeup.

Zac: hey you gotta help me out i need a new psswrd

Wow, he jumped from one subject to another faster than Amelia.

Me: Why?

Zac: did u see that pic of a dogs butt on my IG? ross hacked me

I chuckled. Well, at least I could rest in the fact that Zac hadn't posted the dog picture.

Me: How did you know it was him?

Zac: cuz i'm sherlok holmes baby. privat envestigatr

And a horrible speller too.

Me: Oh, really?

Zac: nahh i told ross my psswrd

Me: Why would you do that?

Zac: hes my bro

Me: I wondered why you posted that pic.

Zac: i will destroy ross in time but i need a new psswrd what do u think? something romantic about us

What does that mean? This boy SO confuses me every day times infinity.

Zac: zakyromeo

Me: How about something with Jack and Rose? Didn't you say you like that movie?

Zac: titanic perfect yes!!! i'll do jackroseizzy cuz it was ur idea

He is so weird sometimes.

Zac: i hate thinking up psswrds for all my different accounts

Me: I always use the same one for all my accounts.

Zac: its a good one? one you wont forget?

Me: iluvcupc8s

Zac: LOL i get it!! iluvcupc8s too!! LOL 😂

I chuckled. He was so easy to entertain. It was adorable.

Zac: kk changing passwords now to jackroseizzy

Zac: ack! need a #

Zac: had to go with jackroseizzy3 cuz 3 names ...

Me: That works.

He didn't text back. I figured he was done, but then I got another one.

Zac: i'm gonna come over after school tomorrow
2 c u
Me: You can't! You had your chance to meet
Sebastian at church and you didn't come.
Zac: ill come next Sunday

Then he sent a picture of his puckered lips, which was becoming his signature sign-off. I put down the phone, both sorry to see him go and kind of relieved to be done. The boy was becoming a huge time-suck in my life. Not that I was complaining. Because #zaclloyd was hunky and texted me sweet nothings. And sometimes a whole lot of nothing to go with it.

When I checked my phone at breakfast, I had a text from Tessa.

Tessa: You told him your password???

A flutter of fear raced through me. I checked my Instagram and saw I had posted late last night. It was a shadowy profile of Zac wearing a baseball hat with a kazoo hanging from his lips like a cigarette. The caption said: "There is nothing more stimulating than a case where everything goes against you. I will solve the secret of the Instagram hacker. The criminal will be brought to justice. ~Detective Sherlock Holmes."

I chuckled, impressed he'd taken the extra time to use correct punctuation, spelling, and capital letters in the caption. I texted Tessa back.

Me: I think it's cute.

Tessa didn't answer.

I was almost late to drama class and ended up sitting on the bean-bag at Tessa's feet. She was sitting on the love seat.

"Did you change your password yet?" she asked me.

"No," I said. "That would be rude."

"Izzy, it was rude of him to hack your account."

"I thought it was funny."

"You won't think it's funny if he does something mean."

"Why would he do something mean?" I asked.

Tessa opened her mouth to speak but stopped herself.

"What?" I said.

"Alex doesn't know my passwords, and he doesn't want to."

"Great. That's you and Alex. Zac and I are different people."

I don't know why she was freaking out over this particular issue. I mean, there were so many other things about Zac she could have made a much stronger case for. The password thing just didn't seem to matter. "It's not a big deal. Knowing Zac, he already forgot it."

At youth group that night, I felt awkward, awkward, awkward. Tessa and Alex were all cozy and whispery. I totally felt like a third wheel and couldn't focus at all on what Zoe was saying in the lesson. *Where was Lauren? And Shay? Hadn't Shay decided she was coming to our church from now on?* I decided then and there to join the robotics marketing team and go every-other week, like Zac had suggested. I wasn't going to torture myself in hopes that Shay might show up, and I wasn't that good of friends with Lauren. Besides, a week away from here would be nice and give Tessa and Alex all the privacy they probably wished they had on a regular basis.

When I got home, I looked up a tutorial for applying mascara and eyeliner. It took me several tries before I found one I liked. I wasn't positive I had the right kind of makeup. Mine was super old—from the time I was in a Christmas dance production in seventh grade. Still, I managed to do an okay job. My eyes did seem to "pop," as Zac said they would.

When I went to bed, I adjusted my alarm to allow for extra time to do my eyes in the morning. I couldn't wait to see Zac's reaction.

Chapter

13

I WAS FINISHING UP in the shower the next morning when I heard the doorknob rattle.

"I'm still in here," I yelled.

Sebastian's muffled scream sent a jolt of fear through me as I realized my mistake. I forgot how getting up early might affect his schedule. My brother functioned poorly without his schedule. I toweled off and pulled on my bathrobe. When I came out, Sebastian was sitting against the wall outside the door, hugging his head, elbow face staring at the carpet.

"I'm done," I said, trying to act like shame wasn't filling me up from inside.

He growled but didn't release his head. I could have started listing Marvel movies. I could have waited until he calmed down. Instead, I walked toward my room. I just couldn't this morning. I had my own life going on, and today was a big day for me.

"Isabella Valadez showers from 6:30 a.m. until 6:45 a.m.," my brother said. "Sebastian Valadez showers from 6:15 a.m. until 6:30 a.m."

"I know," I said, turning to face him. He'd released his head but was still staring at the floor. "I'm sorry I didn't check the time before I showered."

Sebastian growled, then threw back his head so it whacked against the wall.

"Hey!" I said. "None of that."

He did it again, this time growling louder.

I tried threatening him. "I'll get Mamá."

Another thunk. "Josefina Valadez . . ." Thunk. ". . . went . . ." Thunk. ". . . to work." Thunk.

Of course she had. "I'll get Papi, then."

He pounded his head against the wall so hard the paint and drywall cracked.

"Sebastian!" I said. "You're going to hurt yourself. Plus, you're breaking the wall. I'm getting Papi."

"Noooo!" He scrambled to his hands and knees and crawled into the bathroom, slamming the door behind him.

I inspected the dented wall. Papi was going to freak out. Something banged against the inside of the bathroom door, making me jump. Another bang. Sebastian, still hitting his head.

I walked to the top of the stairs and yelled over the railing. "Papi! Sebastian is hitting his head on the door of the bathroom, and he dented the wall up here."

From inside the bathroom came, "Ahhhh!" followed by several loud strikes against the door. My brother had heard me tattle and wasn't happy.

Papi appeared at the foot of the stairs. "What do you mean he dented the wall?"

"He was hitting his head against the wall out here, and it broke through."

The screaming and banging from inside the bathroom increased as Papi came upstairs and inspected the damage.

He sighed. "What set him off?"

"I took too long in the shower."

Papi frowned. "Don't you shower after him?"

"Usually, but today I need more time to get ready, so I tried to get in before him."

"Izzy . . ."

"I'm sorry, okay? But sometimes I need to put myself first!" I stomped into my room and slammed the door behind me. I thought about whacking the back of my head against the door but held off. I'd pushed my luck enough this morning.

I tried to ignore the voices bleeding through my door. Papi and Sebastian fighting it out. I knew I could help—I was good with Sebastian—but it wasn't my turn.

Yet I'd caused this with my desire to look nice for Zac. I reached for my liquid eyeliner. If I was going to do this right, I needed to get started. I twisted off the cap, pulled out the top, and lifted the fine black brush to my left eye.

My hand was shaking.

I took a deep breath and held still. I managed to trace my top eyelid and started on the bottom, but a tear leaked from my eye, taking with it a stream of black eyeliner.

I threw it on the dresser and fell onto my bed, letting the tears come. It was no use. Today was ruined. I'd have to try again tomorrow.

Thursday night, I showered before bed. That way when I woke Friday morning, I would have no reason to go near Sebastian's domain. I ran downstairs, made his pancakes and left them sitting at the table, then I ran back to my room and applied my makeup, just like in the tutorial. I waited until the last minute so Papi wouldn't see my face, and then I raced out the door where Claire was waiting in the truck, the engine idling. She didn't say a word about my makeup on the ride to school. I didn't know if she hadn't noticed or just didn't care.

I went to Zac's locker as soon as I got to school, but there was no sign of him. I finally gave up and went to meet Shay. She must have given up waiting for me because she wasn't there. I found her in the classroom. She noticed my makeup right away.

"Wow," she said. "You look different. Is that for the monologue presentations? I didn't think to dress up."

Right. Drama class. *West Side Story*. "No, I just wanted to try something new."

Shay seemed to accept this. No one else even mentioned my eyes until PE class. Hyun Ki said it looked great, which made me feel good. As she and I were walking with the class out to the track to run the mile, I heard Michael's voice from behind me.

"Izzy! *¡Espera! ¡Déjame ver!*"

I obeyed and turned around. "*¿Qué?*"

Michael's pale brown eyes were fixed on mine—around mine, actually. "*¡Eres muy atractiva!*"

I blushed. Michael had never said I was attractive before. I glanced at Hyun Ki, told Michael, "*Gracias*," and continued walking. Michael fell into step on my other side.

"Why the change?" he asked. "*¿Un novio?*"

A boyfriend? Why would he assume a little eye makeup meant I had a boyfriend? "Just wanted to try it."

Michael shrugged. "Well, he's a lucky guy. And he'd better treat you right, or *Hermano Miguel* will come find him. *Hablo en serio*."

Brother Michael said he was completely serious. Touched by his words, I thanked him. "*Gracias, Hermano Miguel*," I said, "*Hablo en serio*."

We exchanged sincere smiles that quickly turned awkward.

Since we'd reached the track, I started running, Hyun Ki at my side.

"What was *that* about?" Hyun Ki asked as we ran.

"Practicing Spanish as usual," I said, but Michael's sincerity had taken me off guard, and I didn't think mascara was the only reason for it.

———

Drama class went better than I thought it would—in regard to my mascara, anyway.

"Izzy, you look amazing," Amelia said. "I've tried to do my eyes like that, and I can't. I think it's because my lashes are so pale. Or maybe I'm just a failure with eyeliner."

"You did a nice job," Tessa said.

"You look pretty," Shay said. "But you look pretty without it too." She narrowed her eyes, considering—the same way she looked at the horses at Green Tree Farm. "Makeup doesn't make you look prettier, I don't think."

"It's not about being pretty," Amelia said. "Not with theater. If I went onstage right now with performance lighting, I'd look like a white sheet. You have to wear makeup on the stage to give definition to your face under all those lights."

"You know who wears mascara well?" Tessa said. "Zoe."

"Yes!" I said, thinking of how pretty she had looked at youth group the other night. "Hey, where were you, anyway, Shay? I thought you were coming to our church from now on."

"On Sundays," Shay said. "Wednesdays I have to help at the bookstore until Aunt Laura can figure out how to shift the schedules around."

"You're going to their church?" Amelia said, loud enough to turn the heads of the students sitting in the next couch over. "What about my church?"

Shay shrank into the rocking chair, her posture curling.

Amelia scooted to the edge of the couch, getting as close to the rocking chair as she could. "It's because of my youth group, isn't it? Theirs is better?"

"It's more because Aunt Laura made friends with Tessa's mom," Shay squeaked.

Amelia huffed and rolled her eyes. "Whatever." She got up and stormed toward the door, leaving her phone on the couch.

I grabbed it and held it up. "Amelia!"

Tessa pushed my arm down and shook her head. "She'll be back," she said.

But I wasn't so sure.

"Today you will be presenting your monologues on your chosen musical," Ms. Larkin said, looking from face to face. "We will not get through everyone, but those who are ready can sign up on the whiteboard to go first."

I headed for the whiteboard immediately. By the time I signed my name, I was fifth in line. I threaded my way out of the small crowd and went back to our little spot. Tessa and Shay hadn't moved. I shouldn't have been surprised. They rarely volunteered to do anything in this class and would put it off as long as they could. Amelia still hadn't returned, but she didn't have to do the assignment, since she was a TA and had done it last year.

Chad went first. He'd chosen *Dear Evan Hansen* and shared about how he sometimes felt like Evan, like he didn't belong anywhere. I got teary. Twice! I blinked like crazy, worried my eyeliner and mascara might run.

Amber was up next, and she talked about how she felt pressured to be popular and how an off-Broadway performance of *Wicked* gave her a new perspective. "I realized I had my own strengths, and being popular really didn't matter anymore."

Jaiden talked about *The Lightning Thief*. The novels had made an impact on him as a kid. "I wouldn't read until I got hooked on those books," he said. "Now I read all the time."

Gage also presented on *Dear Evan Hansen* but talked about his cousin who had committed suicide. Gage appreciated how the show was helping people start conversations about what others might be going through.

When Ms. Larkin called my name, Tessa whispered, "Good luck!"

Unlike most of my friends, I didn't get nervous presenting in front of groups, and today I had a chance to talk about something that mattered deeply to me.

"A show that has greatly impacted my life is *West Side Story*," I said from the stage. "As a Mexican-American daughter of immigrants, the story's call for tolerance has always resonated with me. Like the song 'Somewhere' says, the immigrants in the story are looking for a place to call home, same as my grandparents were when they came to live in this country.

"Ultimately, *West Side Story* is a love story between two kids from different cultures. Their friends and families are afraid of that love, and their fear leads to death. That same fear is still present in our world today. We must not be afraid to talk and really listen to one another. Only then can we understand. And when we understand, while we might not agree, at least we are able to extend love and compassion to one another.

"In 2009, Lin-Manuel Miranda updated *West Side Story* for its revival on Broadway, and now Steven Spielberg has made a new film version. This musical is a powerful, important story that continues to address issues that resonate with audiences everywhere."

I smiled and bobbed a small bow, my signal to the audience that I was done. The class applauded, and I returned to my seat. Tessa gave me a high five.

Shay said, "That was so good!"

I reclaimed my place on the couch beside Amelia's phone and listened to students share for the rest of class.

When the bell rang, I said, "See you later!" and took off, eager to stop in at the bathroom to check my appearance before finding Zac at lunch. As I pushed into the restroom, I almost hit Amelia, who'd been attempting to open the door from the other side.

"You might want to slow down, Izzy," she said. Her eyes were red and puffy.

"What's wrong?" I asked.

"Like you care."

"I do care," I said, putting my arm around her.

She threw me off. "No, you don't! You and Tessa . . . you did everything you could to get Shay and her aunt to start going to your church, didn't you?"

I lifted both shoulders in slow motion. "They were looking for a church."

Amelia folded her arms. "I don't even know why I hang around with you three. You obviously don't want to be my friend."

My eyes watered. "That's not true. We love you."

"Sure. Except now you three have one another at church. I don't have anyone." She shoved past me and out the door, knocking me into the wall so hard I almost fell over. "Hey!"

Once I caught my balance, I lunged toward the counter, praying my makeup wasn't running. I felt bad that Amelia was hurting, but after everything I'd gone through to look nice for Zac, I would kill her if she ruined my eyes. I grabbed a paper towel but didn't see any smudges. Perhaps it took real crying to do serious damage to mascara. I stared at the girl in the mirror and took several deep breaths. "You're okay," I whispered. Another deep breath. I couldn't solve Amelia's problems right now. It was time to find Zac.

I made my way to the cafeteria. As I worked my way through the lunch line, I kept thinking about what Amelia had said. Had we excluded her in some way? If anything, I felt excluded for always having to watch Sebastian. I knew Amelia didn't like her own youth group because it was small and sometimes awkward. But it wasn't my fault or Tessa's fault if Shay's Aunt Laura liked Faith Community. I felt like I should apologize, but I didn't know what for.

"Hey, gorgeous." Zac's appearance obliterated all thoughts of Amelia.

I beamed at him as we stood almost toe to toe. *"Hola, guapo."*

He looked completely stunned. "You did your eyes. You look amazing." The awe continued to grow across his face. "I knew you would, but dang, girl!" He whistled low, his eyes lit with teasing.

I couldn't stop smiling. "Don't get used to it," I said. "It was a lot of work!"

"Aw, but totally worth the effort," he said, tapping one finger under my chin. "And what did you just say to me? Something Spanish?"

"Hola, guapo means 'Hi, handsome.'" Then I did something bold. Something much more daring than a little mascara.

I kissed Zac.

I kissed *him*!

I totally kissed him, right there in the cafeteria. I didn't exactly know what I was doing. I'd never kissed a boy before, but I guess I figured, how hard could it be? I held my tray out to the side with one hand, stepped up close, and kissed him. Right on the lips. Counted to one Mississippi and stepped back.

For a millisecond he just stared at me, and I thought, *Uh-oh.* But then he flashed The Dazzle, and it was somehow a wider, brighter Dazzle than I'd seen before. I'd done that. I'd made him practically glow. He pivoted to stand beside me, took my tray in one hand, and with his other, grabbed my hand and led me to his table. *Oh, my stars, I was officially with this boy in plain sight for all to see. Score one me.*

Chapter

14

WHEN I GOT HOME FROM SCHOOL, I texted Amelia to see if she was okay, but she didn't answer. I decided not to tell Tessa and Shay what she'd said. I didn't want Shay to feel bad. So I started in on my homework. The problem was, multiplying polynomials was frying my brain. I was barely through half the page when the doorbell rang.

"Ugh!" I really didn't have time for this. I jumped up from the table and ran to the door.

When I opened it, I was shocked to see Zac on my doorstep.

"Hey," he said, flashing me a lazy grin.

My heart picked up a jackhammer and started to do some construction work in my chest. Words came out of my mouth. "What you here?"

Zac chuckled. "I *think* I can translate. You want to know what I'm doing here, right?"

I nodded.

"I wanted to see you." He stepped inside, slid his arms around my waist, and pulled me into a kiss.

Oh. Wowzer. This one was different from the one I'd given him. This time there were no lunch trays separating us, and he was moving his lips while I just stood there, dumbfounded. I decided I should move my lips too, and when I did, Zac somehow pulled me closer until there was no space between us and I became lost in a feeling of elation.

Until I ran out of air, pulled back to breathe, and unintentionally ended the kiss.

Bummer.

Zac gazed down on me, and his Dazzle was different. Intense. He closed his eyes and set his forehead against mine. "You make me feel wild, Isabella Valadez," he said.

What beautiful words! I mulled them over as I managed to catch my breath, and when I did, I caught my wits as well. "Zac, I told you. I have to watch my brother after school."

"Not until 3:50," he said, grinning.

I can't believe he remembered the exact time. "Yeah, but that's only ten minutes from now, and I have homework."

"So I'll help you." He came in for another kiss, but I stepped back.

His idea had merit. "Do you know how to multiply polynomials?" I asked.

He frowned, like he was thinking about it. "I can take a look."

Anything had to be better than me on my own. I shut the door and pushed him toward the living room, desperate for math help.

I fell on the couch and moved my books to the center of the coffee table. Zac sank down beside me. His arm touched mine, and I shivered, inhaling his spicy scent. I wanted to kiss him some more, but that was no way to get my homework done.

Zac peered at my math book for a moment and the problem I'd written in my notebook.

$$(8a - 3)(4a^2 + 3a - 1)$$

"I'm not sure I remember how to do this," Zac said.

"Oh, no, Zac, you have to remember. Please." I wasn't the greatest student. Especially when it came to math. I struggled to pay attention when Mr. Fletcher was teaching. I might be bilingual, but I didn't speak numbers.

Zac scratched his forehead. "I'm pretty sure you use the distributive property."

His math words sounded right. "In English, please? Translate?"

"Well, you take $4a^2 + 3a - 1$ times $8a$. Then you take $4a^2 + 3a - 1$ times negative three."

"Okay, but how?" *Seriously, who would ever need to do this in real life?*

"You need to rewrite it." He took the pencil from my hand and got to work. "So you'd put . . . $8a(4a^2 + 3a - 1) - 3(4a^2 + 3a - 1)$. Then you can simplify it."

Yes, this was looking familiar.

Zac continued to narrate as he worked. "So, $8a$ times $4a^2$ . . . Eight times four is 32. And a times a^2 is a^3. So $32a^3$. Eight times three is 24. And a times a is a^2. And $8a$ times -1 is $-8a$." He continued through the entire problem, then talked about merging like terms as he rewrote the problem again. "So you end up with $32a^3 + 12a^2 - 17a + 3$."

This gave me some serious flashbacks to struggling in geometry class. It was all very familiar, but not quite familiar enough.

"Okay, I sort of understand. Maybe. Could you do one more?" I asked, wincing.

He smirked at me. "You just want me to do your homework."

"That's so not true. I'm a visual learner. One more, please?"

He quirked an eyebrow. He had great eyebrows. "It's going to cost you."

I frowned. "You hungry? I made chocolate chip cookies last night." I started to get up, but Zac grabbed my wrist and pulled me back beside him.

"I will have cookies, yes please, but I actually had something different in mind." Then he leaned close and kissed me.

My mind fogged, my stomach zinged, and all I could think about was how nice his lips felt against mine with his spicy smell all up in my space. Until one of his hands found my waist and started sliding up.

I popped to my feet in a hurry. "I'll get your cookies while you copy the next problem." I scurried to the kitchen, jackhammer working on my heart again, making me all hyper and melty inside. In the kitchen, I took my time, urging my heart to chill out as I arranged cookies on a plate. I suddenly remembered a host of rules I was breaking. No boys in the house when parents aren't home. No friends in the house when I hadn't finished my homework. No friends in the house when I was watching Sebastian. No friends in the house without permission.

I glanced at the clock. It was 3:50. Sebastian would be here any second. I headed toward the couch. Zac had copied the next math problem under the first in his super tidy handwriting. I held out the plate and waited until he took a cookie to lay down the bad news.

"Zac, I'm sorry, but you're going to have to leave. You can't be here when Sebastian shows up. He'll tell my parents, and then I'll get in trouble."

"He'll be cool," Zac said, biting a cookie in half.

I shook my head. "He won't be cool. He'll tell."

Zac ate the other half of the cookie. "I'm good with kids," he said, talking over a full mouth. "You'll see."

"My brother isn't like other kids," I said. "He has—"

The front door opened, and in walked Sebastian, book in hand. I stared, silent, hoping he might go up to his room, which of course he didn't because he never did that. No, as always, he walked to the kitchen, put down his book, and reached for the cookie jar.

"*Hola*, Sebastian," I said, not moving.

"*Hola*, Isabella Valadez." He carried three cookies to the dining room table and sat down.

I shoved the plate of cookies into Zac's hands and then walked to the fridge, feeling like I was in some sort of suspense thriller movie. I got out the milk. I was pouring some into a glass for Sebastian, when Zac said, "Can I have some milk too?"

Sebastian bolted to his feet, chair scraping over the wood floor. His body went stiff. His chin touched his chest, his eyes focused on the floor.

I grimaced.

"A stranger in the house," Sebastian said.

"Not a stranger," I said. "Sebastian, this is my friend from school. Zac Lloyd. He's on Claire's robotics team. He came to help me with my math."

Sebastian seemed to consider this. "Isaac Lloyd," he said. "Address: 412 Richmond Way. Subteam: Programming."

"That's right," I said, wondering when Sebastian had decided to memorize the robotics roster.

"How does he know that?" Zac whispered.

"The robotics roster is on the fridge," I said.

"No friends allowed, Isabella Valadez. Papi said no friends allowed."

"Yes, I know, and my friend was just leaving."

"Come on, bro," Zac said. "Don't you want your sister to do well in math? She's failing her class. She needs my help, or she'll have to repeat tenth grade."

I shot him a glare. *I might not be a good student, but I wasn't that bad off.*

"We won't bother you at all, little bro," Zac said.

"Papi said no friends. Papi said."

"Dude. Does he just keep repeating himself?" Zac whispered.

I put my finger to my lips, hoping he'd shut up. I took Sebastian his milk and set it on the table beside his cookies and his copy of *The Hive Queen*, Wings of Fire book twelve.

"Here's your milk," I said.

"Papi said no friends," he whispered.

"Do you want to play *Minecraft*?" I asked.

While I didn't hear a sound, I could read his lips loud and clear: "Papi said no friends."

I rolled my eyes as I walked toward Zac. "You need to go," I whispered.

He stood to greet me. "But what about my milk and cookies?"

"Another time," I said.

"Promise?"

"Yes! Now will you get out of here?"

Zac glanced over my shoulder toward where Sebastian was sitting, his forehead wrinkling. "What's his problem, anyway?"

"Shh! He's not deaf." I should have told Zac about Sebastian's autism, but I wasn't about to let him stand there and hurt Bash's feelings. "I'll explain later."

"Okay," Zac said. "I'll go. But I want a goodbye kiss."

I bobbed up on my tiptoes and kissed his cheek.

"That doesn't count," he said, hands sliding around my waist. He pulled me to him and crushed his mouth against mine.

Completely off balance, I didn't know what to do but hang on to keep from falling backward over the coffee table. Before I had time to devise a new plan, the sound of breaking glass sent Zac springing away from me.

I whirled around. Sebastian was on his feet, clutching his head in ambulance mode, rocking from side to side and moaning. He'd somehow knocked—or thrown—his book and the glass of milk to the other side of the table where they had hit the wall. Both were on the floor under the table now, the glass in pieces, his book soaked in milk.

Oh no. I shoved Zac toward the door. "Out!" I said. "Now!"

"Okay, okay." He chuckled. "I see short tempers run in the family."

That made me shove him again and put a lot more effort into it. "You need to shut up," I said. "You don't know what's happening."

Sebastian chose that moment to let out a piercing scream. He picked up the chair he'd been sitting on and threw it against the window. The glass splintered but didn't shatter.

Behind me, Zac let out a swear word, which only made Sebastian scream louder.

"Bash," I said, firmly, calmly. "Tell me about Marvel."

Sebastian yelled and picked up the next chair. He tried to throw it, but I grabbed one leg and the whole thing ended up in my hands. I set it down behind me and kept advancing. Bash raced into the kitchen and started throwing whatever he could find. Utensils, a ceramic jar, a bottle of dish soap, several scratch pads, a scrub brush, the salt and pepper shakers. Some of it bounced, some of it shattered. All I could do was inch closer and duck when things flew my way.

"*Thor* came out May 8, 2010," I said. "Am I right, Bash? Help me tell Marvel."

The spicy scent of Zac preceded him stepping into my side view. "How can I help?"

I wanted to tell him to leave, but Sebastian was almost to the silverware drawer. "We need to grab him and hold him down."

"Got it." Zac circled to the other side of the island. Now we had Sebastian pinned between us. He hadn't opened the utensil drawer yet. Instead, he got into the drawer beside it filled with pot holders. These I could take without any pain, so I charged. Zac got there first and tackled Sebastian like some kind of linebacker. The two bodies slammed into me, and all three of us crashed onto the floor in a tangle of arms, legs, and hair. Mostly *my* hair. Sebastian bucked between us, but I managed to get my arms around him. It would have been better if we had wrapped him in a blanket first. Being bundled calmed him.

Zac quickly slid to his knees. "What now?" he asked, and the sound of his voice sent Sebastian into a new bout of kicking and screaming.

"There's a blanket on the back of the couch. Help me wrap him."

Zac's brow crinkled, but he obeyed. Moments later the thick plush fabric was falling over us. Zac smoothed it over Sebastian's back and then somehow managed to tuck it between us, which broke free the grip I'd had on my brother. I jumped to my knees and helped Zac swaddle Bash. My brother was weeping now, and he'd stopped flailing.

Zac met my gaze, and his eyes were wide and panicked. "I messed up," he said.

"Yeah, you did." I pushed back from the blanket burrito that was my now-sobbing brother and stood up. I walked to the door, thankful to hear Zac's footsteps right behind me.

"I'm sorry, Izzy," he whispered. "I should have listened to you. Please don't be mad. I didn't understand."

This caused a deep sigh to well up inside me. I opened the door, holding it for him, and let out the breath. "We'll talk later," I said.

Zac stepped onto the porch and turned back to speak, but I shut the door in his face. I leaned against it, tears welling in my eyes. I stayed there a minute, letting my emotions thaw. Sebastian's cry was now a soft whimper. I started cleaning up broken glass and ceramics, picking up utensils. I poured Sebastian a new glass of milk. Set out fresh cookies. I mopped off his book as best I could and set it on the table, arranged everything just how he liked it.

He was still breathing heavily, so I sat beside him on the floor and leaned against the dishwasher.

"I'm sorry, Bash," I said.

"Papi said no friends," he whispered.

"I know. You're right. I told Zac not to come over, but he wasn't a very good listener. He wanted to help me with my homework." *And apparently make out.*

"Papi said no."

I took another long, cleansing sigh. "I'm sorry, Sebastian."

"Papi said no."

"I was wrong. Will you forgive me? Please?"

A long stretch of silence followed, and I began to imagine how my parents would respond when Sebastian told them about Zac. Not good.

"Okay, Isabella Valadez. I forgive you."

Well, that was a start. "Thank you."

"He's a bad guy."

"No, he was just playing around. He thought he was being funny. He didn't know about our routines and rules because I didn't tell him."

"He's bad. A bad guy."

I didn't want Sebastian to dislike Zac, but there wasn't much I could do about it at this point. Zac had done this to himself by coming over after I'd told him no.

"I want out," Sebastian said.

I unrolled him, and when our eyes met, I smiled. "Well, there you are!"

He smiled back, big enough to show me his teeth. We clasped hands and stood together.

Sebastian gasped. "I broke the window."

"Yeah," I said. "Just a crack, though." Papi would totally have to replace the panes.

Then, to my shock, Sebastian said, "I won't tell Mamá or Papi."

His statement shocked me. "Why?" I asked.

"I don't want you to get in trouble from the bad guy."

Truly, my brother was the sweetest. "Thank you," I said. "I appreciate that."

Sebastian walked toward the table. He sat at his place and reached for his book. He picked up a cookie and dipped it in milk.

All would be well now. Until Papi found out what happened. But Sebastian said he wouldn't tell, and the boy didn't break promises. I guess I'd have to wait and see how this all played out.

I finished cleaning up, then made my way back to the couch and sat down. "I don't suppose you know how to multiply polynomials?" I asked my brother.

But Sebastian was reading now, which meant he was no longer listening to me.

Zac hadn't done any work on the second problem. Weary, I pulled out my MacBook and googled Khan Academy, hoping they might be able to succeed where Mr. Fletcher and Zac had left off.

Chapter

15

AT DINNER THAT NIGHT, everyone was there, even Mamá.

"You did a great job with these *frijoles de la olla*, Izzy," Mamá said of my Instant Pot beans. "I'm so hungry." Seated on my left, she told us about her day and the ongoing drama at the clinic. "I'm starting to think I'm not cut out for resolving staff conflicts."

"Can you hire someone who enjoys that role?" Papi asked.

She shrugged. "The board of directors would have to make that call, but they won't know to make it unless I went to them and complained. I'm afraid that will only make me look bad."

"You're the fourth supervisor in two years," Papi said. "Maybe it's time someone is brave enough to tell the board of directors that changes need to be made?"

"Maybe," Mamá said, sighing deeply. She turned her weary gaze back to me. "I'm sorry about the explosion this afternoon with Sebastian."

I'd told my parents Sebastian had thrown a fit and broken the window. They had accepted it without question. No one asked what had set him off. He'd been having some rough days lately, so perhaps they assumed it was the same old thing. I felt a little bad about hiding the full truth, but Sebastian was keeping his secret, so I wanted to honor that. And cover my tail.

"What do you want to do for your birthday this year, Izzy?" Papi asked.

I'd thought about this already. Last year I'd had my *quinceañera*, and while it had been fun, I enjoyed smaller, more personal gatherings. "Could some friends sleep over?"

Papi nodded. "I figured you might ask that. Your grandparents said they'd take Sebastian if that's what you decide to do."

"We're not going to be home, though," Mamá said. "I have to work."

"What?" I asked. "You can't take it off?"

"*Mija*, as the supervisor of the clinic, I have to step in when things come up. We lost a doctor just yesterday and haven't been able to hire another one, so I have to cover. *Lo siento*."

"What about you?" I asked Papi.

"Last-minute trip," he said. "It's only to Indianapolis, but I'll be gone all day, driving there and back. Won't be home until late Saturday night."

"Neither of you will be home for my birthday?" I asked.

Mamá rubbed my arm and squeezed. "Which is why we're going to celebrate on Friday," she said. "Let's go out to eat. Where shall we go?"

I thought about it. "Nuestra Cocina, I guess?" All I wanted was to be with the people I loved, but I was obsessed with the carnitas and the amazing empanadas at Nuestra Cocina.

"*¡Tu favorito!*" Mamá said. Then she and Papi chattered on, deciding what time to tell Nana and Tata and Leo they should come.

I stopped listening.

After dinner—and dishes with Claire—I texted my squad the news about my birthday sleepover.

> Tessa: Rats! I'm sorry, Izzy. I can't come over Saturday. Mom and I are driving down to Sellersburg to watch Alex's game.

No Tessa at my birthday? Well, that hurt. Not wanting her to feel bad, I typed a cheerful reply.

> Me: ☹☹☹ That's ok. I'll miss you, though.
> Tessa: I'll miss you guys too. I'm sorry, Izzy.

Then two texts came at once.

> Shay: I also have a prior commitment. I'm going with my aunt to pick up a foster dog and bring it back here. Can you do Friday night instead?
> Amelia: Noooo! ☹ A traveling concert is coming to our church and my parents volunteered me to babysit.

My chest tightened. *No one could come?*

> Tessa: I can't Friday, either. I finally agreed to go to dinner with my dad . . . ☹
> Amelia: The babysitting is on Friday too. The traveling concert is here for three nights.
> Me: Well this stinks! Guess that's what I get for planning things at the last minute.

I rubbed my face. I wanted to cry. *No one for my birthday?* But really, I couldn't be sad after this day. *My first kiss!* Then Zac's ambush and more kisses. Thinking about the kisses made me smile until I remembered Sebastian's fit and the way too many hours of Khan Academy I'd had to watch to finish my math homework while making dinner. And the dozen texts from Zac, apologizing profusely. I still hadn't texted back. I hadn't told the girls about kissing him, either. Maybe I should. I started typing it out but deleted it. I couldn't take any more rejection or disagreements today, and I had a feeling Tessa and Shay wouldn't be doing cartwheels at my news. Amelia might, but then she'd probably blame me that no boy liked her right now, like everything wrong in her life was a conspiracy or something.

The text conversation with the girls ended, so I decided to see what Zac had to say for himself. I pulled up his text thread.

> Zac: r u mad?
> Me: Um, let me think . . . Yes.

The three wiggling dots appeared that meant he was typing. It made my heart swell to think he'd been waiting by the phone to hear from me.

> Zac: im srry izzy. i didnt no what u mnt about ur bro

Which was fair. I hadn't told him anything about Sebastian's autism. *Why hadn't I? Had I been trying to hide the truth from Zac?* I didn't want to think so. Maybe I'd been trying to live two lives. Worlds were colliding, and I had no one to blame but myself.

> Me: I should have told you. My brother has autism. He has to have everything just right or he can seriously flip out. Which you witnessed today.
> Zac: i didnt no he was sick
> Me: He's not sick. He just thinks differently.
> Zac: kk ill remembr 4 nxt time

Me: Um, no. There will not be a next time unless you get to know him at church. He's already calling you a bad guy.

Zac: im a bad guy???

Me: Let's see . . . a stranger in our house who kissed me and then refused to leave when I asked him to . . . Yeah, in Sebastian's eyes, you're a bad guy.

Zac: ok ok i hear you. im super srry. imma make up for this no worries girl i got u

This placated me somewhat. I wasn't yet ready to quit on this hunky boy. If he was going to respect my boundaries, he deserved another chance. Plus, I had to admit, his pledge to make it up to me had piqued my interest. But when he didn't text me for over five minutes, I started to think he was done talking for the day. Until . . .

Zac: ur welcome

Then he sent a short video of two tiny kittens, eyes shut, climbing on each other. One was black, and the other was orange and white. My heart somersaulted in my chest.

Me: Ahh! I love them! 🖤🖤🖤 Is Lola okay?

Zac: fat & sleepin all day

Me: 🖤 The kittens are healthy?

Zac: perfct & soft & squirmin all over they were tellin me how they wanna meet u

Me: Sure they were.

Zac: its tru. u gotta come see

Me: I wish.

I wanted to see those kittens so badly, but I wasn't ready to go over there alone. I changed the subject to my birthday woes and told him how my parents were going to be gone and were taking me to dinner on Friday instead.

> Zac: no worries babe i got you i'm gonna take you out
> Me: Really?
> Zac: absolutely! whats ur fave food? where u like 2 go?

Besides Nuestra Cocina?

> Me: I like Khao San Pearl. It's a Thai place.
> Zac: kk yes i know it

A thrill ran over me. *Zac was going to take me on a date. A real date!* Then reality crashed in. I couldn't date until I was sixteen. *Wait. I'd be sixteen that very day.*

> Me: I'll have to see if it's okay with my parents.

And wait until just the right moment to broach the topic.

> Zac: why wouldn't it be?
> Me: I have to check is all.
> Zac: u gonna come see my kittens Jack n Rose or what?
> Me: Someday.

He texted another video of them wrestling.

> Me: AHHH!!! THEY'RE SO CUTE! *dies*
> Zac: they wanna meet u
> Me: I want to meet them too. Which one is Rose and which is Jack?
> Zac: jack is the black one

And just like that, Zac had weaseled his way back into my affections. There had been some serious red flags today, though.

Not listening about Sebastian. His roaming hands. But he'd helped with my homework *and* Sebastian. He'd apologized. *And* he still wanted to talk to me even after witnessing my brother's fit. I'd have to take it one day at a time to see where this thing was going to lead because I seriously wanted to kiss that boy again.

Chapter
16

WHEN I WOKE SATURDAY MORNING, I checked the weather first thing. Perfect! Sun all day with a high of 45 meant the perfect time to concoct my plan titled Operation Kitten Visit. Its success hinged entirely on my ability to improvise while simultaneously carrying out a carefully orchestrated plan. I also might have to fib—just a little, though.

I set Operation Kitten Visit in motion that afternoon with a visit to Shay's house. Shay lived in an apartment above her aunt's bookstore. It was so neat to be able to look out the living room windows to the street below where people were shopping, but the biggest reason I loved coming to her house besides spending time with my friend was her pets, Stanley and Matilda.

I arrived at Shay's house just before two and parked my bike out back. Before I went upstairs, I texted Zac.

Me: You home today? I want to see those kittens.

I'd have to wait and see if and when Zac replied. I pocketed my phone and headed up. I knocked on the door to Shay's place. From inside, Stanley barked, and his toenails clacked over the wood floor as he trotted up to the door with his uneven gait. I heard his tail whack against the door and Shay's muffled voice trying to calm him down.

"Stanley, come here."

I smiled. I loved coming to Shay's place.

The door opened to no one, but when I stepped inside, I saw Shay behind the door, holding the knob in one hand and Stanley's collar with the other. Stanley was a massive greyhound with black-and-brown striped fur similar to a tiger—called *brindle* in the dog world. He had white on his belly and the most adorably animated ears. Once Shay shut the door, she released the hound. He step-hopped toward me, tongue wagging, nose sniffing. He'd recently had surgery on his back leg, making him even more of a leaning greyhound than he'd been before, and I loved him all the more for it.

"Hello, Stanley!" I went to my knees and got right up in his face, scratching his ears. He gave me a kiss, and I said, "Where's your teddy? Huh? Can you go get Teddy?"

Stanley loped away. I didn't even bother to rise. I knew he'd be back in a hurry.

"I'm going to have to take him out for a walk soon," Shay said.

Stanley returned with a stuffed teddy bear in his mouth. I grabbed for the toy, which made him jerk his head out of reach. He looked back to me, chocolate eyes fixed on mine, ears cocked adorably, the bear hanging from his mouth as if waiting for me to try again.

I did. Eventually, I grabbed hold, played a little tug-of-war, and he finally let me take it. I tossed it across the room, and he chased after it. This time I got up and followed Shay into the living room. She flopped down on the couch and picked up a bowl of peanuts from the end table. "Peanuts?" she offered.

"No, thanks," I said. I scanned the room for Matilda, spotting the cat on a rocking chair in the corner. "There you are!" I picked up Matilda, sat on the rocking chair, and settled the tortoise-shell beauty on my lap. "Thanks for warming the chair for me." I stroked her back, and she began to purr.

"She loves you," Shay said, munching on the peanuts.

"I love her right back," I said. "You're so lucky to have a dog *and* a cat."

Stanley returned and danced around me until he realized I was done playing. He finally retreated to his bed in the kitchen, curled up, and gnawed on his teddy bear.

"So Christmas with your grandparents was no good?" I asked.

"Tense as usual," Shay said. "I'm starting to think some people are just plain difficult."

I thought of my brother. "Definitely, but a lot of times, they don't know they're being difficult." Then my mamá popped into my head. "Or they're so set in their ways, they don't realize they're being completely unfair."

Shay's eyebrows arched above her eyes. "Your mom?"

I winked. "Your grandma?"

We laughed, drawn closer by our love for people who made us work for their affections. "I talked to my nana about Mamá once. She said people are sometimes controlling because deep down they're afraid."

"Of what?"

I thought about how Mamá wanted to complain to her bosses but was worried how it would make her look. "I think that part is different for everyone. But maybe they think if they can make everything perfect, then life will be okay."

Shay slid the bowl of peanuts back onto the end table. "That's weird," she said.

"I guess." Though I kind of understood.

Stanley loped over to the door and whined, so we took that as a cue he was ready for his walk. We'd barely made it down the stairs when Zac texted me back.

> Zac: heck yes cme over!
> Me: Okay. See you in a bit.

"It's so nice out," I said. "Do you want to take a bike ride? We could feed the ducks."

"Sure," Shay said. "Sounds fun."

Ten minutes later, we returned Stanley to Shay's apartment. I waited by the door while Shay fed him. Guilt kindled inside at the knowledge of my plan. It was the only way I could see those kittens, though. Shay would *never* agree to visit a boy's house—not even for baby kittens.

Shay returned with a few slices of bread in a grocery sack. "For the ducks," she said.

I led us the long way around to the river. That way, it would seem like stopping at Zac's place was an afterthought on our way back to Shay's. When we reached the park, we walked our bikes over the grass so we wouldn't have to find a place to lock them up. The ducks were thick today and ravenous. Even though I tore my bread into the tiniest pieces, it was gone too quickly.

"I'm worried about Amelia," Shay said.

"About what?" I asked, wondering if Amelia had vented to her about church.

"*Peter Pan*," Shay said. "I mean, I know nothing about casting and all but . . ."

I sighed. "She's not going to get Peter."

"That's what I'm worried about. It's going to kill her."

I wrinkled my brow. "I think sometimes you have to let your friends make their own choices. Sometimes it will work out." I thought about me and Zac and how well things were going. "And sometimes it won't. If Amelia doesn't get Peter and she's upset, we'll just have to love on her until she is happy again." Which made me realize, Amelia needed cupcakes. STAT.

"I guess. We don't want to be bossy like my grandma and your mom."

"Exactly. Amelia would not respond well to that." I was ready to see those kittens. "Let's take a different way back. I want to show you something."

Shay had no reason to doubt my intentions, so she hopped on her bike and followed me up Bloomfield Road and into Zac's subdivision. While I'd never been inside Zac's house, I had ridden past it a few times. On Richmond Way, I coasted my bike into the driveway of 412 and flipped down the kickstand.

Shay stopped beside me. "Who lives here?"

"A pair of adorable kittens I've been dying to meet."

Shay lit up and followed me to the door. "Really? What kind of kittens?"

"I have no idea." I rang the doorbell.

Footsteps inside the house made it creak. Then the door opened, and there stood Zac, shirtless! I looked at Shay, who turned and glared at me.

"Hi," I finally said to Zac. "Kittens?"

"Friend?" Zac said, looking to Shay.

"Shirt?" Shay said, crossing her arms.

Zac chuckled and opened the door wide, motioning for us to enter. Shay raised her eyebrow and didn't move. I hooked her arm in mine and dragged her inside.

"The kittens are in the den," he said as we followed him in.

Zac's house was a wreck. There were piles of stuff everywhere. Empty cardboard boxes were stacked up inside the door. Books and magazines sat in towers on the floor next to an overflowing bookshelf. The kitchen counter was almost completely hidden by dirty dishes and empty pizza boxes. Laundry covered the living room floor, some folded, some still in rumpled piles.

The den wasn't much better. Zac approached a desk cluttered with mail. There was even mail on the office chair, but Zac picked it up and tossed it onto the desk. He sat down, wheeled himself back a few feet, then bent forward, pulling out a laundry basket tucked into the space under the center of the desk. He turned it longwise between us.

I dropped to my knees, cooing over the little kittens. I picked up Jack first since he was trying to climb the side, mewing all the while. Shay instantly reached for Rose. Their eyes were opened now, and I was melting inside over these absolutely adorable creatures.

Jack wasn't solid black. He had a section of fur on his face like the mask the Phantom wore in *The Phantom of the Opera*, and the rest of him was a mottled mix of orange, white, and brown. His sister, Rose, had a patch of black on the top of her head. From there, all along her back and down her tail was a mix of black, orange, and brown.

"They're precious," I said.

"What kind of cats are they?" Shay asked.

"Mutts, I'd guess," Zac said.

I gasped and looked into Jack's deep brown eyes. "Say, 'I am not a mutt, Isaac Lloyd, you take that back!'"

Zac chuckled. "Their mother was a mutt, so they likely are too."

"She looks like a Doll Face Persian," Shay said, speaking of Rose's squishy face while she stroked the kitten's back.

We stayed about a half hour, but when Zac tried to get us to watch *Titanic*, I made our excuses.

"We can't stay," I said. "Shay has to get home and let Stanley out."

"Grandpa not housetrained?" Zac asked.

Shay's cheeks flushed, and she put Rose back in the box. "Stanley is my dog."

"A greyhound," I said. "He's as tall as my waist!" I kissed Jack and snuggled him before reluctantly putting him back with his sister. His soft mewing was so sweet I reached for him again, but Shay grabbed my wrist.

"Stanley is going to be desperate for that walk," she said.

"Right." We said our goodbyes and headed for the door. Shay went out first, but before I could follow, Zac grabbed my hand and pulled me back.

"Don't I get a goodbye kiss?" he said.

"Sure." I pecked him on the lips.

He held me close. "That was a hello kiss," he said faintly. "I want a goodbye kiss." As his lips met mine again, everything became focused, like we were standing on the top of a needle. My knees wobbled. Normally, I might have put my hands around his neck or on his shoulders or something, but with him shirtless, I was too embarrassed to touch him. Thankfully, I was able to rest my hand on a stack of boxes by the door or I might have toppled over.

The only way I finally managed to break free was by stepping into him, so he had to step back to keep his balance. When he did, I lunged back and broke the kiss.

"Bye, Zac!" I was out the door before he had a chance to make another move.

Outside, I pretended not to notice Shay staring at me—or maybe she was glaring. I jumped on my bike and pedaled away. I didn't look back to see if she had followed until I reached the end of the street. She was right on my tail, though, so I continued on, not wanting to talk until I had a chance to calm down. Zac's kiss still had my heart racing.

The cool winter air did the trick, though, and by the time we got back to Shay's place, my heart and mind were back to normal. Shay climbed off her bike and started to lock it up.

"I should probably get going," I said, staying on my bike.

"Yeah, it's getting dark," Shay said.

"Thanks for letting me come over," I said.

"Thanks for coming. I had fun. Mostly." She frowned. "Why didn't you tell me we were going to Zac's house?"

"Because I was afraid you wouldn't want to go."

"I wouldn't have."

"I wanted to see the kittens, but I didn't want to go to Zac's house alone."

"That was the first time you'd been there?"

I nodded and then smiled. "They were the cutest kittens."

Shay beamed. "They totally were, but don't change the subject. I'm mad at you."

"Who can be mad when kittens are involved?"

Shay folded her arms. "It's a bad sign you were afraid to go to Zac's house alone."

I looked away. "I wasn't afraid. I just didn't think it would be wise."

"Because he might answer the door without a shirt?"

Touché. "Well, I wasn't expecting *that*, but he has the tendency to be unpredictable. And I kind of lose myself when I'm with him."

"Sounds scary."

I smirked. "It's a good kind of scary."

She tipped her head and gave me a deadpan look. "Are you even listening to yourself?"

"He's just so dreamy. I'm still trying to figure it out. Please don't tell Tessa and Amelia."

"Now you want me to lie?"

"No," I said, squeezing the handle grips on my bike. "I just don't want you to tell them if there is no reason to. Like if one of them says, 'What did you do yesterday, Shay?' You could say, 'Izzy came over, and we rode bikes to the park and fed the ducks.' You don't have to bring up Zac and his kittens. Unless they specifically asked, 'Shay, did you and Izzy go to Zac's house yesterday?' Then you'd have to tell the truth."

"I can see I'm going to have to pay closer attention to the

things you don't say," Shay said, her eyes narrowing. "You're a sneaky one."

"If Tessa wouldn't make me feel guilty for liking Zac, I wouldn't have to be sneaky."

"She's worried about you because she loves you. And clearly the guy has some kind of magical power over your common sense."

The words triggered something deep inside. Anger welled up and burst out before I could stop it. "Funny how much that sounds like my parents, Shay. Leo and Claire have all the freedom they want, but me? I don't have freedom. I have to make dinner and watch Sebastian. Not a day goes by that one of my parents doesn't ask me to do something that's technically their job." My voice was a watery, whiny mess, and I angrily swiped away the tears filling my eyes. "You don't know how frustrating it is to feel like you have to be everyone's hero. You can't be yourself or make your own mistakes because you're too busy filling in for everyone else and cleaning up *their* mistakes. So what if Zac is wrong for me? Then I'll know. If I get hurt, I'll get over it. But right now, I just want to live my life and make my own decisions and not have to feel like I have to make everyone happy all the time. It's exhausting."

Shay was staring at me, her eyes wide. "Izzy . . . I'm sorry. I never knew you were unhappy doing all the things you do for your family."

"It's just . . . no one ever asks me." I sniffled. "It's expected."

Shay hugged me. "I'm sorry, Izzy. Dating a boy like Zac is nothing I'd ever want to do, but I get why it's important to you. I won't tell anyone we went to visit Jack and Rose. Or Zac."

I cracked a smile. "Thank you," I said, feeling for the first time like I'd successfully revealed part of myself without having to apologize for it. It had felt good. I wished I could do it more often—especially with my parents—but I knew better. Come morning, wild Izzy would be hiding again where she wouldn't make trouble for anyone.

Chapter
17

SUNDAY MORNING, I was sitting next to Tessa and Shay in the teen section of the sanctuary, bulletin in hand, drawing a kitten, which happened to look like Jack. Tessa and Alex were whispering and talking so softly they probably thought I couldn't hear, but I could.

Alex glanced up. "Oh, hey." He was looking past me. Over my head.

Tessa and Shay looked up too, and their eyes widened. I turned around. There stood Zac, wearing black slacks and a dark green sweater. He might as well have been wearing a bow—a belated Christmas present, just for me.

"Hi!" I said, beaming.

"Hey." He motioned to the seat beside me. "Anyone sitting here?"

"Just you," I said.

"Hey, Alex," Zac said. "Shay. And Tessa, right?"

"That's right," Tessa said, frowning. "Hello, Zac."

Zac sat down and took hold of my hand, laced his fingers in mine. "Sorry I missed the morning thing. There's a morning thing, right?"

"Sunday school," I said.

"So where's Sebastian?" he asked.

"With my parents," I said. "He doesn't sit in the teen section." The music started up, and the worship pastor called us to our feet. I stood and tugged Zac up beside me.

"How will I get to meet him?" he asked in my ear as the music got loud.

"After service," I said, then began to sing.

—ɯ—

I spotted my brother in the foyer near the fireplace. Sebastian liked to watch the flames while we talked to our friends after service. Papi was sitting by the fireplace, deep in conversation with Mr. Nelson, probably about cars. I let go of Zac's hand under the guise of throwing out the announcement flyers in the center of my bulletin. When I came back, I was holding my little backpack purse in one hand, my Bible in the other so Papi would notice.

"This way," I told Zac.

As we approached the fireplace, I said a little prayer that Sebastian wouldn't freak out and tell everyone Zac kissed me. Thankfully Shay, Tessa, and Alex were still with us, and Sebastian loved Tessa.

"Hey, Bash," I said. "Tessa wants to say hi."

"Hi, Sebastian," Tessa said.

Sebastian turned his head toward the sound of Tessa's voice. He never really made eye contact with people and ended up looking toward my feet. He wrinkled his nose and growled. Tessa glanced at me, a worried expression on her face.

Papi turned away from his conversation. "Be nice to Izzy's friends, *Mijo*," he said.

"I smell the bad guy," Sebastian said, and then he barked like a dog. "Ark! Ark, ark, ark!"

Oh, my stars. I couldn't believe this was happening. "Sebastian," I said. "There are no bad guys here in church. This is Alex and Tessa and Shay and Zac. Don't you want to say *hola*?"

Sebastian only growled and barked some more.

"*¡Ay!*" Papi stood up from his seat. "Time to go." He nodded to our group. "*Vámonos*, Sebastian," he said, then started for the exit where Mamá was standing with Tessa's mom and Shay's aunt.

My brother followed, barking and growling the whole way.

"That was new," Tessa said.

I winced at her and then at Zac. "Sorry," I said. "You never know what you'll get with my brother."

"It's okay," Zac said. "I deserved that." He put his arm around my shoulder and squeezed. While being the approved side hug for most churches, it still kind of freaked me out. I didn't want it sparking any questions about our relationship. I eyed Mamá, then Nana and Tata, who were talking near the information counter with a group of their friends. At least Papi and Sebastian had gone outside.

"Why'd you deserve that?" Tessa asked Zac, pulling my attention back to the present.

"I stopped by Izzy's place the other day, and her brother didn't take it well," Zac said.

Alex started laughing. "So, *you're* the bad guy."

Zac waggled his eyebrows. "Yep. That's me. I'm a regular Loki."

I punched Zac in the arm. "Oh, you did not just compare yourself to Loki," I said.

"What's wrong with Loki?" he asked. "He's everyone's favorite baddie."

I didn't disagree with that statement at all except I did not want my Iron Man turning into a Loki. That simply would *not* do.

―∽―

That afternoon I frosted chocolate cupcakes with mint marshmallow crème I'd colored green. I'd also made a tray of chocolate candies using a theater face mold. I pressed one theater face atop each cupcake, took a picture of the platter, and then covered it. I precariously balanced the cupcake container on the basket of my bicycle and headed to Amelia's.

Her mom answered the door. Mrs. Bryan looked nothing like Amelia, which was a little weird. She was tall and thin with brown hair piled on top of her head in a messy bun. "Isabella, hello!" she said. "Amelia is babysitting right now. Mr. Bryan and I are in a meeting."

"She didn't know I was coming," I said. "I made her some 'I love you' cupcakes. Would it be okay if I just said hello for a minute? I won't stay."

"You are such a sweet girl. You're welcome to stay if you want to help Millie with Taylor and Ben."

"I'd love to!" I'd never heard of Taylor and Ben in my life, but I adored kids.

Mrs. Bryan opened the door wide. "Come on in. They're down in the basement."

"Thank you." I slipped inside and waved at Felix, Amelia's Labradoodle who was sitting in his bed, head perked up and watching me intently. I fought the urge to go love on him—I was here for Amelia and could visit Felix on my way out. I slipped past a baby gate at the top of the stairs right off the foyer and headed downstairs.

"Tell Millie to share those with the kids, okay?" Mrs. Bryan called after me.

"Okay." The stairs turned halfway down, then widened into a large open space. Amelia was on the floor, playing Candy Land with two little boys. One looked like a preschooler, and the other might have been seven or eight. "Special delivery!" I said.

Amelia twisted around, and her face lit up. "Izzy?" She pushed to her feet. "What are you doing here?"

"I made you cupcakes because I love you. And if it's okay, your mom said I could hang out and help you babysit."

"She doesn't need help," the older boy said. "We're not babies."

I squatted down. "I can see that," I said. "The thing is, I made a mistake when I baked these cupcakes. I ended up with twelve, even though there is only Amelia, Taylor, Ben, and Izzy here right now." I held up one finger at a time to total four.

The boy gasped. "You know me?"

I shrugged, as if equally confused by the magic of my knowledge. "Do you think you and your brother could help us eat these?" I unclipped the latch on the lid and pulled it off, revealing my chocolate mint theater creations.

"Oh, yum!" Amelia said. "Taylor, those look good, don't you think?"

Taylor nodded and bared a wide grin.

"I want a cupcake too!" The smaller boy came running.

Amelia got some paper towels from upstairs and set up the boys and their cupcakes at the coffee table in front of the couch. Then she and I sat on the adjacent couch.

"I'm sorry I yelled at you the other day," Amelia said. "Did you tell Tessa and Shay what happened?"

"No," I said. "I didn't think it was my place."

"Thank you," she said. "I wouldn't have said anything except you came into the bathroom."

"I'm sorry this is hard," I said.

"It's not your fault. It makes sense that Tessa's mom would get along with Shay's aunt. They're close to the same age . . . and single."

Single. So sad. "Tessa said Shay's aunt has really been a good friend to her mom, so Tessa's mom invited her to a women's Bible study group."

"That's so nice." Amelia picked off the chocolate theater face and bit into it, snapping it in half. "How did you make these?" she asked, her mouth full.

"I have a chocolate mold."

"That frosting is like minty air!" She licked the back of the remaining half of the chocolate.

Taylor and Ben had inhaled their cupcakes. They ran around the table, returning to their game of Candy Land, both with chocolate clown mouths.

"Wash your hands first," Amelia said, and both boys headed toward the bathroom, giggling the whole way.

Her instruction to the boys reminded me of the last time I saw Amelia. "Guess what happened after I saw you in the bathroom?" I said, feeling like Amelia and I needed a secret that was just ours.

Her green eyes met mine.

"I kissed Zac."

Her jaw dropped. "What?!"

I grinned and told her the story. "Don't tell Tessa and Shay. They've been worried about me getting too involved with Zac, and I'm afraid they'll freak out on me."

Amelia sank back on the couch. "They totally would. Even though Tessa kisses Alex when she thinks no one is looking."

"Well, Tessa knows Alex's life story," I said. "He has been thoroughly approved as boyfriend material. Zac's past is a mystery."

Amelia raised an eyebrow. "So is yours," she said.

I hummed. "True. I could have all kinds of skeletons in my closet. Kind of wish I did! They'd make for some good stories to shock Tessa and Shay!"

We laughed, both of us enjoying the moment to tease our friends for being such loveable worrywarts.

"Surely Zac will win them over soon," I said. "When you see it happen, demand a kiss report, and I'll tell all."

"It's a deal." Amelia finally bit into her cupcake. "Oh, wow. Izzy, this is so yummy."

She continued to eat, so I ate mine, too. The melt-in-your-mouth mint frosting with a chocolate cupcake really was like eating pure joy.

"Thanks for coming over, Izzy," Amelia said.

"You know I love you, right? That I'm not just saying it?"

She leaned her head on my shoulder. "I know."

"Good," I said. "Please tell me if you're ever feeling left out, okay?"

"I will," she said. "I promise."

Chapter

18

WHEN I GOT HOME, Papi was pacing in front of Sebastian, who was sitting on the living room couch reading a graphic novel.

This was new. "Sebastian reading a graphic novel?" I asked.

"He went to the library," Papi said, arms crossed.

I perked up. "By himself?"

Papi looked pointedly at me. "He told me he looked it up online."

"Carl Jamison taught his sixth grade class to use Google Maps," Sebastian said.

Papi lifted his hands out to his sides, a look of amused shock on his face. "So, Bash looked up the Riverbend Library on the computer in the den and rode his bike over there without asking. He checked out the new Wings of Fire graphic novel."

"Without a library card?" I asked.

"My name is Sebastian Valadez. My parents are Dañel and

Josefina Valadez. My address is 57 Arrow Crest Lane. My phone number is 555-3340."

I couldn't help it, I beamed like a Muppet. "Bash, I'm so proud of you!" At Papi's glare, I added, "Except that you didn't ask permission. That's not okay. You scared Papi."

"Dañel Valadez would say, 'No, *Mijo*, you cannot go,'" Sebastian said. "Dañel Valadez would say I didn't know how to find the library, but Carl Jamison taught his sixth grade class to use Google Maps."

"Well, my *hijo* made his point," Papi said. "Now he's grounded from his bike and will be riding the bus to and from school next week."

Sebastian nodded. "Okay, okay, Dañel Valadez. I am grounded."

I fought back a smile, and I couldn't help but think that Sebastian had won this round. He had proved to Mamá and Papi that he was capable of much more than anyone had believed.

—m—

The following Wednesday night was my first robotics practice. The marketing team was designing costumes to wear at competitions. Since this year's theme was Dragon Horde, the girls had made pennants in our school colors with the team number on them and hooked them to dowels so the team could wave them in the stands. They'd also gathered supplies to make flower crowns with ribbons for the girls to wear and foam to cut swords for the guys.

"What if girls want a sword?" I asked.

"Anyone can have a sword," Laila said. "This is just a general plan."

"I thought the robot was supposed to be a dragon," I said.

"It is," Kerrie added, "but we thought it would be easier to go with a medieval theme for the costumes, rather than trying to dress up like dragons."

"Wings would have been cool," I said.

"True," Laila said. "Kerrie and I wanted to do wings and make dragon tails attached to belts, but the team voted us down."

"Bummer," I said.

I sat there for the next two hours, making flower crowns and swords. I had fun, actually. Laila and Kerrie were nice. Apparently, there were also two boys on the marketing team, Josue and Chris, but they were in charge of fundraising and were out visiting businesses, which was why the girls needed help with the costumes. We tried on our creations. Laila took a picture of me wearing a crown and wielding a foam sword, which I immediately made her text me so I could upload it to my social.

I lost track of time, and when I checked the clock, youth group had already started. I gasped and stood up. I'd forgotten to text Tessa. I had, cowardly, decided not to tell her about joining the robotics team until the last minute.

"What's wrong?" Laila asked.

"I forgot to text my—"

"Isabella!" The sound of my full name on Zac's lips paralyzed me. He jogged up to our table, set down a blue Hydro Flask, and picked up a sword from the piles of crafts. "Check this out!" He swung it like a baseball bat. "Can I have this?"

Laila snatched it away. "You can use one at the competitions, like everyone else."

Zac pouted, though his eyes were full-on Dazzle. "Aw, you're no fun." He grabbed me around the waist with one arm and pulled me against him. "Steal me one of those swords, won't you?" His whisper tickled my ear.

I laughed and shoved him away. "If you think I'll break the rules for you, Zac Lloyd, you're mistaken. My loyalty is to the marketing team."

He clapped a hand over his heart and winced. "You wound me, Izzy."

Mr. Lucas stepped into the room, hands on his hips. "Mr. Lloyd, where should you be right now?"

"At the drinking fountain." He grabbed his Hydro Flask from the table and held it up.

"Then get to it," Mr. Lucas said.

Zac winked at me and took off. I didn't see him the rest of the night. When Claire came to tell me she was leaving, Zac had already left. What a bum.

On the ride home, I saw I'd missed a few texts from Tessa.

> Tessa: Are you here yet?
> Tessa: Can't find you.
> Tessa: Where are you?

I sighed, dreading the conversation I would next have with Tessa in regard to my recent choices. Might as well get it out of the way.

> Me: Sorry I didn't come tonight. I joined Claire's robotics team. Mr. Lucas said the marketing group needed help. I worked with Laila and Kerrie, making costumes for the upcoming competition. Check it out!

Then I texted her a selfie Laila had taken of the three of us.

> Me: I told Mr. Lucas I could only help every other week because of youth group. He said they only need help until the end of February. Their costumes have to be finished by then.

"You seemed to be having fun tonight with Laila and Kerrie," Claire said.

I glanced at my sister. Her face was lit up strangely as the truck passed under streetlights. "It was fun, though there sure is a lot to do."

"Robotics is so much more than most people think."

"I'm starting to see that."

"Do you think you'll stick around?"

"Maybe."

"Didn't see as much of Zac as you hoped?"

"No, but that's okay."

"Mr. Lucas keeps us all busy. Plus, there's a lot to do before the first competition."

"I liked it," I said, "but I'm not sure it's me."

"I get that," Claire said. "It's important for you to figure out what is you."

"Why?"

"It's just, there's a lot of good things you could be a part of in our school. At church, too. But there's not enough time to do everything. You can go crazy trying to do it all. If you can find one or two things that you're good at and bring you joy, that's where you should spend your time. At least that's what I think."

"Drama and baking," I said without hesitation.

She laughed. "Those were the same two I would have picked for you."

"Is it wrong of me to help out the robotics team if I might not stick around?"

"I don't think so," Claire said, "as long as you're honest about it with Mr. Lucas."

"He knows I'm temporary," I said.

"Then we're lucky to have you."

"Thanks." I felt better about the whole thing, until I remembered Tessa hadn't texted me back. The guilt of skipping youth group filled my chest, making everything tight. I told myself it was just a season. It wouldn't last forever. But that didn't make the guilty feeling go away.

—ɯ—

Before going to bed, I bolstered my courage and went out to the garage where Papi was working on the Mustang. I sat down by his feet, which were sticking out from under the car as he lay on his automotive creeper.

"Papi," I said, hugging my knees.

"¿Sí? I'm under the car."

I stifled a giggle. "Um. Yeah. I see you." I took a deep breath, then went for it. "A boy wants to take me to dinner for my birthday. On Saturday night."

"What boy?"

"His name is Zac. I know him from school. He was at church last Sunday."

Papi grunted. "Alex's friend?"

"Yeah," I said, not bothering to correct him. "You always said I had to be sixteen to date, and I'll be sixteen that day."

Papi grunted again. "Your mamá said you had to be sixteen. I said twenty-five."

"Papi!"

His soft chuckle drifted out to me. "Ah, *Mija*." He rolled out from under the car and sat up. His hair stuck up in the air. "Where's this boy want to take you?"

"Khao San Pearl."

"¡Ay! He's a rich boy, eh?"

I shrugged. "He asked what I liked to eat. Since we're going to Nuestra Cocina on Friday, I picked my second favorite place."

He nodded at my logic. "How you going to get there?"

"He has a car."

Papi narrowed his eyes. "What kind of car does he drive?"

I realized I didn't know and shrugged. "I never saw it."

"*Ay ay ay* . . ." Papi shook his head. "How long you know this boy?"

"I met him at church last fall, but we became friends at the robotics Kick-Off day."

"He's on Claire's team?"

"*Sí*," I said.

"Does Claire like him?"

"You'd have to ask her."

He shot me a look that said he wasn't buying that answer for one second.

"Fine." I shared as much of the truth as I dared. "She was mad he asked Natalie for my number and not her. She thinks he's . . . too old for me."

Papi's brows furrowed. "How old is he?"

"He's a senior."

"*¡Ay, niño!*" Papi studied me closely. "You trust this boy?"

"For dinner?"

"You know what I mean."

"I like him, Papi. And I want to do something fun for my birthday."

"You're a good girl, *Mija*. You take care of us all." He slapped my knee two times, as if coming to a decision. "You'd have to go straight there and straight back."

I couldn't believe it. He was actually considering this. "I can do that," I said.

"Normally, I'd demand to meet him first, but I'll be gone all day. I want to talk to him next Sunday at church."

"Okay, Papi."

"'Okay, Papi,' she says." His eyes had their own twinkling dazzle that could only come from a papi like mine. "All right. You can go to dinner with this boy."

I squealed and hugged Papi.

He caught hold of me and chuckled, rocking me from side to side. "*No crezcas demasiado rápido, Isabella.*"

His plea that I wouldn't grow up too fast brought tears to my eyes. All I could do was promise I wouldn't. "*Está bien, Papi. No lo haré.*"

I went inside and up to my room where I plugged in my cell phone and silenced it. My conversation with Papi had left me feeling thankful and pensive. I decided to fast from my cell phone for the night and read my Bible. It had been too long, and if I was going to obey my papi and not grow up too fast, I needed to make sure my priorities were in order. That meant putting God first, before Zac and my friends and my social media.

At first it felt weird not to have my phone close by, but after a while, I got lost in the book of James. I was behind on my devotional reading, and in less than a half hour, I'd read the entire book of James. Chapter 4 hit me the hardest. Its heading said, "Submit Yourselves to God," which was something I hadn't been doing lately. The first paragraph talked about the things that caused fights and quarrels—that we couldn't have what we wanted because we asked God with wrong motives or we didn't ask God at all.

I'd been sneaky lately. I'd wanted so badly to have a boyfriend that I'd lied and manipulated my friends and even my little brother. Well, I had what I wanted now, but whether it would or wouldn't work out wasn't clear. Shay and Sebastian had seen through my lies, and now Tessa had too. Emely, my old youth pastor from our church in Williamsport, had taught us how to pray Scripture. When we found a passage that convicted us or moved us in some way, we could turn those words into a prayer. I did that now with the beginning of James chapter 4.

"God, please help me to trust You. Guard my heart and my actions so You will be honored. Let my faith and trust in You guide me instead of me trying to push my agenda to make things happen. You are trustworthy in everything, and You know what my heart needs. Amen."

Chapter

19

ZAC PICKED ME UP at 5:30 on Saturday. I locked the door behind me before he even had a chance to get out of his bright-yellow Nissan truck—that I had to climb into like some kind of tree house. I'd dressed up for my date, wearing a red stretch-lace dress with a flared knee-length skirt. I didn't wear leggings, but since I didn't own a pair of dress shoes, I wore my knee-high brown leather boots.

"I was going to come to the door," he said.

"Oh, that's okay," I said as I pulled on my seat belt. "No one's home but me."

"Where's your brother?"

"Spending the night with Nana and Tata."

"Who?"

"My grandparents."

"Gotcha." Zac steered out of our subdivision. "Is it just you, Sebastian, and Claire, then?"

"Leo is the oldest. He's in college and has a place across town with some friends."

"Where does Sebastian go to school?"

"Riverbend Middle. He attends a regular sixth grade class. He's very smart. He just struggles with social interactions. He can't read tone in a voice or the look on someone's face. He only understands what is communicated literally. So we have to be careful how we phrase things." I tugged my dress over my knees. "Do you have any siblings?"

"No," he said. "It's just me and my dad here in Riverbend. He's a doctor."

Well, "just me and my dad" explains the messy condition of their house. "What kind of a doctor?"

"Podiatrist. Works on people's feet. Gross, right?"

I laughed. "Hey, feet are important. They take us wherever we want to go. What about your mom? You said you saw *Hamilton* with her in New York."

He looked both ways and then pulled onto the main road. "Mom's a corporate lawyer. She works for a huge firm."

"How long have your parents been separated?"

"Five years. Divorced for the last two. Mom . . . she cheated. A lot."

Oh no. "I'm sorry."

"Yeah . . . it was bad. I caught her, like, three different times."

I gaped at him, trying to process that—how it would have made me feel. "Eww."

"Yeah."

"How often do you see her?"

"Spring break, Christmas, and a week every summer. And that's more than enough."

So sad. "Does she take time off? When you're there?"

"Not really. I spend most of my time with Martin."

"Who is Martin?"

"One of my mom's assistants. He's in charge of entertaining me when I'm in town. You know how I said I saw *Hamilton*? I actually saw it with Martin. Mom can't be bothered to spend time with me."

A little gasp escaped me. *Poor Zac!* My mamá worked a lot, but I knew she loved me and enjoyed spending time with me. "I'm so sorry. That really stinks." Zac clearly needed someone in his life who would be sweet to him. Take care of him. I started thinking about what kind of cupcakes he needed.

He shrugged off my pity. "Honestly, we don't get along. I'm bitter, and she wants to tell me how to live. Thinks I should be a lawyer like her. Dad thinks I should be a doctor like him."

That sounded stressful. "What do you want to be?"

"I don't know. Nothing."

I patted his arm. "Oh, come on. There must be something you like. Computers, right?"

"I guess. I mean, I was always home alone with a computer, so I got good at using them."

He said no more, so I let the conversation die until we were seated at the restaurant and had placed our orders. Zac ordered pad see ew. I chose the yellow curry.

"So," I said, "you're good at computers. Are you thinking of going to college? Majoring in programming or computer science?"

He put his chin on one hand, leaning on his elbow and gazing at me. "Nah. I like graphic arts, actually. Photoshop and Illustrator and stuff like that. It would be cool to get an art degree. Mom and Dad both say that won't pay the bills. It's one of the few things they agree on."

Critical parents were something I understood perfectly. "If it makes you happy, who cares how much money you make?"

"I don't know . . ." He grinned. "I kind of like what money can buy—like my truck."

I laughed. The food came, and he started eating. I stared at him, startled he hadn't offered to pray a blessing over the meal. I felt foolish as I realized how little I knew about this boy, including what he believed about God. Just because he'd come to church a few times didn't mean he was a believer. I closed my eyes and said a quick prayer. When I looked up, he was watching me.

He smiled, his cheeks flushed. "I want to tell you something, but I don't tell many people." He twirled his fork in his noodles.

"Go ahead," I said.

He swallowed before putting down his fork. Elbows on the table, he folded his hands and pressed them against his mouth. "Okay, so . . . I told you I like art. Well, I have another Instagram account, but like I said, I don't tell many people about it because I'm . . ." He wrung his hands. "I don't really want people to know about it."

"Why not?"

He shrugged. "I guess I'm embarrassed?"

I pulled out my phone. "You going to tell me what your account is called?"

He released a long, somewhat tortured breath. "Promise you won't tell anyone it's me?"

I held out my pinky. "I promise."

He laughed and wrapped his pinky around mine. "Pinky swear. Okay, it's @imaginethatartisinme."

I pulled up Instagram and typed in the name. Color flooded the screen. There were a lot of fantasy landscapes like something out of *Lord of the Rings*. Castles, medieval villages, and swampy forests. Lots of animals—cats mostly. Not like Jack and Rose. Monster cats. One image was of a muscled warrior, wielding a sword and riding a sabretooth cat, the pair of them clad in matching black armor. Another image was of a busty fairy sitting on a huge mushroom. I liked the one that showed the back of an elvish-looking woman, looking out over a cityscape, her white hair blowing in the wind. Some of the art was weird. A cat woman kneeling by a birdcage, watching a tiny man swing on the perch inside. A boy floating over a city, holding the string of a balloon that was connected to the moon. A woman with a clockwork key sticking out of her back who was holding marionette strings that were attached to a man walking down a city street. This account was more popular than his other one, likely because he was actually posting things that drew an audience. He had 3,890 followers and was following 1,203. I followed him.

Zac was playing with his food again.

"You're really talented," I said.

He paused, lips pressed together, staring uncomfortably at his food. When he finally looked up, he seemed somehow fragile. "Good enough, you think, for art school?"

Had no one encouraged this boy in his entire life? "Absolutely. You haven't applied to any yet?"

"I missed a bunch of deadlines," he said, frowning. "But Parsons had all this random stuff you had to draw, and I just couldn't find the inspiration. I got into Herron, but Mom said she won't pay for me to go to art school."

This poor boy. "What about your dad?"

"Only if I double major in business. He says all artists are entrepreneurs."

I thought about it. "He's probably right. The more followers I get on Instagram, the more they keep trying to get me to buy ads. A business degree might be helpful."

"It's so boring though."

"Yeah . . . but that's life. Not everything can be exciting."

"Why not?"

I was not the person to tell anyone to be serious in life. "I don't know. I suppose it's up to you. If you want your dad to pay for Herron, I guess you double major. Or you take loans and figure it out yourself. Is Herron expensive?"

"It's Indiana U, so not the most expensive out there."

I put away my phone. "Either way, I think you should go for it. Being an artist, I mean. Life is too short to waste it doing something you hate."

He shook his head, but he was smiling. "I knew you'd understand, Izzy."

We continued our meal, and I savored every drop of delicious curry. On the way home, Zac drove through downtown, then parked right in front of Shay's aunt's bookstore.

"What are we doing here?"

He got out and shut the door. *Weird.* He walked around the front of the truck. Opened my door. He grinned up at me and held out a hand. "Shall we?"

"Oh-kay . . ." I unbuckled my seat belt and accepted his hand. He helped me out and shut my door. Then he offered me his arm, like this was some kind of black-tie, Regency England moment. I took hold and followed him to the bookshop, completely out-of-my-mind confused.

We went inside, and before I could question him again, what felt like a million people jumped out from hiding and yelled, "Surprise!"

I about passed out.

Then I saw Tessa and Amelia and Shay, Hyun Ki and Lilliesha, Alex and even Claire all grinning at me. I started jumping and squealing. For the next half hour all I did was hug my people. It was THE best moment of my life. Hugs are, after all, my favorite, and surprises my second favorite, save for cupcakes.

There were no games or anything planned. Just hanging out with friends from school and eating cake. They had one of those giant Costco chocolate cakes I love, and everyone sang to me.

"Since none of us can bake and we knew you liked Costco cake . . ." Tessa shrugged.

"My aunt picked it up," Shay said.

"Seriously, you guys," I said. "This is the nicest thing anyone has ever done for me. It's absolutely perfect." I hugged them both again. "I was so surprised. There was even a parking spot out front this late!"

Shay laughed. "That was Claire's job. Aunt Laura had a sign in it all afternoon, but when Zac texted you guys were on your way, Claire went out and stood in it for the past half hour."

"My sister?"

"Your sister," Tessa said. "It was great of Zac to help us out. Guess I was wrong about him. He's kind of a catch."

"He is, isn't he?" I squealed again, this time more subdued as I spotted Zac on the other side of the counter, talking to Shay's aunt. "I really like him."

Tessa laughed. "I can tell."

Amelia came rushing over. "I've been waiting to get you away from him." She grabbed my arm and towed me over to our favorite alcove. Shay and Tessa followed. Amelia pulled me onto the love seat, and Tessa and Shay claimed the adjacent beanbags.

"Kiss report," Amelia said. "Now." She crossed her arms and waited, her eyes twinkling with the secret she already knew.

I started giggling, and it was a while before I was able to tell all. To be honest, I didn't tell all . . . I only told most. A girl was entitled to some secrets, after all.

"I can't believe you kissed first!" Amelia said. "Isabella Valadez, you are the bravest person I know."

And the best actress Tony goes to . . . Amelia Bryan!

I shook my head. "We're all brave, just in different ways."

"Who's brave?"

We glanced up, and there stood Zac, which sent us into a fit of giggles.

"What?" he asked, which only made us laugh harder.

Before I knew it, the party was over. I thanked Shay's Aunt Laura profusely for hosting and hugged all my friends again. Then Zac and I left. Strangely, Claire followed.

"Where did you park?" I asked her.

"We're giving her a ride home," Zac said.

"My truck is at Tessa's place," Claire said. "I rode over with them."

"So we'll drop you off so you can get it," I said.

"The keys are in her house," Claire said. "I told Tessa we'd pick it up on the way to church tomorrow."

"Ah," I said, annoyed my sister was spoiling the end of my date. Then, to make matters worse, she and Zac chattered about robotics all the way to our house. When Zac pulled into our driveway and Claire got out, I said, "I'll be a minute."

"Don't be too long, or I'll send Sebastian out to get you," Claire said, all cocky. She shut the door and strode to the house.

"Guess she doesn't know your bro is staying with your grandparents tonight," Zac said.

"Oh, she knows," I said. "She just doesn't know I told you."

"Okay, you have to open your present." Zac reached down to the floor between our seats and pulled up a gift bag.

"That was there the whole night?" I asked, taking it from him. It was not a small bag.

He laughed, almost giddy. "Yep. Right there in plain sight. Open it!"

Tickled, I reached into the bag and pulled out a wad of fabric. "What is it?" I held it up. It was a skirt. A short, full, white-lace skirt with a wide elastic waistband. Or it might be cream or beige. It was hard to see in the dark.

"You said you like skirts," he said.

"I do like skirts." It would actually look adorable with my boots and some leggings and a cute top. "Thank you."

"You hate it."

"No, I seriously don't. It's super cute." I leaned across the cab and kissed his cheek. "Thank you. And thank you for helping my friends plan the party."

"You're welcome, Izzy. Happy birthday." He kissed me again. For a long time.

I finally had to say "I should go."

"Right," he said. "I'll walk you to the door." Where we kissed some more until my sister started flipping the porch lights on and off.

What a snot she was. I finally said goodbye and came inside.

Claire was waiting at the light switch. "You never would have stayed out there so long if Mamá and Papi were home."

"True," I said.

"What'd he give you?"

"None of your business."

She snatched the bag and pulled out the skirt. I could see now it was ivory lace. Very '80s.

She wrinkled her nose. "Is this a . . . skirt?"

"Yep," I said.

"Why?"

I tipped my head to the side, studying it. "I honestly don't know."

She threw it back to me. "For a second I thought I might be jealous of you, but I've snapped out of it. Boys are weird."

Chapter
20

By the time I'd tried on my new lace skirt, changed into my pajamas, and brushed my teeth, my parents had both come home. I went downstairs to say good night.

"Well?" Mamá asked. "How did it go?"

"Were you surprised?" Papi asked.

"Yes!" I beamed, remembering the night. "It was amazing. I wish you two could've come."

"We wanted to, *Mija*." Mamá jumped up and walked toward me. "I want to give my baby girl a birthday hug."

I walked straight into her embrace.

"Sixteen!" Mamá said, squeezing me tight. "Where does the time go?"

When she released me, Papi was standing beside us, ready for his turn. I hugged him, too.

"You'll always be our baby girl," he said.

I smiled, humming my contentment as I lingered in my papi's arms. Sure, I liked gifts, but in my opinion, the best presents were always hugs.

When I got up to my room, Zac had texted me.

> Zac: i can't stop thinking about your lips
> Me: Well, hello to you too. ☺
> Zac: do u even no how beutiful u r?
> Me: Thank you for tonight. It was a great birthday.
> Zac: ur welcom
> Me: And thank you for my present.
> Zac: ☺ maybe u can model it 4 me somtime
> Me: I'll wear it to school next week.
> Zac: kewl but i ment come over and model while I draw u

Wow. Didn't see that coming.

> Me: How would you draw me?
> Zac: on a horse a pegasus i think a black one to match ur hair
> Zac: we wld be flying 2geth over a lake u reaching a hand into the wter ur hair all wild

He'd clearly been thinking this over.

> Me: I like it.

I liked it very much.

Zac came to church again on Sunday, and Papi invited him out to eat lunch with us. Nana grilled him about college, and he told her he planned to go to Indiana U to study business. My whole family liked him, except Sebastian, who still growled and barked if Zac got too close.

That night as I was planning which leggings to wear to school the next day with my new skirt, I remembered what Zac had said about leaving my legs bare. *Could I pull it off?* The skirt was shorter than I was used to, well above my knees, but with my boots, I wouldn't be showing too much leg . . . *would I?*

The next morning, I leapt from bed, took the world's fastest shower, and shaved my legs. Then I returned to my room and got dressed. I'd chosen a red, fitted top to wear with the skirt. As I stood in front of my full-length mirror, I felt . . . exposed. Yet at the same time, part of me felt pretty. I could see myself in Zac's illustration, riding an ebony Pegasus, barefoot, the pair of us flying wild and free over a great body of water. *How could I feel pretty and wild at the same time? Was I too timid to dress pretty?* That didn't make sense. I had plenty of dresses I felt pretty wearing. This outfit was different. It was more somehow. More revealing. More risky. More . . .

Sexy.

The word made me uncomfortable, even inside my head. I put one hand on my hip and struck a pose, like a model on the cover of a magazine. I pursed my lips and tossed my hair over my shoulder.

Then I cracked up.

Until I thought of Zac and how sweet he'd been on my birthday and how awful his mother was to send her assistant to entertain him. He needed me. I began putting on my makeup. I kept it simple. Just the eyeliner and mascara. No eyeshadow or foundation or blush. I did use some lip gloss, but it was colorless. I stepped back, feeling a shock as I regarded myself in the mirror. I looked good. Dare I say . . . gorgeous?

While I was hungry and wanted breakfast, I also didn't want any questions. I stayed in my room until Claire started bellowing for me to hurry up. A glance out my window showed Mamá's car was gone, and I heard Papi in the shower. Time to go.

As I descended the stairs into the living room, I smelled pancakes. Sebastian was seated at the kitchen table, eating a short stack. I'd forgotten to make my brother breakfast, yet there he sat, eating. "Who cooked?" I asked.

"Papi," Claire said. "What are you wearing?"

"Clothes?" I said, still surprised that Papi had cooked breakfast.

My sister was staring at me, her mouth gaping until she finally said, "Is that makeup?"

"Mamá said I could wear makeup."

"Yeah. Like three years ago—but you never have. Is this because of Zac? That's the skirt he gave you, isn't it?"

I sat down on the bench by the door and yanked on my right boot. I needed to be gone before Papi came downstairs. I couldn't risk him saying the skirt was too short.

"Izzy . . . you shouldn't have to change yourself for some guy," Claire said.

I zipped up my right boot and reached for the left. "I'm sixteen now. Puppy-dog leggings are silly."

Before Claire could say another word, I zipped up my left boot and ran out the door to her truck. She had the decency to let it go, which also meant she remained silent all the way to school. That was fine. I got on my phone and checked my social, then texted Zac to meet me at his locker. That I had a surprise.

"Yeah, baby!" Zac said, looking me over as I walked toward his locker. "Now that's what I'm talking about. Girl, you look amazing!"

I grinned, his compliment filling me with confidence and pleasure. "Don't I always?"

"Well . . . sure. It's just . . . I really like lace. Come here." He reached for me, and his hands on my waist made me feel secure—warm and melty inside. He pulled me to him for the best school kiss we'd had yet.

—⁂—

In PE class, we were again playing kickball, and for the first time, I was glad to change into gym clothes. Only two class periods had gone by wearing my new skirt, and I was overwhelmed with the amount of attention that had come with the wardrobe change. Some nice words, but many unwelcome comments from boys and way too much staring.

I took my regular kickball position—against the back wall where there was rarely any ball activity—and listened to the guys talk smack to one another.

"Let's see what you got, Torres," Alex said from the corner of the gym that was home plate.

Michael bounced the ball a couple of times, eyeing his opponent. At the pitch, Alex kicked the ball so hard it shot across the court, right toward Austin, who—rather than grab the ball—squeaked like a mouse and shot out of the way.

"Austin, you wimp!" the first baseman shouted.

Cody sprinted across the gym and scooped up the ball. With perfect aim and timing, he whipped it at Alex. Alex leapt aside, but the ball struck his leg. Donnie grabbed the ball and threw it back to Cody, who lobbed it against Jenna's back as she tried to steal third base. Two outs. Our team cheered. Brie stepped up next. Mika's choice for Peter Pan was tiny but tough. She missed Michael's first pitch but nailed the second. It sailed high through the air in a perfect arc, which Cody caught, putting her out and our team up to kick.

I trudged across the gym, hoping to enact Hyun Ki's strategy of hanging out near the back of the line in hopes of never having to kick. Michael found me there—took cuts actually. Cody cut with him.

"Hey, Cody," I said.

"Hey, Iz."

I smiled at him, wondering what Zac would think if I made Cody some Wimpy Kid birthday cupcakes next month.

"*Hola, Isabella*," Michael said, interrupting my thought. "*¿Qué onda?*"

"*Nada*," I said. "*Todo bien.*"

"I've got to ask," he said, "you dating Lloyd? I saw you with him in the hall this morning." His eyebrows were all scrunched up. He looked hurt. "You pose for him?"

Pose? I narrowed my eyes, oh so confused by this line of questioning. I caught Cody's gaze. He was watching the exchange, frowning. *Had he heard?*

"*Di la verdad*, Izzy," Michael said. "*¿Lo hizo?*"

Flustered, I said, "Did I do what? What are you even talking about, Miguel?"

Michael shook his head and stepped up to the kick line.

Cody was still watching me. "You and Zac?" he asked, his tone incredulous.

For some reason, that annoyed me more than Michael's cryptic questions. I watched Michael kick the ball across the gym and the other team scramble after it. Then I said to Cody, "Is that so shocking?"

"A little, yes," Cody said.

"Why?"

He opened his mouth, then closed it. He seemed to be searching for the right words. He finally said, "You're better than him."

That defused my anger, but Cody didn't know Zac like I did. "Zac is nice."

Cody's gaze darkened, his cheeks too. I couldn't tell if he was blushing or about to blow his top.

"Nichols!" Austin yelled. "You're up!"

Cody stalked up to the kick line. Alex pitched, but as the kickball bounced toward the line, Cody turned back to me. "Be very careful, Izzy. Okay?"

Our team screamed at Cody as the ball rolled past him for a first strike. Cody snapped out of his weirdo phase, grabbed the ball, and rolled it back super-fast. "That was wide, Hastings!" he yelled. "Try again."

Alex grumbled but pitched a second time. Cody kicked the ball so hard it bounced off a ceiling light and shot into the bleachers. While the outfield scrambled to get the ball, I watched Cody jog his home run and wondered what he knew about Zac that I didn't.

Chapter

21

BACK IN MY NEW OUTFIT, I headed to drama class. The first person I saw was Wilson, who'd been talking to Chad when I walked in, then trailed off, like he'd forgotten what to say.

"What?" I snapped. "It's a skirt, people. It's not even as short as the ones the cheerleaders wear. Plus . . ." I twirled so the skirt flew up around my waist. I heard Shay gasp, and when I stopped, Wilson's eyes were even bigger. "I'm wearing shorts underneath."

Half the class had stopped talking to stare. Tessa was giving me her quirked brow. Amelia, hands on her hips, was clearly unimpressed by my performance. They were all crazy.

I stomped to the love seat, crossed my arms, and fell onto the old leather, completely annoyed. "It's a *skirt!*"

"You look very pretty, Izzy," Tessa said.

I fake smiled, grateful, as always, for Tessa's kindness, but I wasn't buying it.

"I don't know," Shay said. "I kind of miss your wild leggings."

"This is stupid," Amelia said. "If no one else will say it, I will. This isn't you, Izzy. You're changing yourself for a boy, and it's dumb."

"Amelia," Tessa said. "Izzy is not dumb."

"That outfit is dumb," Amelia said. "Zac started liking you how you were before. Why change?"

I didn't like the way Amelia was attacking me. "You're just jealous," I said.

"Of that skirt?" Amelia asked. "I don't think so."

"Class!" The sound of Ms. Larkin's voice cut through our fight. "This is theater, not drama. This tension simply won't do. Everyone out into the hallway. Take three deep, cleansing belly breaths, and leave your drama in the hall where it will not affect our work here today. Return in better spirits. Go now."

The whole class traipsed out into the hallway, took their three breaths, and then came back inside. The mood in the room was definitely lighter, but Ms. L.'s little exercise hadn't done anything for the tension between me and my friends. I was still plenty annoyed.

At the end of class, Amelia left without a word. Tessa and Shay moved to sit on either side of me.

"Most everyone says I look good," I said. "Why don't you guys think so?"

"You do look good," Tessa said. "But it's a lot of change all at once. You look like a twenty-five-year-old cover model."

"Not like the Izzy we all know and love," Shay added.

That annoyed me. "I'm still me, but maybe I'm figuring out who I really am."

"Maybe," Tessa said. "I just hope that Izzy doesn't stop being friends with me."

"With us," Shay said.

"I would never!" I said. "You won't stop either, right?"

"Of course not," Shay said.

Tessa shook her head. "Never."

I hugged them both, which made me feel so much better.

—~~~—

When I got home, I was surprised to see Papi in the kitchen, standing over a family-sized box of frozen lasagna.

"Ah, Izzy, I'm glad you're home. Come help your papi figure out how to cook this thing. It says it takes almost two hours."

I walked toward him, my boots clicking over the hardwood. When I was about halfway there, Papi got a look at me. His eyes widened as he took in my appearance. *Uh-oh.*

"What are you wearing?"

I gave him the same line I'd given everyone else. "It's just a skirt."

"Not enough skirt, Isabella. *No está bien.*"

"Papi, if I was a cheerleader, I'd be wearing far less than this."

He crossed his arms and gave me the raised brow. "You are *not* a cheerleader, and even if you were, I would not approve of wearing an outfit like this in public."

Shame crept over me, which made me defensive. "*Papi* . . ."

"*Mija* . . ." He stepped back, looked me over again, and frowned. "The skirt isn't all that bad. But . . . all of it together." Jaw clenched, he shook his head.

"What's wrong with it? I'm wearing gym shorts underneath. That's what you and Mamá always made me do if my skirts were too short."

"No, we made you wear shorts because you were incapable of sitting like a lady in your dresses at church. I was always finding you up trees or under tables."

"Oh." That did sound like me.

"You're not a child anymore, Isabella. This amount of fabric isn't quite enough to keep you modest. What happened to wearing leggings with your skirts? I liked that style."

"It's not really a style, Papi. It's just something I did."

"*Did?* You don't want to do it anymore?"

"I just wanted to try something different."

"For Zac?"

I rolled my eyes. "Why would you say that?"

A smirk. "Because I'm a boy. I know how boys think."

I shrugged. No way I was going to tell Papi that Zac had given me this skirt for my birthday. He'd probably forbid me to see him.

"Your mamá taught you a rule for skirts back when you were in fifth grade and taller than all the boys. Do you remember it?"

I sighed. "A couple of inches below my fingertips."

"Arms at your sides, and longer than your hands. Let's test this one. Go on."

I dropped my hands to my sides. I could feel the bare skin of my legs against my fingertips.

"Too short?" Papi asked.

This was ridiculous. "*Sí.*"

"Okay, then. No more wearing that skirt without leggings. Got it?"

"Yes, Papi." I hugged him. "I'm sorry."

"I love you, *Mija.*" He kissed the top of my head. "Now help me cook this lasagna."

Once Papi and I got the lasagna in the oven, I went up to my room and changed. Zac had been texting, so I lay down on my bed with Fiesta to answer.

> Me: I got in trouble.
>
> Zac: what for?
>
> Me: Papi said my skirt was too short. I'm not allowed to wear it again without leggings.
>
> Zac: no way! that's bogus.
>
> Me: Sorry.

Zac: no i'm srry. didnt no u had a dress code.

Me: Ha ha. Me either. ☹

Zac: !!!

Me: What?

Zac: u frwned. i dont like to see u frwning. not my hppy grl

My stomach flipped inside. *He'd called me his girl. Oh. My. Stars. This boy.*

Me: ☺

Zac: thats btter & heres one 4 u

Then he sent me a selfie of The Dazzle.
I laughed. He knew me so well.

Me: I'm dazzled.

Zac: i should hope so

Then, emboldened by the happy feeling inside me, I lay back on my pillow, made sure my hair was spread out all pretty, and sent him a picture of me, smiling with all my teeth and eyes and every bit of the happiness I felt inside.

Zac: youre gorgeous

He sent me a close-up picture of his puckered lips.
I sent one back, trying not to laugh.

Zac: i srsly cant beleve somone so butiful is my grl

Zac: wish i ws w/u rght now i wanna kiss u so bad

Zac: ur lips tasted lke sugar today it made me hngry 4 an izzy cupcke

Me: Valentine's day is coming. I'll make cupcakes then.

Zac: we shld do smethin 4 v-day

Me: Like what?

Zac: i dunno u could come pose and i'll paint u
a v-day painting

I stared at the word *pose* and remembered Michael's question today in PE class.

"You pose for him?"

What had Michael meant? Had other girls posed for Zac? Him being an artist, I supposed it made sense. But he'd acted like no one knew about his Instagram art account. I searched it again. Sure enough, we had no followers in common. Not one. I studied the images and had to admit the busty fairy on the mushroom looked a bit like Ensley. Could be he'd told her about the account, and then she unfollowed him when they'd broken up.

Cody's warning came to me then. *"Be very careful, Izzy. Okay?"*

If Michael and Cody didn't follow Zac's art account, what were they being all weird about? I loved the idea of posing so Zac could make a digital painting of me on a Pegasus, but considering the magnetic chemistry between us, I did *not* think it was wise for us to be alone together in his house. That was my way of being careful.

I hoped it would be enough.

Chapter
22

FAR FEWER PEOPLE were staring at me on Tuesday since I was wearing my regular clothes. Zac was extra clingy and kept trying to plan a day I could come model. He suggested Saturday, which wasn't technically a problem. I told him I'd check with my parents to see if they needed me to watch Bash. That would buy me enough time to figure out what to do.

Mr. Lucas practically accosted me in the hallway that afternoon. "Izzy, you're coming to robotics tomorrow night, right?"

"Well, actually—"

"Josue and Chris will be fundraising again, so Kerrie and Laila will be working on the costumes alone. They could use all the help they can get, even if you only stay an hour."

"I guess I could stay an hour."

"Wonderful. Thank you so much, Izzy. See you tomorrow."

I walked away, feeling a little flustered. I had decided to help

with robotics every other week, which meant tomorrow I was supposed to go to youth group. I didn't know how to tell Mr. Lucas
no, though. I guessed I'd go to robotics for an hour, then ride my
bike to the church.

Halfway through sixth hour biology I got called down to the
office. There was a problem with Sebastian, and his school hadn't
been able to get in touch with either of my parents. I had the sec-
retary release Claire as well as me, since I'd ridden to school with
her. Claire drove us over to Sebastian's school, and she sat with him
while I talked to his teacher.

"He's been grouchy all day," Mr. Jamison said. "I don't know
what I did to set him off. He called me a *bad guy* a couple of times.
When I told him it was time to go to speech, he lost it. Started
destroying the classroom. I had to clear the room and call for help."

"A bad guy?" It was then I noticed Mr. Jamison's cologne. It
was faint, but there was no mistaking that it smelled similar to the
kind Zac wore. "Are you wearing a new cologne today?"

Mr. Jamison flushed. "Actually, yes. My wife bought it for me
for Christmas. I've never been much for cologne, but she got on
me about not even trying her gift, so I put some on today. You
think the smell set him off?"

I winced. "Sadly, yes. This probably sounds crazy, but someone
Sebastian dislikes wears similar cologne."

Mr. Jamison actually looked relieved. "I won't wear it again.
And I'm glad to know what caused the problem."

"It's just a theory," I said.

"One I don't doubt for a minute. Sebastian has always been
overly sensitive to smells. I'm surprised I didn't think of it myself."

The whole thing was kind of sad. "I thought he was done with
days like these. I keep hoping he'll grow out of it, you know?"

"We all have bad days," Mr. Jamison said. "Having a bad day
doesn't make you a bad person."

"I'm glad of that," I said. "Otherwise, we'd all be bad guys."

—⟋⟍—

Papi got home at 7:37. "Claire still at robotics?"

"Yep," I said.

He walked over to Sebastian, who was rocking in his chair at the kitchen table, reading a Wings of Fire book. "Hey, *Mijo*. Heard you had a bad day. Want to talk about it?"

Sebastian continued to read.

"I'm pretty sure it was Mr. Jamison's new cologne," I said. "He's promised not to wear it to school again."

"*¡Ay, niño!*" Papi said. "That man is a saint, what he goes through. Thank you for your help today, Isabella." He kissed the top of my head. "I appreciate you."

"Mr. Jamison still wants to talk with you."

"I'll call him in the morning. Anything to eat?"

"There's *caldo de pollo* on the stove," I said. "Sandwich stuff in the fridge."

Papi walked over to inspect the soup. "*Se ve apetitoso.*"

I gathered my homework and stood.

"You leaving?" Papi asked. "I thought we could hang out. Watch your baking TV show?"

"Sounds fun, but I have homework. It's been hard to concentrate down here, so I really haven't even made a dent in it yet."

"Okay, school comes first, *Mija.*"

Sure it did. Right after watching Sebastian and cooking dinner for the family. I carried my stuff upstairs and arranged it on the bed. There were a bunch of texts from Zac. I read through them, smiled at how sweet he was, and texted back.

Me: Sebastian had a bad day. Claire and I had to pick him up from school and talk to his teacher. I'm so tired, I want to sleep, but I have so much math homework. ☹

My ringtone, "I Feel Pretty" from *West Side Story*, started playing on my phone. I sighed deeply and closed my eyes. I was never going to finish my homework. I should have ignored the call, but Zac on FaceTime was too big a temptation.

I answered. "Yeessss?"

"Show me the math. I'll help you."

I wasted not one second. I pointed the phone at my textbook, and Zac walked me through the problems until I finished them all.

"Thank you so much!" I told him.

"Anytime, babe. Now, give me a kiss." He puckered his lips at the screen.

I giggled and kissed the phone.

A knock on my door preceded Papi entering my room. "You talking to someone?"

Embarrassed, I held up the phone. "Hi, Mr. Valadez," Zac said, waving.

Papi came closer, squinting at the phone. "*¡Ay!* Technology. Good night, Mr. Lloyd." He lifted his finger to the phone and ended the call.

"Papi!" I said.

"It's late, Isabella. Go to sleep."

My phone vibrated, but I ignored it until Papi shut the door behind him.

> Zac: omg did u get in truble?
> Me: No. But Papi wants me to go to bed.
> Zac: ☹☹☹

Then he sent me a pouty picture.

I sent one back. This started a volley of picture tag with us each trying to outdo the other.

> Zac: what r u wearing?

I sent a pic of me in my PJs, which was a Doctor Who T-shirt and plaid pajama pants.

> Me: Let's see yours. ☺

It took a minute for Zac to text back. When the phone finally vibrated, my screen had gone dark. I could tell Zac had sent a picture but couldn't see it clearly. I grabbed the phone, swiped to open the text, and saw something I wish I hadn't.

It was Zac. Naked.

My stomach twisted. I yelped and dropped the phone. Jumped off the bed and started pacing my room. It wasn't real. It had to be a joke. Some kind of silly meme or something. *Right?*

God, please let it be a joke.

Even if it was a joke, it was a bad joke. Not okay! The sting of tears accompanied a tightness in my chest, which only made me mad. I felt clammy and itchy. I didn't want to look again, but I needed to confirm what I thought I'd seen. Angry, I snatched up my phone.

Ugh. Sure looked real to me.

I closed my eyes, boiling inside. Tears leaked out and down my cheeks. I had to peek again to delete it, but in seconds it was in the trash can where it belonged. I punched out a reply.

> Me: What's the matter with you? Why would you send that?
> Zac: just trying to cheer u up ☺☺
> Me: Is that really you? Or is it a joke?
> Zac: thats all me baby

Double eww! I rubbed my face, completely grossed out, and reminded myself that Zac had always had a juvenile sense of humor, but still . . . Not funny!

My vibrating phone pulled my attention back to the screen.

Zac: u asked what I was wearing . . .

Gross! Who sits around their house naked?

Zac: u had a bad day so relx and snd one back
its fun

Was he out of his mind?

Me: I am NOT sending you naked pictures, Zac.
Zac: ☹☹☹

Oh, my stars. How was this my life right now?

I threw the phone on my bed, beyond frustrated. The picture of Zac flashed in my mind. I growled, paced a bit more, then climbed into bed and pulled the covers over my head. A deep breath and I felt a smidgeon better. Until my phone vibrated again.

Zac: it's fun babe I swear u shuld try it

My bottom lip trembled. *How could I have been so very stupid? How could I even show my face to Tessa, Amelia, and Shay after this? I am beyond humiliated!*

Zac: u don't have to go all the way just show a
little

I blew out an angry breath.

Me: I will not show you a little. I will not show
you anything. I do not take nude pictures because
I'm not stupid.
Zac: ouch

Now I felt bad. But feeling bad was dumb. I had no business feeling bad about any of this. He was the one being inappropriate. I'd just been trying to do math.

Zac: geez izzy. didnt no u were such a prude ha
ha a nude prude

I gasped. "A prude?!" Honestly, I wasn't exactly sure what it meant, so I googled it and found the definition: *An excessively proper or modest person. Old French: honorable woman.*

Okay, yeah. I *was* a prude. And I liked me that way.

I turned off my phone and cried.

Chapter

23

Papi woke me the next morning, shaking my shoulder. "Izzy! You need to get up! You've overslept."

I opened my eyes, confused. "What?"

"Claire is ready to leave."

I leapt from my bed like a jack-in-the-box, sprung. "She's leaving?"

"In ten minutes. She said to hurry up."

Papi left my bedroom, and I scrambled to get dressed. The situation with Zac came rushing back. When I'd shut off my phone last night, I forgot about my morning alarm. I didn't have time for a shower, so I washed my face, brushed my teeth, and put my hair in a ponytail.

Somehow, I managed to get downstairs. Sebastian was in the kitchen, cooking pancakes, Papi and Claire beside him.

"¡Ay! Sebastian! Look at you!" I said, shocked to see him standing at the comal.

"You taught him to cook?" Papi asked me.

"No," I said. "Didn't you?"

"Not me." Papi laughed and patted Bash on the shoulder. *"Sebastian es un muchacho muy inteligente."*

"He must have learned from watching you guys," Claire said.

"Did you eat one?" I asked.

"Yeah," she said. "They were good."

Making pancakes really wasn't that difficult, but for Sebastian to have read the instructions, turned on the stove, and cooked them himself, this was huge.

"Wait until Mamá hears about this," Papi said.

"I'm proud of you, Bash," I said, then kissed Papi goodbye, grabbed two granola bars from the pantry, and followed Claire out the door.

"Late night?" she asked once we were on the road.

"I hate math," I said, though in my head I was thinking, *I hate Zac.*

I turned on my phone, wincing when the texts came through, one after another, buzz, buzz, buzz, buzz.

"Are those texts?" Claire asked.

"Yeah," I said. "My friends were talking too much last night. I finally shut off my phone so I could concentrate."

"Which is why you slept in."

"Yep." Uneasiness swept over me as I saw the only *friend* who'd texted me was Zac. And he'd texted a lot.

Zac: i'm sorry, iz!!!

Zac: srry for calling u prude

Zac: srry for the picture too

Zac: i overstepped

Zac: waaayyyyy overstepped, yeah?

Zac: ☺

Zac: forgive me?

Zac: plz?

Zac: how about u send me a pic of your beautiful
face instead?
Zac: izzy?
Zac: babe?
Zac: i'm really really sorry

My eyes started to prickle, but I stared out my window and blinked hard to keep from crying. Claire started talking about Sebastian and the pancakes and how Mamá and Papi didn't give him enough credit. I'd been saying the same thing since we moved here, but I didn't have the brain power to engage this morning. I just nodded and said the occasional, "I know," to keep Claire from thinking something was wrong.

At school, when Claire and I approached the building from the parking lot, Zac was waiting outside the front doors. I didn't want to talk to him yet. Didn't know what to say.

"Hey, Zac," Claire said. "You guys finish coding the changes we made to the vacuum?"

"Another hour tonight ought to do it," he said.

"Cool," Claire said.

She went inside, but before I could follow, Zac stepped in my way.

"Izzy." He flashed The Dazzle, but it had dulled to me—as had the light in his eyes. "Can't we get past this?" His forehead wrinkled. "I thought you liked me."

"I do like you. But I'm not okay with porn."

"Gosh, Izzy. It wasn't porn. I don't know why you're freaking out about it. Everyone sends nudes. It's no big deal."

Was I overreacting? I didn't think so. "It is to me."

He growled and combed his fingers through his hair. The whites of his eyes were red. "Look, I'm sorry," he said, his voice a soft rasp. He glanced away, as if struggling to find the right words. "I thought it would be fun. I just . . ." He pressed his lips into a tight line. "Can you forget I ever sent it? Please?" The boy looked so upset—so wound up—wringing his hands and fighting back tears, eyebrows all scrunched together.

My heart melted. "I can try," I said.

"Oh, thank you, baby." He hugged me, but I didn't really hug back. Something about his touch felt different. He grabbed my hand and led me inside. Said something about lunch, but I wasn't listening. I was too busy trying not to think about how wrong my hand felt in his.

The day went by in a blur. I tried to brush off what had happened and let it go, but I felt weird around Zac. Whenever I saw him, I couldn't stop thinking about that picture, which embarrassed me. And I couldn't tell anyone what happened, which only made me feel frustrated and completely alone.

After dinner, I put my bike in the back of Claire's truck and went to the robotics meeting. I helped the girls with costumes for an hour, then left for youth group. Thankfully I didn't see Zac.

I sat with Tessa and Shay and Lauren at youth group, as we listened to Pastor Brad's message. He was talking about how God's love was enough. The concept of love confused me. I knew God loved me. And if anyone had asked me last week, I would have thought I was well on my way to falling in love with Zac. What a difference a moment made. Tonight, I felt so far away from God *and* Zac, and I didn't know how to fix either problem. After the message, we broke into girl-guy groups to discuss. Tessa and I ended up in a group with Zoe, who wanted to answer our questions about love. I couldn't bring myself to ask about forgiving a guy who did something wrong—especially not with Tessa sitting beside me. I was on my own to figure out how to deal with Zac Lloyd.

I expected Zac would be on his best behavior from now on, but when he texted me that night, he got all weird again.

> Zac: i can't stop thinking about the pic i sent

Neither could I, and I was really trying to forget. That thing was burned on my brain, and I didn't want it there.

> Me: Don't worry about it. It's fine.
> Zac: thats not it i just dont see why u cant do one so we'd be even just one and ill stop asking

Tears flooded my eyes. *Was he kidding me?* I looked to my Captain Marvel poster, and then I got mad. Turned out Zac was Loki after all.

> Me: Hold on. Let me ask my papi if it's okay.
> Zac: izzy! what? come on! u crazy?
> Me: I'm back. Sorry. Papi said no.
> Zac: hnestly, girl! u gave me a hart attck! just send one ok? i wanna see u too

I know he heard me at school that morning when I told him how I felt. From his reaction, I believed he understood. *Had it been an act? Had he been playing me all along?* My phone buzzed again.

> Zac: what can it hurt? i mean we trst each othr not 2 tell anyone or shw anyone u no? u wont show mine 2 anyone rght?
> Me: I told you. I deleted it.
> Zac: yah, but how can i no 4 sure? its not fair u hav one of me if i dont hav one of u
> Me: I no longer have one of you. I deleted it.
> Zac: yah but u saw me izzy its just nudes not like having sex

Oh. My. Stars! Who was this person? I didn't know him at all.

I hugged Fiesta and fought back a wail of sorrow and anger and disgust and shame. So much shame. Because Michael and Cody had warned me. Somehow they knew. And I'd ignored them.

I shut off my phone and went to bed.

—m—

The next day, I told Claire I was going to meet Tessa at the back entrance to school, so she dropped me off there. I crept through the school all day, avoiding Zac, even eating lunch in Ms. Larkin's classroom. Zac continued to send texts. I didn't reply and didn't see him all day.

The next morning, however, he was waiting outside my first-hour classroom. He grabbed my arm and dragged me across the hall into a water fountain alcove. His roughness so shocked me that I froze, my pulse suddenly rising.

"What is this, Izzy? You're avoiding me?"

"No," I said, which was a complete lie.

"Then why won't you look at me?"

I did, and my eyes started to water.

He swore. "I knew it. Something is wrong."

I ignored his swearing, yet another side of this boy I was just now discovering. "Nothing's wrong, Zac. I'm just busy this week, plus Mamá took my phone when she caught me texting too late. I'm grounded from it until after church on Sunday."

"You're grounded from your phone?"

I nodded.

He puffed an angry breath out his nose like some kind of bull about to charge. "I think you're lying to me, Izzy."

"What? Why would I lie?"

"Good question. Why would you?"

I stared at him, my heart quaking in my chest. He put a hand against the wall beside my head and leaned in to kiss me. I flinched.

He swore and slapped the wall with his other hand. I slid down the cinderblocks, ducked under his arms, and ran into Mr. Lucas's class.

"Don't do this, Izzy!" he yelled after me. The bell rang over his next words, drowning them some, but not enough. "You'll be sorry!"

I sank into my chair, put my head down on my desk, and started to cry.

———◆◆◆———

Shay told the girls about the exchange outside Mr. Lucas's class, so I wasn't surprised when Amelia offered to get me lunch while Tessa and Shay stayed with me in Ms. Larkin's classroom after Drama. I didn't want to tell the girls what was happening, but the moment Amelia returned with my lunch, the words started spilling out.

"I can't believe I thought he was one of the good ones," Amelia said.

"He did seem really nice," Shay said. "Like everyone thinks my birth father is nice, but he's not."

"You haven't been looking at your phone at all?" Tessa asked.

I couldn't! "I'm afraid of what he might say."

"Do you have it?" Amelia asked.

I wiped my eyes. "It's in my bag."

Amelia dug in my backpack until she found my phone. "This okay?" she asked.

I nodded.

Amelia and Shay crowded close to my phone screen while Tessa held my hand.

"I'm sorry, Izzy," she said.

Her kindness made my eyes water. "Everything was going so well . . ." I shuddered.

"Whoa," Amelia said.

Shay looked over Amelia's arm. "This guy has anger issues."

I reached for the phone, curious what he'd been saying.

"Don't," Tessa said.

"Actually, there are some messages here from your dad and from Claire," Amelia said. "Something about your brother."

I snatched the phone. "Oh no! They've been trying to call all morning!" I dialed Papi and waited.

"Isabella," Papi said. "Where you been, *Mija*?"

"Is Sebastian okay?" I asked.

"*Sí*, he's fine. Claire went over to the school and worked it out. Some boy took his lunch money, and he needed more."

"Matt Vega?"

"*Sí*, that sounds right."

"He's the boy who locked up Sebastian's bike," I said.

"Ah, well, don't worry about it. It's taken care of. Have a good day, *Mija*." Papi hung up.

"Is Sebastian okay?" Amelia asked.

I sniffled and lowered the phone to my lap. "Claire took care of it. I can't believe I missed the call. I'm supposed to be there for Bash!"

"You said Claire was there," Tessa said.

I couldn't stop the tears from leaking out of my eyes, and I started a full-on ugly cry. The girls crowded close, and Tessa prayed for me. I felt like everything was falling apart. Zac had let me down. I'd let my brother down. And I didn't know how to fix any of it. Thankfully my friends wrapped me in a group hug that held all the pieces of me together. For now.

Chapter
24

ON FRIDAY and all through the weekend, I heard nothing more from Zac. The following Monday, I had barely crossed the school parking lot with Claire when I could tell something was up. People were staring at me. And not in a good way.

"Why is everybody looking at you?" Claire asked.

"I don't know."

We approached a group of girls. I recognized a few cheerleaders and two girls from the ensemble choir. The moment we passed by, they burst into laughter. A sharp whistle turned my attention toward the parent drop-off area. Two guys were walking toward us, smiling gazes locked on me.

"Looking good, Valadez," said one.

"You should teach your sister how to pose," said the other. "You have a gift."

Pose?

The boys laughed, exchanging handshakes in approval of each

other's gibes. Claire grabbed my arm and dragged me the opposite direction.

"What are they talking about?" she all but growled.

"I don't know!" I racked my memory but could think of nothing.

I left Claire in the lobby and headed toward the humanities wing where Shay was waiting.

"Izzy!"

I turned at the sound of Tessa's voice, saw her jogging toward me. She pulled me over by the front office, and Shay met us there.

"What?" I asked. "Is something wrong?"

"Yes," she said, decidedly. "Why would you post a nude on Snapchat?"

Shay's eyes widened.

"What?!" Shock reeled through me, and I suddenly understood everyone's weird behavior. "But I didn't!"

Tessa closed her eyes and blew out a long breath. When she looked at me again, her eyes were glazed with tears. "I'm glad," she said. "I'd hoped you hadn't."

"What are you taking about?" Panic zinged through me like a pinball in an active game.

Tessa pulled out her phone and opened Snapchat, thumbed her way to my profile, and held up her phone on my stories.

Shay and I gasped together. Sure enough. There I was, topless, lying on my bed at home, brown curls splayed over my pillow. I could even see Fiesta's tail in the top corner. The words "Izzy Valadez" were written in a script font, as if I'd autographed my naked self.

A knot formed in my chest. *How?* "That's not me! I mean, the head is, but . . . I don't understand. Wait." A thought struck me, and chills ran down my arms. "Zac knows my password."

A frown from Shay. "Why does he know your password?"

"Because she told him," Tessa said. "But where did he get this picture? Was he at your house? Did he take a picture of you?"

"I never posed for any pictures!" I yelled, drawing the attention of far too many students.

Tessa gripped my shoulder. "Shh," she said. "Get out your phone and delete it. Right now. Then change your password."

"Right. Right!" I shrugged off my backpack and fumbled for my phone. My hands were shaking. My whole body was tingling. *What if this didn't work? What if Zac had changed my password and locked me out for good?*

But he hadn't. Tessa and Shay stayed beside me while the warning bell rang, as I logged in and deleted the horrid picture—which had been screenshot 164 times!

Tears blurred my vision as I clicked through to my password credentials. I changed the password and checked again that the picture was gone.

"Is it done?" Tessa asked.

I nodded, wiping my cheeks with the sleeve of my TARDIS. hoodie.

"Okay, get to class," Tessa said. "Be strong. I love you."

I sniffled and hugged her. "Love you too."

We parted ways. Shay threaded her arm in mine and escorted me to class. The bell rang as we walked into Mr. Lucas's room. Caydon and Jared stood and clapped, wide grins on their faces. One of them wolf whistled—I didn't know which and didn't care. I slid into my seat and opened my history notebook, pretending to be busy, but my mind was spinning with humiliation and guesses at what must have happened.

Zac must have logged into my account and posted that picture. *But where had he gotten it? Some poor girl was naked all over Snapchat with my face. Because of me! Because I'd made Zac mad.*

Zac had invaded my privacy. He had . . . maligned me! *Wasn't there a law against this? Obstruction of justice?* No, that wasn't it. *Slander! He had slandered my good name. Or maybe slander was words, not pictures. . . .*

Halfway through class, my breath caught as I put it all together. Zac must have created the picture with his graphic arts programs. Photoshop or whatever.

"Ms. Valadez?" Mr. Lucas said, stopping by my desk. "Is everything all right?"

I looked up into his face, and my vision blurred. I shook my head no.

"Do you need to visit the nurse's office?" he asked.

I shook my head.

"Okay, well, let me know if there's anything I can do."

A nod and he walked away. I sniffed and glanced at the desks around me. He must have given us some assignment, but I hadn't been paying attention.

I somehow made it through first and second hours by ignoring stupid boys and giggling girls and dozens of dirty looks, but when I entered the locker room for PE, I found an ugly bra dangling from my locker. I recognized it immediately as the one from the bottom of the lost and found bin. It had been there for years, according to Tessa. Maybe since the 1980s.

"We heard you needed clothes," Jenna Ashcroft said. She was another junior and Brie's friend.

"That bra might be too small," Brie chimed in. "Izzy is *very* well endowed."

Behind me, several girls snickered, as if trying to hold back on my behalf. Some were whispering. Hyun Ki was just standing there, eyes wide.

"She did *what*?"

"I want to see!"

"Who shared it?"

I turned around, annoyed. "That picture was *not* me," I said, glaring at Jenna and the girls behind her with their phones out. "I didn't post it, either. Someone hacked my account."

"Who would do such a thing?" Jenna asked.

"Zac Lloyd would," I said. "He was mad I wouldn't send him a nude, so he decided to humiliate me."

"Are you humiliated?" Jenna asked.

"Wouldn't you be?" I asked.

Jenna shrugged. "*I* thought you looked good."

This brought more giggles.

"You should make some calls," Brie said. "I'm sure someone would pay good money for that picture."

I was so mad, I could spit. Instead, I yanked the '80s bra off my locker and threw it back in the lost and found.

"I guess she doesn't wear bras," Jenna said.

This time no one tried to hide their laughter.

I went back and opened my combination lock, tears blurring the numbers, so I had to try three times before succeeding. I took out my gym clothes and set about changing.

"Girls, look!" Jenna said. "She's going to model for us."

I grabbed my clothes and carried them to the bathroom stalls. Hooting laughter followed me every step of the way. I changed in the privacy of the stall, lingering until it was quiet. When I came out, thankfully the locker room was empty, but someone had shut my locker and reattached the padlock. When I reopened it, I found the '80s bra inside. Annoyed, I shoved my clothes in and locked the lock. Might as well leave the bra where no one could use it to torment me further.

I exited the locker room, arms crossed while I walked, as if such posture could somehow shield me from the stares of my classmates. I dropped to sit at my place on the baseline between Michael and Austin. I could feel their eyes on me as I hugged my knees.

"Yo, Izzy," a boy named Donnie said as he approached. "We should party, yeah?"

I ignored him, but inside I felt like I was disintegrating, like there was a gaping hole where my heart had been, a hole the size of Zac's fist, and the rest of me was crumpling into a heap in that empty space.

Donnie squatted in front of me. "I was surprised when I saw that picture. I was all, man! I had to screenshot that one, you know?"

Screenshot? My vision blurred. Donnie was so close, I could smell his deodorant. I wanted to throw up. Felt like I might.

"Get lost, Donnie," Michael said.

"All right, all right. Don't freak out." Donnie moved on.

Relieved, I risked a quick glance at Michael, who instantly looked away. I turned the other way and found Austin staring at me.

"What?" I said, suddenly angry.

Austin blinked. "Your sister said it wasn't you."

I glared at him. "It wasn't me," I said through gritted teeth. "I would never do that."

"Aw, man! Why you gotta ruin my fun, girl?" Donnie called out.

"Shut up, Donnie!" Michael yelled.

His voice suddenly annoyed me. "You don't have to defend me," I said.

"Of course, I do. I mean . . . as long as it wasn't you. It wasn't, right?"

Wow. Too many eyes on me, judging me. I got up and walked away just as Mrs. DeLeon divided us for a game of kickball. I didn't get more than three steps toward the back wall when she called me over.

"Izzy, can I talk to you, please?" she said.

I walked toward her, hoping she wasn't going to make me stand near any bases. I could never catch the ball when the boys threw it at me a hundred miles an hour.

"Yes?" I said, stopping beside her.

"How's it going?" she asked. "Everything okay?"

No. My life was a shambles because I'd been ensnared by a hunky boy with a Dazzling smile who turned out to be Loki's evil twin, Heart Destroyer.

"I collected a phone last period from a young man. I caught him and his friends looking at an inappropriate picture, and all three of them claimed it was you."

Great. Just great. "It wasn't me, Mrs. DeLeon," I said, trying to hold back the emotions tumbling violently inside me. My voice came out watery and weak. "Someone hacked my account and posted it to get back at me for something."

"Goodness," she said. "I'm afraid to ask what you did to inspire such a horrible thing."

I held it in long enough to defend myself. "I wouldn't text a naked picture," I said.

She put one arm around me. "Izzy, I'm so sorry."

I shrugged, which seemed to be the only response that made any sense. But her kindness and the half hug did me in, and the tears started flowing.

She gave me a moment and then flipped back to teacher mode. "As per our school's cell phone policy, I collected the phone and gave it to the principal. She'll likely be calling you down to the office at some point today to discuss this further."

I couldn't help it. I started to bawl. I'd never been to the principal's office in my life. Not for being in trouble, anyway. Mrs. DeLeon gave me a squeeze. I tried to pull it together, but I caught sight of Jenna and Brie smirking my way and lost it all over again.

"Would you like to go to the office now? Mrs. Ventrella might not be ready for you, but I understand why you might want to get it over with."

This made me cry harder.

"Or you could go sit in the locker room until you're ready to come out and join us. Would that help?"

"Yes . . ." I gasped. ". . . please."

Mrs. DeLeon dismissed me, and I fled to the privacy of the

locker room. I sat on the bench, feeling sorry for myself. I wanted to do something to defend my honor, but I didn't know what. I prayed, but even my prayers felt desperate and clouded by my own shame. *How much of this was my fault? How dumb had I been? How had I missed the signs? There had been signs, hadn't there?*

I changed back into my regular clothes and stayed in the locker room until class ended. Then I headed to Drama early. I couldn't go in, not with my face all puffy. I'd never felt more alone, yet the idea of being with people made me cringe. I couldn't face any more judgmental stares. So I hid in a bathroom near the drama class, too embarrassed to be seen.

I was between sobbing fits when my phone chimed, *"We love you, Miss Hannigan!"*

I pulled it from my backpack.

Tessa: **Where are you?**

If I answered, she'd come find me, and I didn't want to talk. I waited until after the bell rang to go to drama class. When I sat down, the girls all spoke at once.

"How are you holding up?" Tessa.

"You okay?" Shay.

"I say we kick his butt." Amelia.

Ms. L. was talking about the difference between intention and motivation. I tried to listen, to pretend like everything was normal. The phone rang. Ms. L. answered and then motioned to me. "They need you in the office, Izzy."

A hush fell over the multipurpose room. All eyes fixed on me. Someone snickered.

Tessa grabbed my hand and squeezed. "I'll pray," she said.

"Me too," Shay and Amelia said at once.

"Thank you," I said, then headed out the door.

Chapter
25

"Have a seat, Izzy," Mrs. Ventrella said, gesturing toward the chairs in front of her desk.

I took the one closest to the door.

"We have a bit of a situation here, and I'd like to find out what you know about it. Three cell phones were confiscated today from students who were viewing child pornography."

My eyes bulged. I managed to ask, "What does that have to do with me?"

"Child pornography is a sexually explicit visual depiction involving a minor who is less than eighteen years old. All three students claimed the picture was of you, and you are less than eighteen, Izzy."

I shook my head, horrified that the principal thought I was making child pornography. "It wasn't me, Mrs. Ventrella. I mean . . . it *was* me. But it wasn't. I took a selfie on my bed, but I was wearing

231

clothes, I swear." I sniffled. My emotions were building up again. "Someone altered the picture."

"Go on."

So I told her everything, how I thought Zac liked me, how it seemed like we were going out, how we shared passwords, how we'd been texting, how he sent the picture of himself. "He was mad I wouldn't send one back and must have posted that picture on my account."

"That's a serious accusation. Do you have any proof?"

"Well, I didn't post it! And no one else had my password." My mind spun. *Where could I get proof? Did I have any?* "Wait! I have the original selfie I took." I pulled out my cell, hands trembling, and made my way to the text thread with Zac. I scrolled up to find the original photo, passing by cruel words and foul language Zac had never uttered in my presence. I tried not to read the texts he'd written—words I hadn't even looked at until now. I blinked away the tears while scrolling—until I found one of our photo tag sessions.

"I found it." Relieved, I passed the phone to the principal.

Mrs. Ventrella put on her glasses and examined the picture. "This picture does look similar." She leaned back in her chair. "I'm sorry this has happened, Isabella. Because of the nature of the crime, I've had to turn this investigation over to Deputy Packard."

"Crime?" I said, shocked.

"Whether the picture was of you or someone else, it was posted on your social media and distributed on this campus. As I said before, child pornography is a crime. The mere existence of that picture on these students' phones is against the law. Laws broken on our campus are the jurisdiction of our school resource officer. He will want to speak with you at some point. I'll also have to notify your parents."

Great. My eyes filled with tears again. Mrs. Ventrella sent me back to class, but the rest of the day passed by with no summons from Deputy Packard. By the time I got to Claire's truck, I was emotionally wrecked. She was already inside waiting. I climbed in.

"You sent him a naked picture?" she said.

Her accusatory tone triggered my anger. "No!" I snapped.

"Everybody's talking about it. Three people showed me. Shoved their phones in my face before I could even tell them I didn't want to see my sister naked. It's seared into my brain, Izzy."

"Well, it's not me. It's someone else."

"Someone else with your face and your bedspread on your Snapchat story?"

"Yes."

"There's a reason I don't have Snapchat," Claire said. "It's a stupid waste of time. But even I know you can't post pictures on someone else's account."

"If you're done accusing me and want to know what really happened, let me know. Otherwise, I'll be listening to my music." I started digging in my backpack for my earbuds.

"Okay, gosh," Claire said. "Stop freaking out."

"Like I don't have a reason to freak out?" Tears—again!—flooded my eyes, and everything went blurry.

"Just tell me what happened."

I slouched in the seat and wiped at my eyes. "Apparently having a nude picture of a minor on your phone is against the law."

"Duh. The question is, why do you have a nude picture of anyone on your phone?"

"I don't. Anymore." I shook with humiliation as I told her the whole story.

"That jerk. That absolute jerk." Claire sighed and started the truck. She had just turned out of the school parking lot and onto the road when she said, "This is going to get him kicked off the team."

Really? That's all Claire cared about? "If that's what you're worried about, don't. I have no proof. I deleted the picture, so it's my word against his. Your precious robotics team won't lose a programmer because of me."

"That's not what I meant, Izzy. Zac is a senior. I happen to know the coaches were going to recommend him for an award that, if he got it, would also come with a nice college scholarship. I was just saying he blew his chances by being stupid."

"I don't care about Zac and his life plans. I care that he acted like he was someone else. He acted like a nice guy. Sure, if it was just the one nude, then you could say he was 'just being stupid,'" I said, making air quotes to match. "But he . . . he . . . p-p-put time into faking a digital picture of some naked girl and added *my* face! It was methodical. It was meant to hurt and humiliate me because I wouldn't do what he wanted me to do. That's not the rash, *stupid* behavior that happens when someone's not thinking straight. That's . . . evil."

A thick silence followed my outburst. I felt like I should be crying, but I wasn't. It had felt good to say those words. To say the truth of them out loud to someone.

"You're right," Claire said, finally. "He's more than a jerk."

It also felt good to hear Claire agree. "Mrs. Ventrella is going to call Mamá and Papi," I said.

A little groan escaped Claire, and she muttered, "*Ay, niño.* Mamá and Papi are going to freak."

So true. This nightmare was never going to end, was it?

When we walked in the front door, Mamá and Papi were both home, sitting in the living room. At 3:41. On a Monday afternoon.

"*Hola, mis hijas,*" Mamá said. She didn't look or sound happy. "Claire, could you go on up to your room? We need to talk with Izzy."

"It wasn't her fault," Claire said.

"*Gracias*, Claire," Papi said. "We'll take it from here."

He wasn't happy, either.

Claire shot me a sympathetic look and headed for the stairs. I started to cry.

I kicked off my shoes and slunk into the living room, still wearing my backpack and coat. My parents were sitting together on the couch. I fell onto the wingback chair and slumped against the side, weeping softly. I did *not* want to do this. Whatever *this* was going to turn out to be. I hated being in trouble with my parents, but I hated Zac more.

"The principal called me today," Papi said.

"I know." The words came out a mere squeak, followed by gentle sobbing. My body ached from so much crying. I felt drained and empty, yet the tears kept coming.

"Oh, *Mija*," Mamá said, reaching toward me with both arms. "Come here."

I shrugged off my backpack and flew to the couch, falling in between my parents. Mamá put her arms around me and started rocking. I cried some more, but being close to my parents was a comfort.

"We'd like to hear your side of this," Papi said.

I sniffed. "Okay." That was something, at least. I took a deep breath and started talking. It was easier to tell the story to my shoes than to my parents, so that's what I did. Even so, I felt the heat of shame climb my cheeks as I spoke. When I finished, I risked a glance both ways. Mamá looked stern. Papi incredulous.

"¡*Ay, niña*, Izzy!" Mamá said, tugging me toward her. "You should have told us right away."

The thought made me squirm. No way. It had been confusing and embarrassing enough to get Zac's naked picture, but I never thought he would have taken it this far. "I thought once I deleted the picture, the whole mess would be done." How wrong I'd been. "You have to believe me. I thought he was a sweet, funny boy.

If I had thought for one moment that he wasn't, I never would have . . . " I waved my hand, not wanting to share the embarrassing details.

"You're a beautiful girl, Isabella," Papi said tenderly, resting his hand on my shoulder. "There are a lot of guys out there who only care about what they can get beautiful girls to do."

"But I didn't do anything wrong, Papi."

Everything inside me wrenched. *Did I do something wrong? Was kissing him first wrong? Or falling into his long kisses?* I blushed again as I thought about how he'd talked me into skipping youth group to help with robotics.

Papi raised a brow. "You trusted a boy you didn't know. That wasn't necessarily *wrong*, but it was foolish. He took advantage of your naiveté, tried to draw you in, making you think he liked you so he could get pleasure out of you. Does that sound about right?"

I cringed at the sound of my papi saying the word *pleasure*. *Stars.* "Maybe." *Had that been what Zac was doing?* "I thought he liked me."

Mamá scoffed. "He liked you because he saw you as a girl he could easily manipulate."

I blushed, embarrassed I'd been so gullible. So desperate to be liked by a cute boy that I would believe every word he said.

"The kind of boy you should want to spend time with is one who wants to be your friend first," Mamá said.

"Who will respect the rules of your family and home," Papi added. "Not try to get you to break them, and not become vindictive when you say no." Papi tapped me under the chin. "I'm proud of you for telling him no."

Tears dripped down my cheeks, but I smiled, my heart just a bit lighter at Papi's praise.

"And most of all, a boy who will respect your purity," Mamá said, her expression both gentle and urgent.

Papi looked past me to Mamá, who nodded. Their ability to communicate without speaking always astounded me.

"Do you remember the contract you signed when we allowed you to have a cell phone?" Papi asked.

"Yes. But I didn't send any pictures!"

"I believe you. But being responsible for how you use the phone was on that contract. Do you think you acted responsibly?"

I hung my head. Of that, I was painfully aware. "No," I said in a very small voice.

"From now on," Papi said, "you may not have your cell phone in your bedroom."

"No one but Papi and me are allowed to have your passwords. No one." Mamá sometimes liked to repeat herself to make sure I got the point.

"Okay," I said.

"As per the contract you signed," Papi said, "the cell phone comes to me for one month." He held out his hand.

I dug the phone out of my backpack and handed it over. Feeling both loss . . . and an odd sense of relief.

"Give me your laptop as well," he said, his hand outstretched.

I pulled it from my pack and handed it to him. "But, Papi. I don't use my laptop for social media. I need it for school. How am I going to do my homework?"

"When it's in this house, the laptop can stay on the dining room table," he said. "You are also no longer allowed to communicate with Zac."

"Not a problem," I said, an involuntary shiver of horror passing through me.

Papi started to fiddle with my phone. "Password?"

"It's *cake*," I said. "2253."

Papi tapped on the phone. "Okay. The password . . . is . . . gone."

I sat there, humiliated but also relieved everything was out in the open. To have peace with my parents.

"Now, where is this picture?" Papi asked.

I cringed, remembering it. "I told you. I deleted it."

"Doesn't mean it's gone," Papi said. "You check the deleted files?"

A chill ran over me. "You can do that?"

He cocked an eyebrow, like he didn't believe me, but when he saw the expression on my face, he said, "*Sí*, you can." He tapped around on my phone a while, but then jerked his head, a twisted expression on his face. "*¡Ay, niño!* It's still here."

I started to cry, so, so embarrassed that Papi had seen *that* picture.

Papi offered Mamá the phone.

"I do *not* want to see that picture, Dañel," she said. "Oh, *Mija*." She began rubbing my back. I leaned on her, comforted by the gesture.

"This is good," Papi said. "Now Deputy Packard can have the evidence he needs."

"He called you?" I asked.

"*Sí*. We will be meeting with him tomorrow," Papi said.

"Can he tell who sent the picture?" I asked.

"It came from Zac's phone number. He can also tell the type of camera that took the picture. Properties will say iPhone 12 or Samsung or whatever. After that, I don't know. They can't exactly do a lineup for something like this."

My eyes bulged. "Papi!"

"Dañel!"

Papi started to chuckle. "*Lo siento*. That was inappropriate." But he was still laughing when he walked from the room.

—ᨒ—

School was hard the next day, but my friends stood by me and continued to spread the truth that Zac had accessed my account and uploaded a fake picture. I again avoided people by eating lunch in the drama classroom. Thankfully I didn't see Zac all day.

After school, my parents and I met with Deputy Packard. Once we were seated in his office, he got right down to business.

"Isabella, Mr. and Mrs. Valadez, I'd like to start by letting you know I retrieved Isaac Lloyd's cell phone today and searched it. I found no trace of any inappropriate images." He nodded to a slender cell phone on his desk.

"That's not Zac's phone," I said.

Deputy Packard picked it up and turned it over, inspecting it. "You're sure?"

"Zac has an iPhone 11," I said. "I know because it's the exact same cell phone my friend Amelia has. They even have the same phone cover."

The deputy wagged his head and sighed. "Some students buy burner phones to protect their real phones from being searched. It could be what Mr. Lloyd did."

"We brought you Izzy's phone," Papi said, taking it from his pocket. "I found the original image the boy sent in the deleted images and recovered it. Will that help?"

"Indeed. I'll make note of the picture, the type of phone it was taken with, the date it was taken. Did it come through a text or another app?"

"Text," I said.

"Is the text thread still there? Or did you delete it?"

"It's still there," I said. "He sent a lot of angry messages since sending the picture."

"I'll transcribe those as well," Deputy Packard said. "Even if there is no way to prove Mr. Lloyd sent the picture, the texting thread will add context."

Papi tapped the back of the phone. "I removed the password so you can have easy access."

"Thank you. I'll get this back to you as soon as I can. I'm sorry for the inconvenience."

"Not at all," Papi said. "Izzy's grounded from the phone for the next month anyway, so she wasn't going to be needing it."

Chapter
26

THURSDAY AFTERNOON, Sebastian didn't come home. I rode my bike to the middle school, but his bike wasn't there. Mr. Jamison said he left school in a good mood, and JoAnn hadn't seen him. I rode home, glancing down every side street on the way, wondering where he might have gone and why. *To the library again, perhaps?* I hoped I would find him waiting when I got home.

I didn't. My first inkling was to call Papi or Claire, but I no longer had a cell phone. Papi had a house line in his office, so I went up there. The only problem was, I didn't know any phone numbers. The realization of just how much I relied on my phone made me sick. I caught sight of the file cabinet. Surely the phone numbers would be on the phone bills. I opened the top drawer and started digging. I was halfway through the second drawer when the house phone rang.

I grabbed the receiver. "Hello?"

"This is Officer Joyce Fenner with the Riverbend Police Department. May I speak with Mr. or Mrs. Valadez, please?"

"They're not here. Is this about my brother? He's missing."

"Who am I speaking with, please?"

"Isabella Valadez. I'm Sebastian's sister. He didn't come home from school, so I went looking for him, but I can't find him anywhere and I don't have my cell phone so I can't call my parents, and I don't know what to do!"

"We have your brother here at the station on East Third Street," the woman said. "What school does he attend?"

"Riverbend Middle," I said.

"You are welcome to come sit with him until I can get in touch with your parents."

"I'm on my way." I hung up before it occurred to me to ask how Sebastian had ended up at the police station. I ran downstairs, dumped the contents of my backpack on the floor, then grabbed Sebastian's Nintendo Switch, the charging cord, and a Wings of Fire book that was sitting on the kitchen table. I also threw in a Ziploc bag of chocolate chip cookies from the freezer in case he was hungry, then took off on my bike as fast as my legs could pedal.

On the way, dozens of thoughts assailed me. I should have left a note at home. I should have ridden by Tessa's house and asked her to go find Claire at the school. In between each thought, I released desperate prayers that Sebastian was okay and no one had been hurt.

I didn't stop pedaling until I reached the station. Inside, a receptionist directed me down a hallway. "Fourth door on the right," she said.

I raced down the hall until I found the office. There sat Sebastian, stiff as a board on a chair across a desk from a female police officer.

"Sebastian!" I said, running to his side.

He stood up. "I want to go home, Isabella Valadez. I want to go home now."

I wanted to hug him—needed to! But while hugs made everything okay for me, they did the opposite for my brother. I patted him a few times on the arm. "We have to wait for Papi," I said, shrugging off my backpack.

Sebastian screamed and threw himself onto the floor, elbow-faced.

I crouched beside him. "Tell me Marvel," I said. "*Iron Man*, May 2, 2008. *The Incredible Hulk*, June 13, 2008."

He moaned a little and then picked up where I'd left off. "*Iron Man 2*, May 7, 2010. *Thor*, May 6, 2011. *Captain America: The First Avenger*, July 22, 2011."

"I brought you your Switch and a Wings of Fire book. What would you like?" I unzipped my pack, dug out the Switch and the book, and offered them to Bash.

He dropped his elbow face and considered the options. "Okay, Isabella Valadez." He took the Switch, sat up, and flipped it on, still rocking back and forth.

I let out a long breath and claimed the chair Sebastian had abandoned. I smiled at the woman. "Thank you for taking care of him. Where was he?"

"We should probably wait for your father to discuss what happened," the woman said. "I'm Officer Fenner, by the way."

"Izzy Valadez." My hands were shaking, and the tears were desperate to come. *Stars! I'd been crying too much lately.* "Were you able to find a phone number for my parents? My sister Claire is at the high school. I could ride over there and use her cell phone."

"Your father is on his way," Officer Fenner said. "After I talked to you, I contacted the middle school, and they gave me your father's contact information."

Relief washed over me and flushed out the tears I'd been holding back. "*Gracias a Diós*," I whispered.

"It's going to be okay," Officer Fenner said, passing me a box of tissues.

I took a tissue and dabbed at my eyes.

"This kind of thing happen a lot?" she asked.

"Never," I said. "I mean, Sebastian is my responsibility after school until my parents come home. We've only had a couple of problems before, but they were small, everyday things for Bash." I watched him playing his game, overwhelmed with gratitude. That was when I noticed his fingers were scraped up.

"Bash, what happened to your hands?" I asked.

"No more bad guy," Sebastian said.

I sniffled. "What? What bad guy?"

Sebastian's gaze focused somewhere past my left ear. "I fixed it, Isabella Valadez. No more bad guy."

My stomach knotted, and I turned to Officer Fenner. "What is he saying?"

She looked sympathetic. "I'm sorry, but I need to wait for a parent or legal—"

"But he's my responsibility!" I said, tears leaking down my face. "Did this involve Isaac Lloyd?" He was the only *bad guy* Sebastian knew.

The officer shifted, uncomfortable it seemed, though she still said nothing.

If Zac had hurt Sebastian . . . I folded my arms and hugged myself, hoping that might somehow hold me together until Papi arrived. Thankfully, I didn't have to wait much longer. The sound of my papi's voice down the hall filled me with relief.

"Sebastian?"

"Papi!" I leapt off my chair and raced into the hallway. I met Papi halfway, hugged him tight, and dragged him into Officer Fenner's office. "She wouldn't tell me anything until you got here."

Officer Fenner stood and offered her hand to Papi, who shook it, then stroked my brother's hair back from his face as he sat on the chair I'd abandoned.

"Oh, *mi hijo*," he said. "What will we do with you?"

"What happened?" I asked.

Officer Fenner directed her words to Papi. "Mr. Valadez, your son was picked up for trespassing and assault." She went on to say Sebastian had ridden his bike to Zac's house, let himself inside, and attacked him. "Mr. Lloyd was not injured badly and does not want to press charges. He said there was some kind of misunderstanding between him and your daughter?"

Misunderstanding?

I lost it. I sat down on the floor beside Papi's chair and sobbed. *This was my fault! All my fault. My brother had been right to call Zac a bad guy. And he'd somehow found his way to Zac's house to defend me!* I was overcome by a mixture of self-shame and love for my brother. I vaguely heard Papi get angry and tell Officer Fenner about Zac's texts and the Snapchat hacking incident. I heard Officer Fenner say something back about Sebastian needing to stay away from Zac. When Papi stood and told Sebastian we were leaving, I wiped my face and picked up my backpack.

"Thank you, Officer," Papi said as we walked toward the exit.

"You're welcome, Mr. Valadez. And don't forget what I said about making a new schedule for your son. His caregiving shouldn't be the responsibility of any minor."

I asked Papi several times on the way home what Officer Fenner meant by making a new schedule for Sebastian. He said we would talk about it later. When Mamá came home, she and Papi disappeared into their bedroom. We could hear them yelling. Sebastian was reading at the kitchen table. Claire came and sat beside me on the step at the foot of the stairs, and I filled her in on what happened at the police station.

"I asked Bash how he knew where Zac lived," Claire said. "Guess what he said?"

"The robotics roster on the fridge," I said.

Claire raised an eyebrow. "He told you?"

"No, but he recited Zac's address the day he met him." I left out the part about that happening in this house.

"Wild." Claire sighed. "She's right, you know. That cop?"

"About what?" I asked.

"They shouldn't be asking you to watch him all the time."

Defensiveness rose up inside me. "But I'm good with him. Usually."

"That's not the point. She wasn't trying to say you failed him. She was saying he's their kid, not yours. It's one thing to watch him a couple of times a week, but they ask too much of you."

Did they? Deep inside I screamed, *Yes! Of course, they do. They always ask too much. But was that fair?* We were a family. We had to take care of each other.

I wished I could text my squad. "I still can't believe Bash tried to beat up Zac."

Claire snorted, fighting back laughter. "Every time I picture it, I can't stop laughing."

I imagined my little brother throwing fists at Zac, who was almost six feet tall. I grinned. "I bet Zac was surprised."

"Can you imagine? When Bash comes at you in one of his furies?" Claire shook her head. "That isn't fun for anyone. I don't care how tall you are."

I put my arms around my sister and laughed silently against her shoulder. It really was quite funny, yet sad at the same time, and preciously heroic of my brother to fight for my honor.

At the top of the stairs, my parents' bedroom door opened. Claire and I jumped up and ran to sit on the couch in the living room. Papi and Mamá came down and sat with us.

"We have to talk, *mis niñas*," Papi said. "There will be some changes in this house. Isabella, you will no longer be responsible to wait home for Sebastian after school every day."

"I'm sorry," I said.

"*¡Ay!*" Papi silenced me with a look. "You are not in trouble, *Mija*, or to blame for what happened. Moving to Riverbend was a big change, and you have helped make this transition so much easier for all of us. But Officer Fenner . . . what she said made me realize you have done more than your share to help this family, and we have been taking unfair advantage of you."

"I don't mind," I said.

"Liar," Claire said. "Tell them the truth. This is your chance!"

I stared at her, shocked she would contradict me.

"Be honest with us," Papi said. *"Por favor."*

Tears blurred my view of Mamá and Papi. "It does feel unfair sometimes," I said, my voice small.

"What does?" Mamá asked.

"Uh . . ." I was shaking. It felt like I might break if I said all the things inside me. Still, like Claire said, this was my chance to speak for myself. "I feel like you're always too busy for me. I have to take care of everyone, make dinner and breakfast and be here for Sebastian. I can't have friends over or have a pet because of him. I can't go anywhere on weekdays because of him. I'm tired of trying to do everything for everyone else and never anything I want." And, I said more quietly, "And I'm tired of feeling like I don't have a mother."

Mamá looked liked I'd slapped her.

"I'm sorry." I covered my face with my hands to hide my tears.

"I didn't know you felt so burdened," Mamá said. "Or that you needed anything from me." She put her hand on my knee. "Isabella, I am sorry. Will you forgive me for taking advantage of your strength?"

I nodded and leapt against Mamá, hugging her tightly. She rocked me back and forth. In that moment, it felt good to know my place as daughter.

"We will be changing our schedules," Papi said. "I will start

working from home, part time. No more travel. And your mamá . . ."
He looked to Mamá. "Josefina?"

"I am going to resign as the director of the clinic," she said. "We don't need the income, so we both can afford to cut back at work and take on more at home."

"*Gracias*," I said.

"We know that will be hard for you both," Claire said.

"At first," Papi said. "But once we find our new routine, it will be much more rewarding."

Chapter
27

I THOUGHT HAVING Mamá and Papi home more would make everything better, but school was still mortifying. After Sunday school the following week, I approached Zoe, desperate to talk to someone about my problems at school.

"Zoe," I said, and I'm pretty sure my voice had a tremor in it, "Do you have a minute to talk?" *Calm down. Calm down.*

"Sure, Izzy. What's up?"

I glanced behind me to make sure the room had fully cleared. "I don't know if you heard about me and a picture on Snapchat. Uh . . ."

"I'm your Snapchat friend, Iz."

My cheeks flooded. "Oh, right. So, you know."

"I talked with your mom. I know it wasn't you."

"Right. Good. I'm glad Mamá told you." Though I kind of wasn't. I mean, what if Zoe hadn't been my Snapchat friend?

Was my mamá walking around telling people my most embarrassing moments?

"To be fair, your mom didn't come to me. I went to her when I saw the picture. I was concerned. It's my job to keep an eye on you girls."

"Why didn't you say anything?"

"Your mom explained what happened. I figured you'd had enough uninvited attention and would talk to me if you wanted to talk. And here you are."

"Oh. Thanks."

She smiled. "How are you doing, Izzy?"

The question breached my shield of stoicism, and tears rushed to the edge of my eyes. "Not so good, actually. It's hard to go to school. I feel like everybody has seen that picture and believes it was me. And even though lots of people know the truth, I still feel . . . falsely accused."

"Truth doesn't spread nearly as fast as gossip, does it?"

I shook my head and sniffled.

Zoe reached behind her to grab a tissue box from the bookshelf and handed it to me.

"Thank you." I yanked out two and dabbed my dripping nose.

"I'm sorry for what you're going through," Zoe said. "I can imagine it's terribly difficult—and embarrassing."

"How can I get past it? I feel like my reputation is ruined."

"Aw, sweet girl. It might be bruised for the moment, but God has a way of bringing the truth to light—even if it takes time."

"I feel so *stupid* for making such a huge mistake."

"Everyone makes mistakes. But some people hate making mistakes so much that they become quite adept at pretending to be perfect. And part of keeping up that façade of perfection is judging others for their mistakes. Because if they're perfect, then they would *never* make a mistake like that, right? So these people deflect attention from their mistakes onto someone else, casting judgment on them. At the very least, they separate themselves from the sinner, so they'll look pretty good in comparison. Sound about right?"

I wiped my eyes and nodded.

"All that judgment and finger-pointing doesn't matter. Sure, if *feels* like it matters because how people treat us tends to affect how we see ourselves. But we don't have to give others that power over us. They don't get a say. Remember what God tells us. We are already forgiven of that poor choice, that sin, that mistake. We are loved. Always."

Zoe held up her Bible. "Being a Christian isn't about being perfect and never making any mistakes. It's about trusting God and letting Him transform us into the person He created us to be." She opened the Bible and showed me Romans 8:31. "'What then shall we say to these things? If God is for us, who can be against us?' He is our Savior. Our only Judge. He even calls us friend. Do you believe that?" She closed the Bible, her dark brown eyes searching my face.

I nodded. Stuff I've known forever—but somehow had let slip from my reality. "It's a good reminder, but God's treatment of me is not what I'm afraid of."

"I was getting there," Zoe said. "If you know God loves you, despite your mistakes and your sin, then what other people think of you doesn't matter. It only matters what God thinks of you." She patted her Bible. "*God* is for you, Izzy. GOD. The almighty God. You can trust Him with all aspects of your life. Your value—your worth—it comes from Him."

Gratefulness washed over me.

Zoe took my hands in hers, turned them palms up. "Walk around with your hands open, Izzy. Let all your problems rest on them, exposed to God. All your hopes and dreams too. If you're going to trust God with everything, you need to keep your hands open. Let God be in control of everything that concerns you." She curled my fingers into fists. "We have a tendency to walk around tightfisted, holding on to our worries and fears and hopes and dreams. We grip them until our knuckles are white, making things worse. Until we let go and give it over to God, He can't fix it for us, because He never forces us to do anything."

I took my hands from hers. "Give my desire for a boy to like me over to God? That's what you're saying?"

Zoe smiled. "That's part of it."

"My reputation. Letting God take care of my reputation."

She winked. "Ooh, good idea."

"But it won't change what people think."

"Probably not, but who cares about what people think, anyway? The people who matter know the truth about you, Izzy. *God* knows the truth."

She was right. But it would take time for this truth to sink in and practice to let go. "Thanks, Zoe."

She hugged me, prayed for me, promised to check in, and then hugged me again. I could get used to visiting this lady. I liked her a lot.

I felt better after confiding in her but didn't feel *fixed* or anything. I mean, it was easy for her to say what others thought of me didn't matter. While I knew she was right—I really did—I also knew I still had to go to school with people like Jenna and Donnie, who would say rude things to me. But Zoe was right. Jenna and Donnie—and anyone else like them—what they thought about me didn't matter. I needed to remember that.

As the days passed by at school, some students still made comments about the photo, but most had moved on. I went back to the cafeteria for lunch, and my squad sandwiched me in so they could protect me if anyone tried to say something. Even Alex sat with us, which was really sweet. Friday, I was sitting between Tessa and Lilliesha, with Amelia, Shay, and Hyun Ki sitting across the table. Alex sat by Tessa, of course.

"I watched *The Greatest Showman*," Tessa said with a shrug. "It was okay."

"What? No!" Amelia said. "It was amazing."

"Because Hugh Jackman is the best," I said.

"Exactly." Amelia gave me a high five.

Tessa laughed at us, and then her gaze shifted to two girls standing at the end of the table in their cheerleading outfits. Ava and Malorie from the girls' ensemble choir. Both looking at me.

"Hi," Ava said, her voice a near whisper. "Can we talk?"

"Anything you have to say to Izzy, you say to all of us," Amelia said.

Ava glanced at Malorie, who urged her on with a nod and raised eyebrows.

Ava leaned over the table and whispered, "We want to talk to you about Zac."

The sound of her voice and the look on her face told me this was not some pathetic attempt to mock me.

Amelia raised her voice. "Like I said . . ."

"It's okay," I said, turning to Lilliesha. "Scoot down?"

Lilliesha did, dragging her lunch tray with her, and I motioned for the cheerleaders to squeeze in. Ava sat beside me with Malorie on her right.

"So?" I asked. "What's up?"

"We met Zac last fall at a party," Ava said.

"We were stupid," Malorie said.

I realized where this was going, and my heart sank. "No," I said. "You were played by a professional player."

Ava nodded, but her frown looked so hopeless, I felt bad for her.

"What happened?" I asked.

"A lot of things I wish hadn't," Ava said.

"Zac hooked up with Ava at the party," Malorie said, "but he begged her not to tell anyone."

"I didn't tell a soul," Ava said.

"So I had no idea," Malorie added. "Meanwhile, Zac is friends with my brother Paul, and Zac came over to my house one day with a bunch of guys. One thing led to another . . ."

"Let me guess," Tessa said from across the table. "Zac told you not to tell anyone."

"Yep," Malorie said. "But I've never been good at secrets. I caved and told Ava."

"We got in a huge fight," Ava said.

"We didn't talk for two weeks," Malorie said.

"Until I heard her brother and Zac talking one day at school," Ava said. "Paul said Malorie's name. He was mad Zac had uploaded pictures of his sister to Dropbox."

I shivered. "What Dropbox?"

"So we got our friend Cody to ask around," Malorie said.

I perked up. "Cody Nichols?" *Please don't say he was involved. Please, oh, please!*

"Yeah," Malorie said. "We know him from basketball. Well, he found out Zac and Paul and Ross and some other guys . . . they made a Dropbox account online, and they collect pics of girls and post them there."

I was stunned.

"Shut up," Amelia said, dropping her burrito onto her tray.

"It's true," Ava said. "They charge boys money to access it."

"Eww!" Tessa said.

The mere idea of boys ogling my fake picture made me feel icky. *How much worse for girls whose real pictures were on there?*

"We thought you should know," Ava said.

"It's why Zac dates so many girls," Malorie said. "Especially younger girls."

"And why he's all about taking pictures and getting girls to pose for him."

My entire body was shivering from a sudden chill. I had so many questions, so many thoughts vying for attention. None of them mattered but one.

"We have to tell Deputy Packard," I said.

Ava paled. "Oh, I don't want to get in trouble."

"I don't care if I get in trouble," Malorie said. "If my brother keeps doing stupid stuff like this, he's going to end up in jail. I'll tell all."

"I'm not asking either of you to do anything," I said. "I'm meeting with Deputy Packard today, so I'll tell him what I heard— but not from who. I'll let you know what he says."

Ava's fearful expression shifted into a devious grin. "It would be so great if they got caught."

"Yes," I said. "Yes, it would."

—m—

When I told this new information to Deputy Packard, however, he did not seem to share my enthusiasm for quick arrests.

"Thanks for letting me know."

"That's it?"

"I appreciate the tip, I do. But without evidence, it's akin to gossip."

"Akin?"

"It's gossip I've heard before, mind you. Off the record, I don't doubt it's true."

"Then what's stopping you from going after them?"

"I have been going after them, but believe it or not, most high school boys aren't quick to confess they've had anything to do with illegal porn sites."

I growled.

"I need proof, Ms. Valadez."

I folded my arms. "Well, I don't have proof."

He lifted his shoulders and hands in a "sorry" gesture.

"If I found you a boy who would help, would you keep him out of trouble?"

"As much as I could. But I wouldn't be able to keep his identity a secret forever. He'd need to make a statement, and eventually, the guilty parties would know who ratted them out. Not many guys are eager to be *that* guy, either."

"The only reason the girls I talked to know about the Dropbox account is because they asked a boy to sniff around," I continued. "They said Zac gave him the prices."

"If this boy would be willing to make a statement, that would be enough to implicate Zac. I could then likely get a subpoena to search his computers and other devices."

I pursed my lips. "Okay, I'll ask him."

"No way."

"No?"

Cody wouldn't look at me. He went about unnecessarily straightening some wooden spoons on display at the checkout counter in Paprika's.

I forced myself to ignore how his hair curled around the bottoms of his ears. "Why not?"

"I don't want to get involved, okay? I had no idea what was going on when I asked Zac about it. I was just trying to help Malorie because she was crying, and I felt bad."

"What if I cried? Would that make you feel bad enough to help?"

He threw me a little half grin that made my stomach dance. "Izzy . . ." He sighed.

"Pllleeaassseee?" I crooned, thinking the little half grin had been a sign I was wearing him down.

But he glared at me and yelled, "No!" so loudly that two customers over by the pots and pans stared at us. "Look," he continued in a regular voice. "I can't talk about it anymore, okay? I'm sorry. I'm not trying to be a jerk here. I just can't."

"So you think it's okay for Zac and his friends to keep weaseling nude pictures from naive girls?"

"Will you please keep your voice down?"

"You think it's totally fine they post those pictures online and get dumb boys to pay to access them?"

"Of course not," he growled.

"Yet you'll do nothing."

"I don't do nothing. I've told dozens of girls to stay away from Zac and Ross. That they're bad news."

"How noble of you."

"I told *you*. Think back to how well you listened to my warning."

"Oh, yes, and such a clear warning it was, too, Cody. You said to be very careful. You could have said a lot more a lot clearer. So don't think your vague warnings are saving girls from anything because they're not."

His peachy cheeks flushed. "I have to work." He pushed through the little swinging half door enclosing the pay counter and stalked over to the register.

I started to follow him but then stopped myself. I was so worked up, I felt like crying. I needed to retreat to my corner. Get a pep talk before coming back for round two. I left the store and ran through the rain to Grounds and Rounds where the girls were waiting.

"Well?" Tessa asked.

"He won't do it."

Tessa and Shay groaned.

"I'm not surprised," Amelia said.

I glared at her, annoyed.

"He's on the basketball team," Amelia said, "the track team. He's ASB treasurer. Everybody knows him. If he blabbed to the cops, he'd lose all that."

"No, he wouldn't," Tessa said. "A few boys might be angry, but the girls would love him."

I set my chin in my hands and stared out the window at the rain pounding the streets.

"Do you want to order something, Izzy?" Shay asked. "I'm going back for a refill."

I glanced at her. "No thanks."

She got up and walked to the counter. I refocused my attention on Tessa, on her phone. I glanced at Amelia, who was also staring at her phone. The phone that looked just like Zac's phone. If only I could get my hands on Zac's phone. His real phone.

An idea blossomed. "Deputy Packard needs evidence," I said. "He can't move forward in his investigation without it."

"We know," Tessa said.

Shay fell back into her chair and tucked her wallet into her pocket. "What do we know?"

"That Deputy Packard needs evidence," Tessa said.

"I know where to get it," I said. "But I'm going to need your help."

Three sets of eyes fixed on me.

"I'm in," Tessa said.

"Me too," Shay said.

Amelia narrowed her eyes at me. "You have a plan? A real plan that doesn't involve coercing boys?"

"This is a girls-only operation," I said, "and you, Amelia, are the most integral part of my plan."

Amelia smiled. "Then let's do this."

Chapter 28

WITH LESS THAN A WEEK until their first competition, the robotics team met after school every day to perfect their robot, so it was all very intense. I was counting on that. On Zac being totally distracted.

Another integral piece to my sting operation was having an inside man. Since none of my good friends were on the robotics team, that left one person: Claire. I thought long and hard about how to broach the topic and even asked my squad for ideas. None of it had been necessary. The moment I asked, she said, "I will absolutely help you take down that dirtbag." Score one for sister power.

I chose Tuesday night for our sting. Claire said her design and build subteam had finished and passed the robot over to the programming subteam on Monday. Zac and the other programmers were under a lot of pressure to quickly write the code needed for the robot to do what they wanted it to do.

Tessa, Shay, Amelia, and I hung out in the drama classroom while we waited to hear from Claire. She texted to say Zac's phone was in his back pocket—not where we needed it to be. But she was working on it, she said. So we waited.

"What if he's so busy, he never checks his phone?" Shay asked.

"Claire said he would, so he will," I said.

"Do they really text each another at practice?" Tessa asked. "I'd be in so much trouble if I had my phone out at swim practice."

"Robotics is a different kind of club," I said. "They use an app called Slack to talk to each other. Even the coaches use it. It's kind of like having their own social media forum. It lets them have threads for different conversations. Claire said they're supposed to keep it handy at practice in case one of the mentors on a different subteam shares important information."

My phone vibrated in my hand. *"We love you, Miss Hannigan!"*

"You should really silence your phone," Amelia said. "We're on a stealth mission here."

"Good point." I silenced it as I read Claire's text.

Claire: His phone is now on the table.

"It's a go," I said. "Let's do this."

Amelia went in first. She was friends with Jeremy and in the same science class, so she was going to ask him about some major project they were working on together. I was to wait exactly two minutes and then go in.

"Are you nervous?" Tessa asked me.

"Not really," I said. "I feel like this is what I'm supposed to do."

"It does feel like God has His hand in this," Tessa said.

"How so?" Shay asked.

"Using my mistakes to catch Zac," I said.

Tessa smiled at me. "Zac was a fool to underestimate our Izzy."

"He was," I said. "But we haven't won yet. Let's not get cocky."

"It's time," Tessa said.

I took a deep breath and grabbed Tessa's and Shay's hands. "Please help us, Jesus. We need You. Amen."

"Amen!" Tessa and Shay chorused.

"We'll be right behind you," Tessa said.

I left the multipurpose room and headed for the STEM wing. It took me a minute to orient myself. To my right was my destination—the computer lab. I opened my hands, palms up, and headed for the open door.

I spotted Amelia's wild red hair and her mustard-yellow cardigan first thing. The lab had four long tables holding computers. Amelia was half sitting, half leaning on the front of the fourth row—Zac's row—talking to Jeremy, who was working kitty-cornered to Zac. I quickly counted five more people working on computers.

I was standing right behind Zac, actually. I paused for a minute to admire his amazing hair, and then I spotted his cell phone sitting on the table about two feet from where Amelia had stationed herself. My stomach did a little flip. It was game on.

"Zac," I said. "Claire said you'd be in here." I waited until he turned his head, then strode toward him, smiling.

This seemed to confuse him. "You talking to me?"

"Yes, I'm talking to you, silly." I noticed the bruise under his left eye.

And just like that, with Zac looking my way, Amelia deftly made the switch. I wanted to turn and run, but we needed to buy a little more time.

I touched my eye, in the same place Zac had his bruise. "You have a little something right here. Turns out Sebastian is a pretty good judge of character."

"I don't have time for this." He turned back to his computer.

"Is he here?" This from Tessa, who'd come in behind me.

I pointed. "Right there. Zac Lloyd, professional scoundrel."

"Wait," Amelia said, putting both hands on the table beside

Zac's computer and leaning down to face him. "*This* is the guy Sebastian beat up?" Amelia could project better than the rest of us, and her question drew the attention of everyone else in the computer lab.

"What's *your* problem?" Zac asked Amelia.

"You're my problem," she said. "You embarrassed my friend when you hacked her Snapchat and posted some photoshopped picture like it was her."

"Who was she, Zac?" I asked. "Someone from Riverbend or from your old school?"

"I don't know what you're talking about," he said.

"I bet he has other pictures on his phone," Tessa said, lunging for Amelia's phone.

Zac scooped up the phone and tucked it into his back pocket. "I don't think so." Then he called Tessa a word I would not repeat.

"Is there a problem here?" Mr. Lucas entered the computer lab, looking serious.

"These girls are bothering us," Zac said.

Mr. Lucas panned the room, paused on Amelia, passed right over Shay to Tessa, and landed on me.

I grinned. "Hi, Mr. Lucas."

He cocked one eyebrow. "The marketing subteam is meeting in the usual place," he said.

"I'm sorry, Mr. Lucas. I'm not here to help tonight. We'll leave." I grabbed Tessa's and Shay's arms and pulled them toward the exit. Amelia was right behind us. Before we got too far away, I heard Mr. Lucas speak.

"Let's see how your code is looking, Mr. Lloyd."

We ran. The moment we were back in the safety of the multi-purpose room, Amelia handed me the phone.

Tessa squealed. "I can't believe we did it!"

"You girls were amazing," I said. "Thank you."

"You were amazing!" Shay said.

As I held Zac's phone in my hands, I felt exhilarated and a little terrified. This phone was the key to justice, but I didn't want to know what kind of shocking horrors might be on it. I said a little prayer, then punched in the numbers to spell out the password we had created a couple of weeks ago.

Relief coursed through me when the phone opened up. "Stars, it worked!"

The girls cheered. Amelia punched her fist into the air. "Zac Lloyd is going down!"

I barged into Deputy Packard's office, holding up the phone. "I got it!"

He pushed up from his chair and came around his desk. "And this is . . . ?"

"Zac Lloyd's cell phone."

"How do you know?"

I was about to blurt out the story of our entire scheme, but he was giving me a look that, for some reason, made me hold my tongue. "Well," I said slowly, "it was sitting on a table in one of the computer labs. My friend Amelia has a bad habit of picking up things that aren't her own."

Deputy Packard grunted. "I'm well aware of Ms. Bryan's kleptomaniacal tendencies. But what made you think it belongs to Zac?"

"Well, I told you how he and I had shared passwords. I tried it, and it worked." I switched to the Contacts app. And there it was. *Isaac Lloyd* at the top. A photo next to his name. I held up the phone for the deputy to see. As I did, my eyes caught sight of the Dropbox app. I opened it. A list of files came up. There were only three. One said Government Project, but the other two were images that, even though they were super tiny in the list, looked to be of naked girls.

I wasn't familiar with Dropbox. A menu on the bottom said: Home – Files – Create – Photos – Account. I clicked on photos, and the screen filled with image files, most of them of girls in sexy poses or various stages of undress. I thumbed the page upward, scrolling, scrolling, scrolling. My mouth went dry.

"Izzy?" Deputy Packard said.

"Uh . . ." I held out the phone so Deputy Packard could see the photo collection for himself. "I think this phone has some other incriminating evidence on it besides the photo he posted on my Snapchat. Should I leave this with you?"

"I'll hang on to it, yes," he said, reaching out.

I placed it firmly in his open hand.

—⁂—

I sprinted back to the drama classroom and told the girls everything.

"I can't believe the Dropbox was right there on his phone!" Tessa said.

"I'm so glad this is over!" Shay said. "I couldn't sleep last night; I was so worried about today."

"It's not over yet," Amelia said, grinning. "I seem to have lost my cell phone, and I'd really like it back."

Chapter
29

THIS TIME when the four of us walked into the STEM computer lab, Mr. Lucas was up front working with Natalie.

"Call it again, Izzy. I might have left it in here." Amelia walked to the place she'd been standing before. "Jeremy, have you seen my phone?"

"No," Jeremy said, not even looking up from his computer.

"Zac, did you see it?" Amelia asked. "I think I left my phone in here."

Zac ignored her.

"Zac?" Amelia sang.

"For the love . . ." Zac raised his voice. "Will you people leave me alone?"

A phone started ringing. Zac jumped, a confused look on his face. He drew the phone from his pocket. I inched close enough to see a picture of us four girls smiling on the screen.

"Oh! Zac, you found it!" Amelia said, reaching for the phone.

Zac moved it out of her reach, frowning at the screen. "What the . . . ?" He looked at me, eyes narrowed. "Did you hack into my phone and change the picture?"

I smiled sweetly and batted my eyes. "I would never hack into anyone's phone and plant a photo on it."

"Unlike some people we know," Amelia said.

"Girls," Mr. Lucas said, walking toward us. "You're back."

"Sorry, Mr. Lucas," I said. "But Zac has Amelia's cell phone."

"I do not!" Zac roared.

"It's ringing right now," Shay added.

Mr. Lucas joined us, noticed the picture of us girls on the lock screen just before the phone went to voicemail.

Mr. Lucas reached for the phone. "Isaac, may I have a look, please?"

"What? No. It's mine."

"It will only take a minute to confirm whose phone it is."

Zac pressed his thumb against the screen. It flashed the picture of us girls, and then it displayed the password screen. Zac punched around some more and tried his index fingerprint. Punched in his passcode. Twice. Three times.

"Can I have my phone, please?" Amelia said, holding out her hand and tapping her foot impatiently.

"This is nuts," Zac said, eyes scanning the table, the floor.

Amelia snatched the phone from his hand. It instantly responded to her thumb print. She held it up, the four of us smiling big from a picture we'd taken in drama class. "See?" she said to Mr. Lucas. "It's mine." Then she flipped to the Contacts app where her name and image appeared.

Mr. Lucas seemed appeased. "Do you agree, Isaac?"

The Dazzle was gone. Zac's brow was so furrowed, he looked to be in pain. "Yeah. It's hers. But where is mine?" He ran his fingers through his hair. "I had it right here. Like, a half hour ago. Claire told me to check Slack for Mrs. Mosely's thread."

"I have a bad habit of picking things up and losing them," Amelia said. "I probably grabbed yours when I was in here before. If someone found your phone, they probably took it to the lost and found. That's where I usually find mine."

"Or they might have taken it to Deputy Packard's office," I said. "I mean, if the main office is already closed."

Zac looked at me then, no Dazzle in his eyes, just dark suspicion and panic. He jumped up and raced past Amelia and out of the room.

I clapped my hands over my mouth to hide my grin from Mr. Lucas. We calmly left the computer lab, the four of us smiling from ear to ear. Once we were in the hallway, we piled together for the biggest group hug ever.

Zac wasn't at school on Wednesday. Deputy Packard called me into his office during fifth hour to tell me he was able to get plenty of evidence off Zac's phone. He would eventually be filing charges against Zac and possibly a couple of other boys, whose names he did not reveal. I was totally relieved until he said I needed to come in with my parents and record a statement on camera.

"The phone is evidence enough to implicate him, but your testimony, and the testimony of anyone else who will come forward, will help to make sure charges are brought against him."

Was that what I wanted? Zac to go to jail? "Do you think that's necessary?"

"These boys broke the law in a serious way. If they don't face consequences now, they might continue on this path and do something worse when they're older. The consequences will hurt, yes, but if they learn from them, they have a chance at a new start."

His words made sense. "I'll help however I can." Even though I was terrified, it was the right thing to do. I had found my voice, and while it was still difficult to speak up sometimes, I refused to stay silent when it mattered.

The next day, rumors were flying about a handful of suspensions. Lilliesha heard the boys had been selling drugs. In second hour English, Jason Corina was telling his friends that the boys had robbed the cafeteria cash register. In PE class, Hyun Ki told me she'd heard they'd assaulted some freshman on the track team. Michael had it closest. I heard him tell Donnie, "They're going down for harassing girls and selling porn."

I heard over twenty names implicated that day, but only a handful did I hear over and over again: Isaac Lloyd, Ross Miller, Shawn Edwards, Paul Neil, and Daniel Nichols.

Cody Nichols's brother.

I was so shocked, I prayed for the Nichols family, which then prompted me to pray for all the boys and their families. Even Zac. I was sure his parents would be disappointed in him. I certainly had been.

When I checked my email in science class, my calendar app had sent me a reminder that Cody's birthday was tomorrow. Well, if anyone needed a pick-me-up right now, it was my very own Captain America, especially considering I'd tried to guilt him into turning on his brother. When I got home, I used the computer in the den to google "*Diary of a Wimpy Kid* characters" and began to resize some images in Paint to use as stencils. It was cupcake time.

The next day after school, I knocked on the Nicholses' front door. I knew Cody was home because I'd seen him drive by earlier.

Riku answered. "Izzy, *konnichiwa*!" He gasped. "For me?"

I laughed. "Is it *your* birthday?"

Understanding registered in Riku's eyes. "I'll get Cody. Come in!"

I stepped into their foyer. I'd never been inside their house before. It was pretty similar to ours, only they had a lot more sporting equipment sitting . . . everywhere. I guess that's what came with a house full of boys.

"Izzy, hey." Cody walked down the last three steps and approached me, Riku on his heels. "What's up?"

"I brought you some birthday cupcakes—as promised," I said. "And as a peace offering."

His gaze settled on the plate in my hands, and I so enjoyed how his eyes widened as he took in my latest creations. "These are amazing!" His mouth gaped open with a grin. He looked so cute right now. I kind of wished I wasn't holding the plate so I could take a picture. "You really made these?"

"Yep. And I posted a video on my IGTV, so these are basically famous cupcakes." I'd had to borrow Claire's phone to make and post the video, but Papi said it was okay. This once.

Cody chuckled. "Seems a shame to eat famous cupcakes," he said as he took the plate from me.

"I can always make more."

"Thank you, Izzy."

"Happy birthday. I hope it was nice, despite, you know . . ."

"It was nice. My parents are taking us all out to dinner. Also, um . . ." He swallowed, noticed Riku was standing right there, watching our every move. He glared. "Hey, beat it, you." He winked at Riku, who rolled his eyes.

"Okay, okay, I'm leaving now for your privacy. *Maji ka!*"

Cody grinned as Riku stalked off toward the kitchen, grumbling under his breath.

"What's *maji ka* mean?" I asked.

"Oh, something like *really* or *gosh* or—"

"Oh, my stars?"

Another All-American grin. "Sure." He took a deep breath, studying his cupcakes. "So anyway . . ." Head still bowed, he glanced up. "I'm sorry I didn't help you. I knew. But I just couldn't . . . I didn't know what to do."

"You are 100 percent forgiven," I said. "You did what you had to do. I totally understand, and I probably would have done the same thing if I had been you."

"Really?"

"Of course. Family comes first." I shrugged. Though I might have told my parents.

"I couldn't go to Deputy Packard. Not on my own brother. Does that make me a horrible person?"

"It means you love your brother," I said. "Don't be so hard on yourself. It all worked out in the end."

He narrowed his eyes. "How did it work out, anyway?"

I cocked an eyebrow. "God handled it."

He seemed to accept this. We stood there. Our eyes met, and we both looked away, suddenly becoming awkward.

"Well, I should go," I said. "Just wanted to bring those by and say happy birthday."

"Thank you, Isabella."

Oh, my stars, I liked when he said my full name. *Play it cool, girl.* "You're welcome."

I turned to let myself out but stopped when Cody said, "Wait."

I turned back as he slid the cupcake plate onto a slender table beside the door. Cupcakes safely down, he clasped his hands together like he was fighting to keep something in.

Finally, "Um . . . this might sound weird, but I'm a hugger. Do you mind? It kind of gives me closure."

Sweetest. Thing. Ever.

He ran a hand through his hair. "I mean, I'm not trying to like, be a creeper or anything, I swear. A side hug works."

Okay, now that *was the sweetest.*

"I totally get it," I said. "I'm a hugger too."

So we hugged, and he smelled even better up close. Felt good too. Human touch was so powerful. It symbolized acceptance, connection, forgiveness, friendship. Cody's hug meant a lot. It meant he and I were going to be okay.

The hug ended far too soon. I could have stayed there for a half hour or so. But all good things come to an end, and soon enough I found myself walking home, one plate of cupcakes lighter and a huge smile on my face.

—⁓—

The girls and I were sitting at Grounds and Rounds on Saturday, hanging out before Alex and Tessa's date. They were both so busy with her swim practices and his basketball schedule that they'd had to plan an evening out.

"I can't believe there were five guys in on the Dropbox scam," Amelia said.

"I thought it would only be Zac and Paul," Tessa said. "Alex said Daniel got kicked off the basketball team."

"No wonder Cody wouldn't help you," Shay said.

"Think he knew his brother was involved?" Tessa asked.

"He must have," Amelia said. "It didn't make sense he'd go out of his way to help Malorie and Ava, then stop caring."

A moment of silence descended as the girls thought about Cody. I was the only one not frowning as I remembered our closure hug. I should probably tell the girls about that. Without a phone, I hadn't been able to give them the play-by-play of my life.

"You going to say anything to Cody?" Tessa asked me.

"Already did."

"When?" Amelia asked.

I told them about the birthday reminder, the cupcakes, and the closure hug.

"That is precious!" Tessa said.

"You should go after him, Izzy," Amelia said.

Shay groaned. "Can't she let a few weeks go by first?"

Amelia's eyes were slightly wild. "So someone else can snap him up? No way!"

"Actually," I said. "I'm with Shay on this one. I'm not interested in chasing any boys right now. The friend zone is the perfect place for me and Cody. He's got a lot going on in his family, and so do I. Plus, I'm still grounded."

"Baby steps, Izzy," Tessa said. "If it's meant to be, it will happen."

I liked that. "I think so too."

"Did Alex say anything else about this, Tessa?" Amelia asked. "I mean, does he know if the boys have been charged?"

"Not yet," Tessa said. "Deputy Packard is still questioning people."

I sat back in the booth. "Ah, my first boyfriend. What a sad story."

"He wasn't your first boyfriend," Tessa said.

I looked at her, curious what she meant by that.

"Because he wasn't really your *friend*," she finished.

Amelia sighed. "I sure thought he liked you, though."

Zac, I had decided, was a sad, confused person. I liked to think he regretted how he treated me and would miss me from time to time. "Who's to say he didn't?" I asked. "I mean, he did spend a lot of time getting to know me."

This made Amelia scowl. "Looking back, were there any signs you missed? Signs that he wasn't as amazing as we all thought he was?"

Funny how Amelia had completely forgotten that Tessa and Shay had taken a long time to get fully onboard with Zac Lloyd. Still, I thought about her question. "Actually, there were lots of signs. I just didn't want to see them."

"Like what?" Amelia asked.

"He contradicted himself. He would compliment me on my leggings, saying how cool I was not to care what people thought about them, but then he tried to get me to stop wearing them. Bought me that skirt."

Tessa gasped. "He bought you that?"

I nodded. "For my birthday. Also, he texted more than he talked in person. Always told me I was beautiful and tried to get us texting about things that led to pictures. He told me about his art and asked me to pose."

"Do you regret ever knowing him?" Shay asked.

"Of course not. Meeting those kittens made the whole thing worth it," I said with a grin.

Amelia and Tessa groaned.

Shay shook her head at me while fighting a smile. "They were sweet, but if you needed a kitten fix that badly, I would've asked my aunt to foster a cat that's expecting."

My eyes widened. "You can do that?" I asked.

"Sure. People do it all the time."

I sipped my hot chocolate, trying to imagine a box of kittens in Sebastian's spot under the piano. The bell over the door jangled, and Alex approached our table holding the familiar white paper sack of La Petite Boulangerie.

Tessa saw it too. "You went to the bakery?" she asked.

He grinned down at Tessa. "Sweets for my sweetheart," he said. "One chocolate peanut butter macaron."

Amelia and I glanced at each other, then sang, "Aw!"

The tops of Alex's ears turned pink.

"Alex! You're blushing," Amelia said, which elicited another "Aw" from me.

Alex shifted from one foot to the other. "You ready?" he asked Tessa.

"Yep," she said, giving us all a reprimanding scowl that was really more of a smirk.

"Have fun!" Amelia said.

We watched the couple exit the coffee shop and make their way down the sidewalk hand in hand. They were so cute.

Alex treated Tessa like she was special—valuable. Because she was.

And so was I.

Amelia, Shay, and I parted ways a few minutes later. I unlocked my bike from the rack outside and headed for home, still thinking about Tessa and Alex and comparing what they had to me and Zac.

If I ever found another boy who wanted to spend time with me, I deserved to be treated with the same kind of sweetness and respect that Alex showed Tessa. *Could I control that, though?* I had no power over what boys did or didn't do. But I could choose my own actions. I could be wiser next time, that was for sure. God valued me, so I needed to set better standards for myself. Standards that showed I valued myself as much as God did. That meant not changing myself to please other people. It also meant being strong enough to speak up and say no when I needed to.

As I coasted into our driveway and put away my bike, I felt incredibly thankful to feel comfortable in my own skin. Zac had caused me to doubt who I was. That was a mistake I wouldn't make again. No matter what life brought my way—no matter what anyone thought of me—I knew I was exactly who I was. And I liked me.